D0122638

AN AMATEURS NOVEL

# LAST SEEN

## THE MURDERER NEXT DOOR

SARA SHEPARD

FREEFORM BOOKS
Los Angeles New York

First Edition, November 2018
10 9 8 7 6 5 4 3 2 1
FAC-020093-18264
Printed in the United States of America

This book is set in 11-pt. Bembo and Sackers Gothic/Monotype;
Natura/House Industries; Sevigne/Fontspring
Designed by Marci Senders

Library of Congress Cataloging-in-Publication Data
Names: Shepard, Sara, 1977– author.
Title: Last seen / Sara Shepard.
Description: First edition. • Los Angeles ; New York : Freeform, 2018. •
Series: [Amateurs ; book 3] • Summary: When Aerin is kidnapped by a killer she knows all too well, her friends Seneca, Maddox, and Madison have four days to solve a series of related cases in order to secure her release.
Identifiers: LCCN 2018005848 • ISBN 9781484742297 (hardcover)
Subjects: • CYAC: Mystery and detective stories. • Kidnapping—Fiction. • Cold cases (Criminal investigation)—Fiction.
Classification: LCC PZ7.S54324 Las 2018 • DDC [Fic]—dc23
LC record available at https://lccn.loc.gov/2018005848

Reinforced binding

Visit freeform.com/books

THIS LABEL APPLIES TO TEXT STOCK

*To Clyde*

# BEFORE

**IT WAS SO** dark in the shed. His underwear was wet, and his skin itched. It smelled awful in here—a little like the mouse that had died under his family's porch that one time. And he could hear the ocean going *whoosh-whoosh-whoosh*, but he didn't know where the sound was coming from. He hadn't actually *seen* the ocean since coming here. It wasn't like he was on a fun vacation.

He moved right and left, bumping into plastic beach buckets, rusty bikes, and a busted pool float. He'd never been allowed to play with any of it. He kept thinking about all the creatures that might be crawling over him. Centipedes. Spiders. Maybe even a mouse. His throat tightened. The smell of that dead mouse had gotten worse and worse every day—first it smelled like puke, then something even more awful. When his dad finally pulled it out with a shovel, there were only bones. He'd screamed, and his dad had run over to him to give him a hug. *I know, buddy,* he said. *It isn't pretty.*

Would he ever *see* his dad again? Was *he* going to turn into that mouse?

His heart started to pound. He pressed his face into his knees. In times like this, times when he got really scared, the only thing that helped was to disappear into the Harry Potter books he loved. If he were at Hogwarts instead of trapped here, if he had magical powers like Harry and his friends, he'd strike down the woman who'd done this to him with a magic spell. She'd shrivel up and disappear. And then? Then he'd run. He'd run *fast*, away.

The door creaked open. He stood up, suddenly not able to breathe. The light made his eyes hurt, and he brought his bound hands to his face.

She stared at him. She wore that big flowered dress, the one that fit her once but didn't anymore. Her hair was a tangle of orangey-blond around her face. When she was just his teacher, she'd reminded him of the friendly scarecrow from *The Wizard of Oz*. Now she was more of a Halloween skeleton.

"I—I'm sorry," he stammered. "I'll never do it again, I promise."

She sniffed and gave him an ugly look. Once upon a time, he hadn't felt stranger danger with her. He'd thought she was a normal, friendly, happy person he knew well, a person who told funny jokes and gave him Junior Mints after a lesson and talked to him about the Harry Potter books—she said she loved them, too.

They never talked about Harry Potter books anymore.

"C-can I go back there?" he said, gesturing to the house across the yard. He could see it through the crack in the door. "I'm thirsty."

She wrinkled her nose. *"I'm thirsty,"* she mocked. "Whose fault is that?"

His cheeks burned. How long had he been trapped in here? When she first shut him inside, he'd wanted to scream, but then he worried she'd do something even *worse. You better watch it,* she was always saying. *I could really make things bad. You should be happy about how kind I'm being.* She also told him that his parents were glad he was gone, and they weren't searching to bring him home. No one was. No one cared.

She shook a finger at him. "You should have thought about what would happen before you did it. But you didn't, and you broke my heart. All I've done for you, and this is what I get. You *leave* me. You make me look like a fool."

"I—I said I was sorry."

He knew he should have never tried to escape . . . but it had felt so good. Out there on the sidewalk, he'd turned from the helpless victim into a hero in one of his books—into Harry Potter himself. The air had smelled so fresh. The hot summer sun gave him strength. When he'd knocked on that door two houses down, he'd been sure the people staying there would save him.

Now she moved closer, her face almost touching his. Her breath smelled like coffee, just as his mother's always did when she leaned over his bed to wake him up for school. It made him so homesick to smell it, and yet he always kind of *wanted* to smell it, too, just so he could remember.

When she reached for him, he flinched. But instead of hitting him, she petted the side of his cheek. "My sweet, sweet boy. I love you. You know that, right?"

"Uh-huh," he whispered. But he felt icky for saying it.

"Except you've been so very bad. And bad boys need to be punished."

The door crashed shut so hard that the whole crappy plastic shed rattled. “Wait!” He lurched forward, tripping over his tied-up ankles. “Wait, no, *please*! Let me out! I’ll never do it again! I *promise*!”

“I’m sorry, honey.” The metal padlock clicked into place. “But this is how it has to be.”

# ONE

**SENECA FRAZIER STOOD** in the way-too-chilly, upscale lobby of the Reeds Hotel in Avignon, New Jersey, staring in horror at a text message she'd just received.

*Don't bother looking for us. We're outta here.*

"Impossible," Maddox Wright whispered. Maddox rubbed the bridge of his nose, which was peeling from sunburn, and pushed his grown-out brown hair out of his eyes. "You really think it's from Brett?"

Seneca was clenching her jaw so hard it felt like her teeth might grind to powder. "It has to be. But what the hell does it mean?"

Seneca, Maddox, and Maddox's stepsister, Madison, plus their friends Aerin Kelly and Thomas Grove had been embroiled in a game of cat and mouse with Brett Grady for the past week. Ironically, once upon a time, Brett had also been their friend, a member of their cobbled-together investigative team—they'd met on a crime-solving website, Case Not Closed, which acted as a gathering place for people who loved digging into cold cases. Their first case had been to figure out what had happened to Helena Kelly, Aerin's sister, whose bones had turned up in a park years after her mysterious disappearance. During that investigation, they'd trusted and respected Brett. He had great insights. He'd been a good listener, and he'd stuck by them to the very end, when they believed they'd found Helena's murderer—Marissa Ingram, the wife of the man Helena was having an affair with.

Little did they know at the time that he'd steered that investigation exactly where he wanted it to go. *He* was the one who'd murdered Helena, not Marissa Ingram. But he'd disappeared before Seneca had made the connection. And that wasn't all Brett had done. . . . Through subtle hints he'd dropped, Seneca was almost positive he'd killed her mother, Collette, as well. That he'd been so close to her, right in front of her face, *taunting* her—it made her blood sizzle in her veins.

She wanted to catch Brett. She *needed* to catch Brett. It felt like her life's mission now. But Brett was like a phantom—he changed his looks as easily as he changed his name. Finding him was easier said then done. This past week, he'd resurfaced and put the group through their paces to find Chelsea Dawson, his latest victim . . . only to twist the scene to make it look like the Instagram-star Chelsea had kidnapped herself in order to gain more followers. Seneca and her friends had looked like fools when they tried to explain to the cops that Brett, who had been going by the name Gabriel Wilton around Avignon, was behind it all. It also didn't help that Brett had staged a fiery car crash that killed "Gabriel." Who knew who Gabriel actually was—not Brett, clearly, but an innocent person whose life didn't deserve to be cut short by Brett's vicious game. As far as the cops were concerned, Chelsea's case was closed—and Seneca and her friends were liars.

And now here was Brett, teasing her again with this text. *I win, you lose!* Seneca pressed her nails into her palm, wanting to scream. Every day that passed, her desire to capture Brett turned more desperate. She needed to get this guy—for her mom, for his other victims, for herself, if only to ask him why. Why her mom? Why Helena? Why *anyone*?

She canvassed the lobby, wondering if Brett had been here, if they'd walked right past him at any point. This hotel had been their HQ, though now that Chelsea had been found, Seneca and the others planned to head back to their respective homes—Madison, Maddox, Thomas, and Aerin to Dexby, Connecticut, and Seneca to Annapolis, Maryland—and reconvene their search for Brett after a few days. The lobby had a cheerful tiki theme and was bustling with sunburned tourists. A group of raucous college-age boys drank tequila shots at the thatched-roof bar. Outside, a bunch of valets in Hawaiian-print shirts rushed to cars pulling up to the roundabout drive, and bellboys pushed carts of luggage through the automatic doors.

Seneca stared at the text again, her hands fluttering to the bare spot at her throat. She was so used to fiddling with her mother's *P*-initial pendant, but Brett had burned it beyond recognition a few days ago. She felt so naked without it, as though she'd parted with a limb.

Why had Brett sent this message? Just to tease that he'd gotten away again . . . or for some other reason? His use of pronouns—*us* and *we're*—felt like a clue. Did Brett have someone with him? His "sister," Viola, maybe? She'd just found out that Brett called her "sis"—Amanda Iverson, Brett's boss at the real estate company when Brett was posing as "Gabriel," beach bum and Realtor-in-training, had clued her in. Seneca needed to find this Viola person. She'd already begun racking her brain, trying to figure out how they might be able to track her down. Only, why would Brett brag about Viola when, as far as Seneca knew, he wasn't yet aware that she knew of Viola's existence? It didn't quite fit.

"Ready to go? Madison's here." Maddox pointed out his sister's shiny dark hair by the elevators. She was dragging two giant, overloaded pink suitcases behind her. She'd changed into a neon floral minidress and cork-wedge sandals.

Seneca was about to tell Madison about Brett's cryptic text, but Madison spoke first, holding up an iPad in a Louis Vuitton case. "Aerin forgot this. She still here?"

"She left to meet Thomas." Seneca glanced at the front entrance. Thomas Grove was Aerin's brand-new boyfriend and an ex-cop; he'd helped them hunt down Chelsea and Brett. This morning, he'd received news that his grandmother was in the hospital and that he needed to return to Dexby. Aerin insisted on going with him; Thomas was picking her up in the hotel driveway.

She dialed Aerin's number, eager to talk to her for reasons beyond the left-behind iPad. She needed to clue everyone into this text, pronto—Brett's words seemed more ominous with every passing second. Maybe Aerin or Thomas, with his police experience, would have some insight.

But the call went to voice mail. Seneca dialed Thomas next; he answered on the first ring. "Thomas? Put me on speaker. Aerin needs to hear this, too."

"Oh." Thomas sounded surprised. "Actually, I'm still about five minutes away."

"Wait, what?" Seneca cocked her head, not understanding.

"I haven't picked Aerin up yet. I got stuck in traffic. I shouldn't be long, though."

"Huh." Seneca stuck her head out and peered around the hotel's driveway, searching for Aerin's silky white-blond hair, her long tanned legs, the black designer handbag looped over her elbow. She wasn't there.

Seneca's skin started to prickle. She looked at Maddox and Madison worriedly. "Thomas isn't with Aerin," she whispered. "And she's not in the driveway, either."

Maddox frowned. Madison's eyes darted. "Maybe she's in the bathroom?"

Seneca eyed the bathroom door across the lobby. She would have seen Aerin coming or going from there. She pressed the phone to her ear again. "Thomas, can you meet us inside? We'll find Aerin. There's something I need to show you."

After she hung up, she dialed Aerin once more. Voice mail. A hot feeling was spreading across her stomach, but she tried to breathe steadily. This didn't *mean* anything. There had to be an explanation.

She looked at the driveway again. Still no Aerin. She noticed a lanky young bellman standing by the valet stand. The guy seemed bored, leaning his head against the wall with his eyes closed. A shiny name tag read *Hunter*. He snapped to attention when she approached.

"Did a girl just pass by here?" Seneca asked. "Seventeen. Pretty. Blond hair. You wouldn't have missed her."

Madison showed Hunter a picture of Aerin from her phone. The kid's lips curved into a suggestive smile. "Oh yeah. I saw her. She got into a car a couple minutes ago."

Seneca felt a jolt. "*What* car?"

The kid tried to think. "I think it was white? A sedan?"

Seneca frowned. Thomas's car was a white Ford sedan . . . but Aerin wasn't *with* Thomas. Could it have been a cab? But the cabs around here all seemed to be standard taxicab yellow. "Where did she go? Did you see?"

"Toward the bridge, I think." He nodded confidently. "Yep, definitely toward the bridge, because they cut off someone making the left. Really peeled out of here."

Then Hunter became distracted with an SUV full of people that had just pulled into the drive. Seneca turned to Maddox and Madison. Alarm bells were going off in her head. By the look on Maddox's face, she could tell that scared, paranoid thoughts were churning through his mind, too. That didn't surprise her—she and Maddox had bonded long ago over private messages on the Case Not Closed site, confessing all kinds of things, weirdly in tune with one another's thoughts.

Seneca called Thomas back. He picked up right away. "Who called you to tell you that your grandmother was in the hospital and that you needed to come home to Dexby?"

There was a pause. "My nana's doctor," Thomas said. "Why?"

"Have you ever spoken to him before? Like, do you know what his voice sounds like?"

"No . . ."

"Seneca, what are you getting at?" Madison narrowed her eyes.

Seneca held up her finger in a wait-a-second gesture. "Thomas, call her doctor back. Ask if your nana's really sick."

Madison looked confused. "You think the doctor is lying?"

Maddox swore under his breath. Seneca looked at him; by his ashen expression, she could tell he was toying with the same theory she was. Brett's text danced in her mind. *Don't bother looking for* us. Could the *us* be . . . ?

A dangerous scenario unfolded in her mind: Brett had posed as Thomas's grandmother's doctor and lied about her condition. Then he'd pulled up to the driveway in a car that looked exactly like Thomas's and taken Aerin . . . while the rest of them were inside, mere feet away, unaware.

She pressed her phone to her ear. "Call him, Thomas. Please."

"Okay," Thomas said. "I'll call you back. Or actually, I'll *see* you in a couple minutes—I'll be turning onto Sea Breeze soon."

The call ended. Seneca shifted her weight from foot to foot. "Ten bucks says that doctor never called him," she murmured. "Ten bucks it was Brett, disguising his voice."

*"What?"* Madison asked, gaping. "Why?"

Wordlessly, Seneca showed her the text on her phone. Madison crowded in to look, and the color drained from her cheeks. "This is from . . . ?" She trailed off in horror.

Seneca nodded.

"And you think he's *outta here* . . . with Aerin?"

The pieces were starting to slide into place. Throughout the search for Chelsea, Seneca had questioned Brett's every move. Why had he taken her specifically? Could he really have a vendetta against every woman who rejected him, or was there something else at play here? And why had he given them clues on how to find Chelsea . . . and, finally, why had he let Chelsea *go*? Brett was the kind of criminal who left no witnesses—he didn't want his victims to tell anyone about him. And he had no interest in clemency.

"Guys, maybe Chelsea wasn't Brett's endgame," she said in a choked voice. "Maybe *Aerin* is."

Madison was trembling. "We have to call the police. *Now.*"

Seneca peered into the hotel lobby. Maybe they should tell the management, too—they probably had a surveillance camera in the driveway and had caught Aerin getting into Brett's car. But she didn't see a single staff member anywhere. She stared at her cell phone, eagerly awaiting Thomas's call back. Then, as she looked up, she caught sight of Thomas's white Ford rounding the corner onto Sea Breeze Drive.

Even from a distance, she could see the frightened, confused look on his face. He'd made that call, she knew. His nana wasn't in the hospital. The doctor hadn't told him to come home.

*Brett* had.

There was something strange about Thomas's car, though. Thick black smoke poured from its tailpipe, obscuring the air behind it. Seneca knew nothing about car maintenance, but it didn't seem good. The traffic light turned green, and Thomas hit the gas. The smoke billowed. A strange *pop* sounded. And suddenly, horrifyingly, the car burst into flames.

"Oh my God!" Seneca darted toward the automatic doors.

The air outside smelled like burning fuel. Flames leapt from Thomas's hood. Most people were running away from the fire, but a few brave souls were running toward it. Seneca pressed her hand to her mouth as she reached the sidewalk. Thomas's door had opened, and he tumbled out and crumpled to the ground.

"Thomas!" Seneca screamed, but he didn't raise his head. Fear cut jaggedly through her. How had this happened? How could a car just *explode*?

Two men in volunteer fire jackets sprinted toward Thomas's body. "Get back, get back!" they screamed at Seneca, Maddox, and Madison, who'd rushed up behind her. Seneca bit down hard on her fist.

A police officer had appeared and was starting to divert all traffic to a side road. The fire department arrived and sprayed the car down. Ambulance sirens wailed. Onlookers to Seneca's left began to murmur. "Did anyone see what happened?" a woman asked.

"It just exploded!" someone else said. "Scared me half to death!"

"I've heard you can't trust that model year," a third voice murmured.

Seneca was starting to get woozy from the smoke. *Was* Thomas's car just a lemon? But Thomas was a meticulous guy. She couldn't imagine that he'd let important car maintenance go to the point where his vehicle would explode. Paranoia nagged at her. She clutched Maddox's arm. "I don't think this was an accident."

Maddox and Madison nodded numbly. *And just like that, Brett has cut our numbers to three,* Seneca thought with dread. Of course he wiped out Thomas—as an ex-cop, he had a lot of resources to hunt Brett down. *And* he and Aerin had just started dating. Seneca couldn't forget the dreamy looks Brett had given Aerin back in Dexby. He'd liked her. Maybe liked her a *lot*.

So Brett wanted Thomas out of the way, then. He wanted Aerin all to himself. And he wanted them never to be found.

"Okay, now we're *definitely* telling the police." Madison spotted a broad, squinty-eyed cop who'd appeared to direct traffic. She took a few shaky steps toward him, but then Seneca's phone started to buzz. She looked down at the number, and her breath caught in her chest. *Impossible.* The person who had sent the *Don't look for us* text was now *calling*.

"Wait, Madison." She grasped her friend's arm. *"Don't."*

Madison gave her a startled look. Maddox started to protest, but then Seneca showed them the phone's screen. "It's the same number as before. The same number that sent that text."

Madison blinked. Maddox's lips parted slightly. The phone kept ringing.

"*Answer* it," Maddox finally urged.

With a thumping heart, Seneca pressed the green phone icon, then put the call on speaker. "Long time no talk, my friends," sang a familiar, haunting voice over the din of sirens.

*Brett*.

# TWO

**BRETT GRADY,** a name he'd gotten used to calling himself, kept his hands at ten and two on the steering wheel, his cell phone wedged between his ear and his shoulder. Years ago, when he'd taught himself to drive, he didn't know how the phrase *ten and two* had leapt into his brain or how he'd known that it was the proper orientation for your hands. From his dad, maybe, when they used to ride go-karts? From a TV show? Still, he prided himself on always following the rules of the road to a T. Never speeding, never making crazy moves across lanes, always staying under the cops' radar. He'd passed three patrol cars today already, but they hadn't stopped him. Why would they? He was a model citizen. If those cops did notice Aerin's limp form in the backseat, they probably just figured she was his girlfriend and had decided to take a nap.

He was tickled by this tableau and decided to run with it for the few moments it was taking for Seneca Frazier to mentally get her shit together on the other end of the phone line. If a cop *did* stop Brett, he would see Brett and Aerin as a couple on a long road trip. *She's my one and only,* Brett would tell the officer, smiling sweetly at her passed-out form in the back. *We finish each other's sentences. We order for each other at restaurants. We've had tons of play-fights about songs on the radio, and I guess all that wore her out.* And actually, Brett really *did* know all those things about Aerin. She wouldn't want to listen to "Call Me Maybe" because it reminded her of her murdered sister, for instance. And if they stopped for pizza, she would like it plain, with barely any cheese.

See? He wouldn't even have to fake it.

"Are you still there?" he finally asked Seneca. His phone had gone silent. Brett wasn't surprised. Seneca was probably stunned that he'd called her directly.

There was some fumbling, and then Seneca came back on the line. "Yes. Wh-where are you? Is Aerin okay? And Thomas's car *exploded.* That was you, wasn't it?"

"So many questions." Brett could picture Seneca, with her curls and determined eyes. She probably thought she was going to entrap him, make him slip up, which felt insulting. They knew each other so well by now—she should understand that he *never* made mistakes.

He'd already known about Thomas's car accident. An app on his phone played the local police scanners; he'd heard the emergency call. Apparently, Thomas was still alive and had been taken to the hospital. Not the best outcome, but Brett hoped the injury was enough to scare the others. His nose wrinkled at the thought of that brawny, brainless interloper smiling at Aerin, touching Aerin, *kissing* Aerin . . . and Aerin kissing back. And also? *Brett* was the fifth person in their little sleuthing group. Thomas Grove couldn't crime-solve his way out of a paper bag.

"Aerin's great," he said brightly, glancing at her in the backseat.

She was slumped over, her head bent at an unnatural angle, a bubble of spittle at the corner of her mouth. Her skirt was hiked deliciously high on her thigh. "We're having a really nice time together."

"Let's talk to her, then," a new voice demanded.

Brett grinned. *Maddox.* He could just picture the guy standing next to Seneca, all coiled-up muscle and easy, jock-boy good looks. He was a little hurt by Maddox's harsh tone—he'd been a great friend, the type of guy he could chill with while playing *Resident Evil 7.* He thought with a mix of fondness and sadness about how admiringly Maddox used to laugh at his jokes. "Uh, Aerin's a bit indisposed at the moment," he said. "But she's good. Scout's honor."

"Where are you taking her?" Seneca demanded.

"It's a secret." He smoothly moved into the left lane to pass, spying yet another police car lurking behind an overpass. *Just a guy out for a drive. Just a couple on a trip. Doo-dee-doo.* "Though if you scratch my back, I'll scratch yours."

"Why would we do anything for you?" came yet another voice. It was Maddox's cute, perky sister, Madison. Interesting. So they'd *all* stayed. Well, except the one he needed to get rid of.

"Because we're old friends," he singsonged. "Aren't we?"

Silence. Brett squeezed the steering wheel tightly, then let go. He'd been kind of kidding, but kind of not. He really missed his old group. It killed him that they were all together, hanging out, brainstorming as a unit . . . and he wasn't in on the fun.

"Check your CNC messages, Seneca," he said. "I've sent you a case I've been interested in. I tried to figure it out . . . but I didn't get very far. That's where *you* come in."

He thought of the link he'd sent her just a few minutes before when he'd pulled up to refuel. *Nine-Year-Old Catskills Boy Goes Missing.* It had only happened two months ago, but a Case Not Closed file had already been opened on the kid. It was despicable how lazy cops could be, how quickly they could give up if things were just a teensy bit confusing. Did anyone in this world use their heads anymore? Did anyone care about justice?

His phone beeped. Brett glanced at it, then felt a leap in his chest. He pulled over—there was no way he was getting caught texting and driving!—and stared at the screen. The software he'd set up blinked a message. *User is ready to connect. Do you want to connect?*

Brett clicked yes. A map of Avignon, New Jersey, appeared. He'd downloaded this program from the darknet and loaded it onto Seneca's phone the night he'd broken into her room at the bed-and-breakfast in Avignon. Now, because his and Seneca's phones had connected for more than three minutes, the software had activated, and it was triangulating her phone's GPS coordinates and allowing him to track her every move. This was Brett's little insurance policy. He wanted to make sure his puppets were doing exactly what he wanted at all times.

"I don't get it," Seneca said, presumably after finishing the CNC article, which described how Damien Dover, a shy, musical nine-year-old boy, had disappeared from his New York hometown two months before. "Did you kidnap this kid, too?"

Brett scoffed as he pulled back into traffic. "You know I'd never kidnap a child."

"Why do you want us to look into this? It's a waste of time."

"A kid is missing, Seneca. That's a terrible thing. Don't you want to help?"

"Why didn't *you* solve it?" Seneca challenged. "You're the expert."

"You flatter me," Brett said, grinning. "Like I said, I *did* look into it. But then I had other things to do. So I'm delegating."

"How do we know this boy's even still alive?" Maddox asked.

Brett drove past a farmers' market sign in the shape of a dopey smiling eggplant. "I don't know for sure, but I'm hoping he is. And you're going to find him for me."

"Uh, no, we're not." Seneca sounded irate.

"That's the deal. You solve this, you get Aerin back. But no cops. If I find out you've talked to the cops, you'll never see Aerin again. And, oh, I want updates every day. If I don't hear from you, or if I don't think you're working hard enough . . ." He trailed off, letting them fill in the blanks.

"How do we know you haven't already done something to Aerin?" Madison demanded.

"Good point," Seneca said. "Put Aerin on the phone. Prove she's okay."

Brett's skin flushed all the way to the roots of his hair. *Guys, it's me! Your old pal! I saved you from a burning building, Seneca! Do you really think I'd hurt our precious girl?*

He knew it was insane to presume they'd think like that—he'd just rigged Thomas's car to go *kaboom*. Still, he'd hoped that they'd at least acknowledge that they *knew* him instead of talking to him like he was some random nutjob on a Most Wanted poster.

He glanced at Aerin's limp, sleeping form again. She looked so peaceful, the fear on her face gone. She'd been a bad girl, and she made him so angry and disappointed like so many other women he knew, but he also loved her, and the pull of love was greater than the pull of hate.

"I'm looking right at her," he said into the phone. "She's fine."

"Prove it," Seneca demanded. "Take a picture of her."

"No way. You're going to have to trust me. So start investigating. The clock's ticking."

"What do you mean?" Seneca asked. "You're giving us a time limit?"

"Let's see, today's Friday." A semitruck whooshed by him on the shoulder. "I'm going to give you three days to crack this. So until Monday."

"Three days?" Seneca sounded horrified. "You want us to solve a cold case in *three days*?"

"Eh, you guys are experts. I believe in you. Now, chop-chop! Get going!"

Then he pressed END, tossing the phone onto the passenger seat. Aerin sighed, and he glanced at her in the rearview mirror. Still sleeping. Still unaware. He tried to run through what she might say when she woke up. Let's face it, it probably wasn't going to be *Oh, how lovely! A trip, just the two of us!* It was going to be *Seneca's going to find me. Then you'll be sorry.*

And what would Brett say to that? All his kindness would vanish. He'd see her again as the girl who'd chosen another guy over him. *Sorry, but you're wrong,* he'd tell her. *Seneca and the others aren't even looking for you anymore. I've got them busy doing something else.*

# THREE

**"UNBELIEVABLE." MADDOX WRIGHT** watched as Seneca said this over and over, making wide circles around a very big floral display. "Unbelievable. Un-be-*freaking*-lieveable."

They stood in a flower shop inside the Avignon Hospital, a bright, sand-colored building that had banners of smiling, healthy people all over the walls and a man playing a classical tune on a grand piano in the lobby. Thomas had been brought here by ambulance. When they'd checked in about Thomas at the front desk, the triage nurse said that he was being evaluated and they couldn't see him yet. Because the waiting room was too crowded, they'd retreated into the chilly, plant-filled room that smelled a little too much like a funeral home. Now they were staring at one another, still trying to process what had just happened.

Thomas's explosion kept playing over and over in Maddox's mind like a Boomerang video on Instagram: his car pulling forward through the light, the smoke billowing out of the tailpipe, and then . . . *fiery inferno*.

But the conversation they'd had with Brett really had its claws in Maddox. This had gotten so personal. Well, it had *always* been personal—the Kellys had been family friends of his growing up, and it devastated him that the same monster that had murdered Aerin's sister had taken Seneca's mom away *and* manipulated all of them into being friends with him.

But now Brett had taken *Aerin*? Maddox had grown to adore her since they re-met this year. He tried to picture what she must be going through, but all he saw was scary, paralyzing emptiness. It was almost too painful to think about. He felt guilty, too—if he'd just done . . . *something* . . . maybe he could have prevented this. Why hadn't someone gone outside and stood with her to make sure all was okay? The second they dropped their guard, disaster stuck. There was no way he would take his eyes off Madison or Seneca again.

In a letter he'd written to the group just days ago, Brett said he'd had drinks with Aerin's sister, Helena, in New York, and her rejection of him might have inspired him to kill her. Was that why he'd taken Aerin, too? Any fool could see that Brett had fallen head over heels for Aerin back in Dexby. But Maddox had thought he was so harmless at the time! He'd actually felt sorry for the guy's lack of game! And now, this past week in Avignon, Brett had probably watched her in secret—and *seen* Aerin and Thomas together. The same crazy alarm bells that had rung with Helena must have gone off again. Maybe he was punishing Aerin for not choosing him.

Was he going to kill her, too?

The flower shop was so chilly, and Maddox jogged in place to get his blood pumping. It was hard to believe that just a few hours ago, he'd actually thought this whole mess was . . . well, not *over,* exactly, but at an impasse. For a few minutes, he'd figured he'd be returning home to Dexby to get ready for his freshman year at the University of Oregon, where he'd been recruited to run track and compete at the Olympic trials. He'd begun to mentally plan for buying new off-to-college boxers at Abercrombie and doing a fartlek workout around his neighborhood tomorrow. He'd thought that *maybe* they'd return to Avignon to revisit the search . . . but with Brett tying the mystery up so neatly and cleanly, would they really find any answers about him?

What an *idiot* he'd been. As long as Brett was out there, this was never going to be over. He *had* to stay here now with Aerin gone. All of them had postponed their trip home the moment they'd gotten off the phone with Brett, actually. Seneca, in her typical balls-to-the-wall way, had called her overprotective father and blurted, "Dad, I'm nineteen years old, and I can do what I want, and I'm not coming home quite yet. I'll call soon." *Mic drop.*

"Any luck?" Seneca asked, nodding at Aerin's iPad, upon which Madison was furiously tapping and swiping.

"Still trying to log in," Madison mumbled between shaky breaths as she leaned against a refrigerated case of roses. The woman behind the counter was staring at all of them blandly, disinterestedly, as though panicked individuals who had no interest in buying flowers hung out in the shop every day.

The group had strategized about how they might gather clues as to where Brett had taken Aerin. They doubted they could just call her and ask, or even send a secret text—surely Brett had already taken Aerin's phone away. But maybe Aerin had composed an SOS in those first few moments of getting into the car. Was it possible?

Aerin had an iPhone, which meant her texts and photos might be linked to her left-behind iPad, which was in Madison's lap. When Madison finally remembered Aerin's password to unlock the screen—she'd used Aerin's phone once or twice, and Aerin had recited it to her—she hadn't found any photos that had loaded to the cloud from the last hour. As far as Aerin's texts, she hadn't yet authorized them to show up on the iPad. But if they could figure out her iTunes password, the texts would load onto the device.

"I'm going to try that Viola person, too. You know, Brett's 'sister'?" Seneca typed on her phone. "Maybe she knows something about where Brett went." Maddox watched as she pulled up a new e-mail, using the address for Viola the Realtor had given her. "I wish we had a phone number," she muttered. She searched Viola's e-mail address in Google for personal details, but the inquiry yielded nothing.

"Maybe we could question people in Avignon about what they knew about the guy they knew as Gabriel, too," Maddox suggested. "Maybe he had another beach house somewhere?"

"But everyone thinks Gabriel died in a car crash." Madison didn't look up from typing.

"Uh, well, obviously *that's* a lie." Seneca pushed her phone back into her pocket, having finished the e-mail to Viola. "Unless Brett was calling us from beyond the grave."

When she sighed, Maddox saw pain flashing across her face. What had it felt like to hear Brett's voice just now? It was her mother's *murderer*. . . . He couldn't even imagine. He opened his mouth, desperate to say something to console her, to make it better, but he had no words.

Suddenly, Madison let out a *yes*. "Got it. Aerin's password is *CapnCrunch*."

"How did you figure that out?" Seneca asked.

"She used the same password for this fashion-consignment app we downloaded a couple days ago." The iPad made a *bong*; Aerin's texts loaded.

"Well?" Seneca asked impatiently. "Anything?"

Madison filled her cheeks with air, then blew out. “Nope. No text drafts.”

“Ugh.” Maddox grabbed his foot and started to stretch his left quad, then his right. Moving felt good, so he leaned over to touch his toes, feeling the muscles in his back release.

“What are you doing?” Seneca snapped, staring at him.

“I haven’t run in a couple of days,” Maddox admitted, still upside down. “I’m starting to get stir-crazy.”

“But she did send something to her mom about forty-five minutes ago,” Madison interrupted. She had moved to the part of the store that featured a whole bunch of Get Well Soon helium balloons. “And we noticed she was missing, what, an hour ago?”

Maddox stood from his stretch, feeling overwhelmed. It was hard to believe so much had happened in sixty minutes.

Madison tapped the screen. “Her text said *Me too, see you soon*. And then her mom goes, *Have a great time in LA!*” Madison wrinkled her nose. “Wasn’t Aerin going back to Dexby?”

Seneca wrinkled her nose. “Yeah, that makes no sense.”

“Aerin doesn’t write back to her mom saying one thing or another,” Madison went on. She scrolled back through previous texts. “Nor do they talk about LA before this.” She twisted the bracelet around her wrist. “Is this some future trip we don’t know about?”

But then Seneca shook her head. “Maybe Aerin *wasn’t* going to LA. Maybe Brett hacked Aerin’s e-mail and wrote about the trip. He planted that idea in Aerin’s mom’s mind.”

Madison’s eyes widened. “Brett didn’t want Aerin’s mom instantly freaking out about where she was, so he made up a story that she was leaving town for a while. So her kidnapping was premeditated?”

"Definitely premeditated." Seneca absently touched one of the balloons in the shape of Mickey Mouse and then gasped. "Could that be why Brett told us we have until Monday to solve that other case? Maybe that's when Brett-as-Aerin told her mom she was coming back."

"So if we solve it by Monday, he returns Aerin to us, and all is well." Madison tried to talk this out. "But if she doesn't, her mom starts to get worried and calls the cops. Though by then Brett and Aerin will be long gone, and we'll have to confess that we knew Aerin was missing all along and didn't do anything about it, and . . ."

Maddox stared miserably into the hospital atrium. Nurses wheeled a woman and a newborn to the exit. The pianist was playing the theme to *Star Wars*. Doctors in scrubs strolled past with coffees. Life was moving on while Aerin was trapped. It was incalculably cruel.

He felt in over his head. Brett was *crazy*. And last time, when they didn't tell the police right away, Brett twisted the story to suit his needs, *and* he got to escape. If they could just call the cops, they'd have real evidence on him this time—a surveillance photo from the hotel. And the cops had actual forensic techniques, way more than Maddox and the others had access to—especially with Thomas out of commission. The cops might be able to find a fingerprint or element of DNA that they missed. And they could investigate "Gabriel's" car crash, too. It wasn't that Maddox didn't love sleuthing—it was a huge adrenaline high, and he was thrilled when pieces of a case came together. But this all felt so precarious—lawless, even. They were *kids*. They weren't equipped to handle this.

There was another reason Maddox wanted to call in the police, and she was shivering among the floral arrangements, dressed in a breezy, floaty dress and beat-up Vans and wearing that cute,

I'm-thinking-really-really-hard expression. Seneca Frazier was the girl of Maddox's dreams. *Literally:* Every time he dropped into sleep, Seneca floated into his fantasies; each dream was sexier than the last. He felt she knew every version of him—the investigative side, the nerdy side, the insecure side. His friends from school only knew the jock side—everything else, he'd worked hard to cover up. He thought he knew her well, too—and he wanted to know her even better.

A little over an hour ago, he'd gotten up the guts to kiss her. It had felt beyond amazing, but it hadn't been enough. To him, a measly eleven-second kiss (yep, he'd mentally timed it) was the equivalent of downing a Gu energy packet after a long road race. And now that it had finally happened, he was reluctant to dive back into more danger. If Brett took Aerin and hurt Thomas, couldn't one of them be next? What if that was Seneca? Or his sister? Or *him*? No, he'd rather call the cops, hide away somewhere, let someone else handle it.

Except they couldn't. Here they were, *again,* handling it on their own.

"So I guess we jump on this other case, right?" Madison broke the silence. "This Damien kid?"

Seneca pinched the space between her eyes. "I feel for him, I really do, but I don't know if we have time."

Maddox felt alarmed. "But . . . don't we *have* to?"

"This is Brett's master plan. He's going to make us run around like chickens with our heads cut off while he plots something awful we don't see coming." Seneca looked hard from Maddox to Madison. "Think about it, guys. Aerin's kidnapping was premeditated—we already figured that out. So when did Brett plan for it, and how did he carry it out without tipping us off? It all happened while we were searching for Chelsea. While we were focused on her, Brett was securing the place where he'd take Aerin, and grabbing a getaway car that looks just like Thomas's, and figuring out how to fake his death, and watching Aerin's every move. If we look into Damien, we might fall into that trap again . . . and who knows what he has planned next."

Maddox shifted from foot to foot, still thinking about Brett picking them off one by one. Maybe Seneca had a point . . . but it seemed foolish to just ignore Brett. "He said that if we don't solve the Damien case, he'll hurt Aerin. Can't we try to solve it *and* find them?"

Seneca made a face. "I don't like dividing our efforts."

"But Brett gave us a way to get Aerin back. Shouldn't we at least try to find Damien?"

Seneca scoffed. "Since when has Brett been a man of his word?"

Maddox stared at his phone. The CNC message thread about the case was on the screen. Damien Dover, a quiet, introspective nine-year-old who loved Harry Potter, hadn't come home from school on a Thursday afternoon two months before. After searching and interviewing, the townspeople noticed that Damien's piano teacher, Ms. Sadie Sage, had vanished, too. Then the police found a surveillance camera image that was dug up from a Trailways bus station of Sadie and Damien standing together the night he was taken. They were together . . . going *somewhere*.

An Amber Alert went out, but not a single soul called in a tip. After only a month, the police held a press conference saying they'd failed. "So weird," Maddox said out loud. Why had the cops given up so easily?

He peered through the interior double doors marked *ER,* across the atrium. What were the doctors doing to Thomas in there? Would he be okay? Then he turned back to Seneca. "I think we have to do both things. Remember how Brett said that he wanted updates? What if he gets pissed when we don't have any information for him? Sure, maybe he's bluffing, but do we really want to toy with Aerin's life?"

Seneca pulled her bottom lip into her mouth and stared blankly at a huge spray of pink and purple flowers. After a moment, she let out a huge sigh. "You're right. I just hate that Brett's in the driver's seat again."

"I do, too." Maddox was glad she'd come to her senses. Sometimes, with Brett, she could get irrational, laser-focused, forgetting everyone and everything around her. He understood when she got that way, he really did—he'd go crazy, too, if he were battling the maniac who'd murdered one of his parents. It was his job, he figured, to bring her down to earth, show her the big picture.

"Excuse me?"

Maddox turned. A tall, sandy-haired male doctor in blue scrubs had crossed the atrium to find them. "You're here for Thomas Grove, right?"

"Yes." Seneca stood straighter. "Is he okay?"

The doctor pressed his lips together. "He has multiple fractures, a broken arm, facial contusions. He's also suffered a few second-degree burns, some smoke inhalation, and a possible concussion. But if his MRI is clear, he'll be on his feet in a few days."

Maddox swallowed hard. A few *days*? Then again, it could have been much, much worse. "Can we see him?" he asked in a wobbly voice.

"We have him sedated. It's best if he sleeps." The doctor gave them a kind smile. "Call the hospital tomorrow morning. He'll probably be more lucid then."

"Thanks," Seneca said gratefully. Everyone shook his hand. The doctor nodded and pivoted back toward the ER doors. Maddox felt relieved . . . but also unsettled. Where did they go from here? How would they start looking for Damien? Then he thought about Brett and Aerin together. Where were they going? What was churning in Brett's brain? If only they could talk to someone who knew the *real* Brett, not his aliases. He stared at the lettering on the hospital sign until his eyes blurred. Suddenly, an idea came to him like a bolt, and he straightened up.

"Wait a minute." He pointed at a large hotel directory that hung behind the piano guy, who was now playing, appropriately, "Piano Man." "Chelsea Dawson was brought here. We should talk to *her*. She spent hours locked up with Brett. Maybe he gave a hint about who he is, and where he might be going, or . . . something."

There was a spark in Seneca's eyes, too. "God, you're so right." She reached over and squeezed Maddox's hand. "Good thinking."

"Thanks." His stomach felt like it was swinging from one of those rope vines on *American Ninja Warrior*. He wanted to pull Seneca close. Just for a couple of minutes. Just to further define what they'd become. And to tell her, in no uncertain terms, how protective he felt, and how much her safety meant to him.

But it was time to go back into the hospital and ask some questions. Maddox's stomach twisted at the thought of coming face-to-face with Chelsea again. Just this morning, she'd been stuck in a house with Brett, forcibly obeying his every whim, probably scared out of her mind. It was the same situation, he realized with a shudder, that Aerin was in right now.

Even more reason to find out how Chelsea was doing, coming through it alive.

# FOUR

**WHEN AERIN KELLY** woke up, it felt like her tongue weighed a thousand pounds. There was a terrible taste in her mouth, too—sort of like tin, sort of like a rubber tire—and her neck was twisted at an uncomfortable angle, like she'd spent the night sleeping on a boulder.

She blinked a few times, deeply disoriented. What time was it? Where was she? A heavy blackout curtain covered a window, letting in only tiny slivers of gray light at the borders. A large, boxy air-conditioning floor unit rattled. The floor was carpeted, and the walls and ceiling were painted a flat white. The whole place smelled overwhelmingly like mint. Something *else* had smelled like mint recently—but where? The inside of somewhere. A *car.* A newly cleaned car, fresh and minty and horrifyingly wrong.

And then she remembered.

It hit her like a hammer to the back of her skull. *The hotel driveway. Dropping my bags in the trunk. Climbing in to that minty upholstery smell. And then . . . Brett.*

As her vision focused, she noticed a dark figure in a ball cap standing by a door. Her heart jumped, and she slithered toward the headboard, gutted with fear. She tried to scream, but the sound came out muffled. She raised a hand to her mouth but realized her wrists were bound together with plastic zip ties. When she touched her lips, she felt several strips of duct tape across them, sticky and strong.

She squealed, trying unsuccessfully to rip it off. Brett pounced and clamped her wrists to the headboard.

"Now, now." Oh God, his *voice*. It dripped with sarcasm. "If you're good, I'll take off the tape. But if you scream, not only will we have to leave it on, but I'm also going to have to tie your hands to the bed. You don't want *that*, do you?"

Aerin's pulse thrummed at her throat. She had never felt so afraid and disgusted in her life. Here was the man who'd haunted her dreams since she'd discovered he'd killed her sister. The man who'd insinuated himself into her life, who'd befriended her, flirted with her, almost *kissed* her, before she realized who he really was.

It sickened her that she'd so unwittingly gotten in the car with him at the hotel. She'd *thought* he was Thomas—the white Ford was exactly the same, and Brett's profile behind the tinted windows in his baseball cap hadn't given her pause. By the time she'd realized her mistake, it was too late. And now she wondered: Was she Brett's goal all along? Maybe that was why Brett had lured them all to Avignon—kidnapping Chelsea was a fun game, but it was really Aerin he wanted. Was that somehow possible? He *had* had a crush on her. He *had* seemed shaken when she rejected him, and wasn't it the girls who rejected him that he went after?

"Promise me you won't scream?" Brett asked in an eerily calm voice. Aerin frantically nodded yes.

"Are you *sure*?" Brett urged. Aerin nodded again.

Brett slowly pulled the tape from Aerin's skin. When the tape was free, Aerin let out a cough. "Where are we? What day is it? Does anyone know we're here?" She pictured Seneca and the others at the hotel. Thomas would tell them Aerin hadn't shown up. They would find her. She *knew* it. Her four best friends were crack investigators—they could solve anything.

Brett snorted. "Doubtful." Even in the dim light, Aerin could tell he was smirking. "It's nice to hear your voice, Aerin. I've missed you. Did you miss me?"

Aerin held in a joyless laugh. Was he insane?

Brett reached out and traced his fingertip along Aerin's calf. His touch felt like sandpaper, like a million tiny needles. She wanted to slap him, but there wasn't much she could do with bound wrists. And so she lay, helpless, staring at his finger as it made a figure eight across her skin.

Tears welled at the corners of Aerin's eyes. Brett didn't deserve to touch her.

She felt his fingers travel to her kneecap, and then his other hand touched her cheek. Was this what Brett had done to Helena, too? She pictured Brett hovering over her sister in her last moments, stroking her cheek, saying bullshit about how *nice* it felt, how he hoped they'd be *friends*. She wanted to throw up.

He was going to kill her. That was how this was going to end.

"Can you say you missed me, too?" Brett asked, cupping her chin.

Aerin cringed. Helena's murderer wanted her to talk sweetly to him? *Seriously?* "No," she said, shaking her head.

Brett's fingers froze on her jaw. "Excuse me?" His voice was a little sharp.

She glared at him. "I'm not going to do that."

He squeezed her jaw hard. Pain and surprise rippled through

Aerin's body, and she let out an ugly scream. Brett wrenched Aerin's face around and she was forced to make eye contact. In the tiny bit of light that came through the blinds, she saw the soullessness in his eyes.

"Did. You. Miss. Me?" he whispered, his voice low and calm.

Aerin felt her chin wobble. "Y-yes, okay, I missed you," she blurted, filling with shame.

Brett let go of her and shoved her back to the pillow. Aerin curled into a ball, her throat tight, her jaw aching.

She pictured Seneca and the others again. Were they still at the hotel? Had they figured it out? Of course Seneca wanted to find her—Seneca would never give up.

There was one question, though. Would she find her in *time*?

# FIVE

**NO ONE SPOKE** as they walked quickly through the hospital atrium, around the guy playing the grand piano, and to the information desk. With every step, Seneca felt more and more anxious. All she could think about was that Aerin was trapped with Brett. What was he doing to her? Was she scared? She prayed Chelsea would have an important clue that would guide them toward him. Chelsea had spent almost a week with the guy—she had to know *something.*

Or if not, maybe Viola would. She checked her phone, hoping Viola had gotten her e-mail and wrote back. But she had no new messages.

From behind the information desk, an aging man with tufty gray hair appraised the group. "Only two people are allowed to see psych patients at a time," he said in response to their request. "One of you will have to wait downstairs."

"I'm going," Seneca volunteered. There was no way she was twiddling her thumbs for the next thirty minutes. She wanted to hear the intel on Brett firsthand.

"I'd rather *not* go," Madison said, looking relieved. "Hospitals give me hives."

Maddox and Seneca looked at each other. "Guess it's us, then," Maddox said.

The psych ward was on the fourth floor. Seneca pressed the elevator button and waited. The doors slid open, and she and Maddox stepped inside. As the doors closed, they turned to each other at the exact same time.

"Hey." Maddox gave her a nervous, crooked smile.

Seneca's jaw twitched. "Hey."

"You okay?"

She took a breath. ". . . No."

Maddox put his arm on her shoulder and pulled her into a hug. Despite the chaos, there was a tiny flutter in Seneca's chest. She looked up, into his eyes. God, she wanted to kiss him. She wanted to forget this nightmare for a few seconds . . . but her brain wouldn't let her.

She pulled away.

"Seneca?" Maddox said.

"I'm sorry," she blurted. Maddox looked embarrassed, and she quickly backpedaled. "Not that I'm saying we shouldn't . . . you know. I just . . ." She blew her bangs off her face, hating how awkward she sounded. "Let's see where we get with Chelsea, and then go from there. Okay?"

Maddox held up his hands as if to say, *Don't shoot.* "All I was doing was hugging you."

Seneca felt a prickle of annoyance. Maddox sounded defensive. She didn't want to argue about this right now. "We should be taking this situation as seriously as possible, don't you think? We don't have time for distractions."

Maddox watched the climbing numbers. "Who said I wasn't taking Aerin seriously?"

"No, I know you are, I just . . ."

The elevator dinged, which put an end to the argument, though Seneca still felt unsettled. A sleepy-eyed receptionist wearing scrubs the color of pea soup looked up at them curiously. Seneca straightened her shoulders and walked over. "Hi. We're here to see Chelsea Dawson."

"Names?" the receptionist asked.

Seneca gave her and Maddox's names. The receptionist typed something, then frowned. "Sorry. You're not on the approved visitors list."

Seneca sniffed. "I really think she'd speak to us. Can you at least ask?"

"If you're not on the list, there's nothing I can do."

Maddox shifted from foot to foot. Rolling her shoulders, Seneca leaned toward the receptionist until their faces were level. "Look," she said in a low voice. "Miss Dawson was kidnapped. We rescued her. I'm not leaving until you ask, okay? You're going to have to drag me out the doors."

The receptionist looked alarmed, then annoyed. Seneca still didn't break eye contact. Her heart banged in her chest.

Finally, the receptionist reached for the phone. It was a crapshoot whether she was going to call a nurse or security, but then Seneca heard her say, "Dr. Lowenstein? I have some people up here who . . ." She spoke the rest in a voice too muffled for Seneca to hear.

Seneca straightened and turned around, meeting Maddox's gaze. He was agape. "You're going to get us kicked out," he whispered, though he seemed impressed.

Seneca shrugged. "Not necessarily."

The receptionist hung up the phone with a *clunk* and glowered down her nose at Seneca and Maddox. "Chelsea has agreed to speak with you, but we ask that you be brief. Someone will be out momentarily."

"Thank you," Seneca said. She shot Maddox a satisfied smile, then ambled over to him and squeezed his hand. He squeezed back. And just like that, the tension between them disappeared.

A nurse in gray scrubs—couldn't they find cheerier uniforms for the psych ward?—retrieved Seneca and Maddox and escorted them through a locked door. They passed an empty day room filled with tables, bookshelves, a TV, and a soda machine, and then a small pharmacy window, and then into a warren of patient rooms. Seneca resisted the urge to peek through each door—she'd never actually been to a psychiatric floor before, and the patients here didn't make her feel apprehensive, exactly . . . more like curious. What differentiated people sick enough to be in the hospital from those on the outside? Sometimes she worried *she* needed to be in one of these places. Especially the last couple of months, when she'd been hunting for Brett.

The nurse opened a door marked with the number *16* and pushed inside, revealing a nondescript room with a twin bed, a large window, and a pitcher of water on a small side table.

"Here are your visitors, Chelsea," she said, then stepped into the hall.

Chelsea Dawson was propped up on the bed wearing ripped jeans and a white T-shirt. Her eyes had a glazed look, and the corners of her lips angled down in a frown. Her fingers twitched in her lap, pulling at imaginary threads on her jeans, and her light blond hair was greasy at the roots. This certainly wasn't the same glamorous, lively It girl with half a million Instagram fans. Seneca's heart broke. That was Brett's fault. Just another life he'd destroyed.

"Hey," Seneca said gently, stepping closer. "How are you feeling?"

Chelsea looked slowly from Seneca to Maddox. "It's you guys." Her voice was feathery and uncertain. "You found me today."

Seneca nodded. "We'd been looking for you. We were really worried."

"Really?" Chelsea picked at the hem of her jeans. "I thought nobody cared. Nobody cares *anymore*, that's for sure."

The news had painted Chelsea as a fraud, a liar, and a narcissist. Thanks to Brett's machinations, they all thought she'd staged the kidnapping to gain social media notoriety.

"Well, *we* care," she said. "Are they treating you okay here?"

"I guess."

"Has your family come to see you?"

Chelsea lowered her eyes and shrugged. "My family . . . it's weird right now."

Seneca waited for more explanation, but none came. Was it weird with her family because her family also thought she'd lied about being kidnapped? But if that was the case, why hadn't they listened to Chelsea's side of the story? Seneca hated how air-tight Brett had made Chelsea's disappearance: He'd chosen a person who was already seen as narcissistic and flighty, made her look like the girl who cried wolf. How disempowering that must feel to have no one believe you. How utterly hopeless.

The nurse stuck her head back in. "Guys, you have ten minutes."

Seneca blinked. Only ten minutes? She had hoped to ease into this interview, get Chelsea comfortable first. It seemed callous just to barge in and ask questions. Annoyed that she didn't have a choice, she eased closer to Chelsea's bed. "I'm sorry to do this, but we have a couple of questions about what happened to you. Is that okay?"

Chelsea squinted. "Are you the police? Because they already asked me questions." She made a face as if to say, *and a lot of good* that *did.*

"No, we're . . . investigators. But we want to help you. And we think you can help us."

Chelsea's gaze dropped to her sheets. A commercial for Dunkin' Donuts blinked mutely on the TV in the corner. "Some of the counselors told me I shouldn't think about it. No one kidnapped me. It's all in my head."

Maddox scoffed. "You know that's not true."

Chelsea glanced toward the door nervously. "But denying I was ever kidnapped might be the only way I'm going to get out of here. They want me to admit I'm self-absorbed. That I set everything up because I crave attention. Maybe it's better just to go along with it."

The bright overhead light was starting to make Seneca's head hurt. Poor Chelsea was trapped in a nightmare. Everyone in her life, even doctors, were trying to tell her that Brett wasn't real.

"Look," she said sternly. "I'm no doctor, but you *were* kidnapped. If you help us, we might be able to find the guy who did this to you. Then you'll be able to get *real* treatment instead of whatever this crap is."

Chelsea began to chew on her bottom lip. Seneca could see the ambivalence rolling across her features. A bell rang somewhere on the floor. Nurses passed back and forth in the hall. Finally, Chelsea breathed in. "Okay. What do you want to know?"

Seneca breathed a sigh of relief. "Well, let me first tell you that we know Gabriel, too."

Chelsea blinked slowly. *"How?"*

Seneca and Maddox glanced at each other. *How,* indeed. Then Maddox shifted forward a little. "It's a long story, but he hurt all of us. He murdered our friend's sister."

"And my mother, too," Seneca said, her voice cracking.

Chelsea's eyes widened. "Are you serious?"

Seneca nodded, then stared at Chelsea's fingers as they tightly clutched the bedsheet. Blue veins popped out on the back of her hand. "Are you sure you're okay with us talking about this?"

"I think so," Chelsea said, though she didn't stop grabbing the sheet.

"Okay, so now Gabriel . . . well, he's kidnapped our friend, Aerin," Seneca said slowly. She checked for a negative reaction from Chelsea. The horror tumbling back, maybe. But Chelsea just stared at them, her mouth set, her eyes wide, almost like she felt vindicated, in some weird way, that it had happened again. That she *wasn't* crazy. That Gabriel truly was a monster.

"But we can't go to the cops or he'll kill her," Seneca went on. "And we have nothing to go on to find this guy, so we were hoping you could help. Anything you could tell us about him when you guys were in that house would be huge. If there's anything he told you, any way he acted, a strange habit he had, patterns he kept—"

Chelsea cut them off. "Wait. Isn't Gabriel dead?"

Once again, Maddox and Seneca looked at each other. How to say this, exactly? Was Chelsea going to freak? It was so unconceivable.

"He faked his death," Seneca finally blurted. "He put someone else in his car that looked enough like him."

For a moment, Chelsea just blinked. "So then he's still out there?" Her chin wobbled. "What if he finds me in the hospital? What if he hurts me for telling the cops about him?"

"He won't," Maddox insisted. "We'll make sure."

"Absolutely," Seneca seconded. "We promise."

Chelsea widened her eyes. "So he has a totally different look now?

What if he's already nearby and we don't know it's him? What if he's a nurse at this hospital?"

"He's not," Seneca assured her, though Chelsea's point wasn't a bad one. What if Brett *was* hiding in plain sight again? And how *were* they going to keep him from sneaking in and tormenting Chelsea? Then again, Brett sort of had his hands full right now with Aerin. He'd be foolish to come back here and face his victim. Besides, hospitals had cameras. Security. Strong narcotics they could inject Brett with if they caught him.

Then again, the doctors didn't believe Brett was real.

Once Chelsea seemed to have calmed down, Seneca took a deep breath. "Let's talk about before Gabriel kidnapped you. How long did you know him? Did he tell you anything about his family, where he was from?"

Chelsea's gaze fixed on a marker board across the room. Only the date was penned at the top, nothing else. It took her a while to answer. "We knew each other for two years before he . . . you know." She lowered her eyes, a look of shame and fear crossing her features. "I only saw him in the summers, when my family came for vacation. He might have lived in the condo year-round . . . I'm not sure."

Seneca tapped her lip. "Did he ever mention family? Maybe a sister?"

A light came on in Chelsea's eyes. She snapped her finger. "*Yes.* This one time, he said his sister taught him to play Monopoly. And he mentioned a few times they were close."

"Did he ever visit her? Do you know where she lives?"

Chelsea shook her head. "I don't think he visited her—or at least he never told me about it. But they sometimes talked on the phone."

"On a cell?"

"Actually, on a landline. I thought it was super weird that he *had* a landline, actually—I mean, who has one anymore? But he was always complaining that the cell reception wasn't great in his building."

Seneca thought about when she'd been in "Gabriel's" condo—he'd let them chill there one afternoon when he had to go to work, and it horrified Seneca now that they'd spent so many hours in Brett's private space and still *had no idea he was Brett*. She didn't recall having any cell issues in the condo, but maybe Brett used a different wireless carrier.

"Do you remember what they talked about?" she asked.

"Definitely not. He shut himself in the bedroom whenever he talked to her." Chelsea seemed to think about this for a moment. "Come to think of it, that was a little strange. I always wondered why he did that."

Maddox crossed his arms over his chest. "Did Gabriel have any unusual hobbies or interests?"

"I can't think of any interests except for surfing. He wasn't very good at it, though. Not like Jeff or the other guys. I always found that funny—the waves would pound him. But some people love things they aren't good at, you know?"

"I love playing mini golf, but I generally suck at it," Maddox agreed. "So you guys were close, right?"

"Yeah." Chelsea ducked her head. "Stupid me, huh?"

"Not at all," Seneca assured her. "Gabriel's a master at tricking people into thinking he's a safe person to be around. He did it with us, too."

"And what did you guys do together, as friends?" Maddox asked.

Chelsea shrugged. "Hung out. Went to this make-your-own frozen yogurt place a lot. Went to this other place where you paint your own pottery. I made him a mug." She looked away, embarrassed. "He was always up for listening to my problems—maybe *too* much." She laughed self-consciously. "I told him all kinds of stuff. Complained about my boyfriend, or school, or my family. He was so good at just sitting there and . . . *absorbing* it."

Seneca gripped the arms of the orange plastic chair beside Chelsea's bed. When Brett had helped them on the Helena case in Dexby, he'd listened to her problems, too. When she'd talked about her murdered mom, he'd sat there quietly, never interrupting, a big sponge sopping up her pain. Little did she know at the time that he was licking up every miserable crumb of her confession, probably thinking, *Ha. I caused this pain. I did this to her. I'm the freaking king of the world.*

"And when you hung out, was it always in Avignon?" Seneca asked. "Never in another beach town, or somewhere inland, or in another beach house?"

"Nope," Chelsea said. "Mostly we were on the deck of his condo. Rarely anywhere else."

Seneca knew that deck well. She and Maddox had sat there, too—face-to-face with Brett as Gabriel, and they hadn't even realized it. "So how about after he kidnapped you? Did his personality change?"

There was a *ding* in the hall that almost sounded like a timer going off. Chelsea stared at the door for a moment, then looked at Seneca again, her expression grave. "He did a total one-eighty." She shivered. "It was like I was meeting a totally different person . . . just with his same face. He was in total control. Icy. Terrifying."

Seneca exchanged a loaded look with Maddox. That was what Brett did time after time, wasn't it? Earn someone's trust, then snap, becoming his true self. And then he disappeared and did it all over again.

She leaned forward. "Did he ever say why he'd kidnapped you?"

"I asked. I wanted to know if I'd done something wrong. But he never said. He just talked about my Instagram followers." She laughed ruefully. "He kept wanting me to dress up and take pictures for Instagram, show everyone how pretty I was."

Seneca gritted her teeth. Of course Brett did that—it was all part of his plan to make people think that Chelsea had faked the kidnapping.

Chelsea started to wind a tendril of hair around her finger. "I will say this, though. He didn't actually treat me that badly. I had food. I had clean clothes. And he kept saying things like, *Aren't you happy about your new dress? Don't you like the shampoo I got for you?* Like he was trying to make it the Four Seasons of kidnapping situations."

"He wanted you to like him, even when you were his victim," Seneca mused aloud. "He wanted you to feel grateful, maybe. Like he was doing you a favor."

Maddox scoffed. "Some favor."

"And then there was this weird thing when he turned on the TV. The news was on, and it was a story about Gabriel Wilton being a suspect in my kidnapping. And I turned to him and was like, *They've got you* . . . but Gabriel was so collected. He said, *No, they don't*. He didn't seem bothered at all. It made me realize: Maybe this wasn't the first time he'd done this. He was so confident, so certain he was going to go free." She peeked up self-consciously. "Does that make any sense?"

"Perfect sense," Seneca said, feeling chills go up her spine. Brett was so confident about everything, wasn't he?

"Is there anything else you remember Gabriel doing the week he held you in the house?" Maddox asked. *"Anything?"*

Chelsea shook her head. "I don't think so. I'm sorry."

"One more thing," Maddox said. "Did Gabriel ever mention someone named Damien Dover . . . or maybe Sadie Sage?"

Chelsea thought for a moment. "Neither of those names sounds familiar."

Then the door creaked open. The same nurse pointed at the clock on the wall. "Okay, people. Time's up. Miss Dawson needs to rest."

Seneca turned back to Chelsea regretfully. She hated dropping all this on the poor girl and then leaving her a mess. It seemed like new circles under Chelsea's eyes had formed even since they'd been here. Her shoulders drooped. Seneca had no idea what kind of drugs the doctors had her on, but it was clear their interrogation had worn her out and put all sorts of new fears into her mind.

She brushed her sweaty palms against her dress. "Thank you. This meant so much. And don't worry, okay? We're going to find him. We'll make everyone believe your side of the story. And we'll make sure he never hurts you again."

"Uh-huh." Chelsea looked like she was about to burst into tears.

Noticing a pen and paper by the bed, Seneca scribbled down her cell phone number and e-mail. "If you want to talk, call or write. I'm serious. We know what you're going through. We don't want you to feel alone."

"Thanks." Chelsea gave a weak smile and clutched the pad to her chest. "Maybe I will."

They backed out of the room quietly, then headed for the exit. Once they were alone by the elevators again, Seneca breathed out, feeling even more despair than she had before. "Poor thing."

"Seriously." Maddox ran his hands over the back of his head as they stepped into the elevator.

The doors slid shut, and the motor began to whir. "Brett giving Chelsea the royal treatment strikes me as odd. Do kidnappers usually care for their victims like that?" Seneca said as the car passed from floor three to floor two.

"Maybe if they love them, they do," Maddox turned red at the word *love*. Seneca looked away, wondering if Brett thought he loved Aerin, too.

When they reached the main floor, they found Madison sitting on a chair near the entrance, her gaze intent on her phone screen. She leapt up when Seneca and Maddox approached. "Well, Chelsea confirmed Brett has a sister," Seneca announced. "But we didn't really learn anything new about *him*."

"But that's good," Madison said. "The sister is real. Maybe Viola knows something."

"They could be working together," Seneca said cautiously, explaining how Chelsea said Brett used to talk to Viola behind closed doors. "We need to reach her." Anxious, she composed a new message to Viola, piggybacking on the one she'd sent only an hour before. *I know we don't know each other, and I apologize for all these e-mails, but seriously, we need to talk to you about your brother. It's very important.*

Her phone made a *whoosh* as the e-mail was sent. "I wish there was another way to contact her except for this random e-mail address," she sighed. "For all I know, these messages are going to her spam."

Madison snapped her gum. "If we could access Brett's phone records, maybe we could research all the numbers he called and find Viola that way."

Maddox's eyebrows shot up. "Chelsea saw Brett talking to Viola on his landline in his condo. Do we know anyone at the phone company?"

"I'll check one of our channels at CNC," Seneca said. The site was filled with crime-solving junkies, many of whom had careers in law enforcement, medical examination, and private investigation. "I think RedBird94 might be able to access phone records."

"Sweet," Maddox said.

Seneca felt better, too. She could still hear Brett's voice echoing in her ears—teasing, laughing, totally in control. But if she had her way, he wouldn't be in control for long. She was going to find him. And maybe, just maybe, this would all finally be over.

# SIX

**"THAT'S IT, MADDOX,** I'm never going on a road trip with you again," Madison grumbled as the Jeep pulled into a parking lot in Catskill, New York, the following morning. "Since when did you acquire such road rage?" She slid out onto the blacktop. "I really thought you were going to drive *over* that Fiat on the highway."

"He was in the passing lane going forty-five," Maddox snapped. "Who *does* that?"

He felt so off today. It was because of all the running he'd skipped. His head felt murky and messy, and he could almost feel his legs tugging on him like a bored dog, asking why they couldn't go out and play. It hadn't felt quite right to go for a jog this morning, though—running was such a life-affirming activity, with all those big strides and his filling lungs and pumping heart, and it felt like a slap in the face to poor, cooped-up, traumatized Aerin. He worried Seneca would find the activity petty, too. Like he wasn't taking things *seriously*.

Except now his teeth were gnashing and he couldn't stop digging his nails into the fabric of his cargo shorts—he probably *should* have logged a couple miles. Running had always kind of been his Prozac.

He opened his car door. The air felt crisp and cool, like autumn had already arrived. Green mountains rose up around them, and every half mile there was a marker for another hiking trail. Unfortunately, earthy, woodsy places like this would forever remind Maddox of Camp Spruce Creek, where he'd gone between the ages of nine and twelve. The experience had been dreadful: rodents scurrying in the cabin walls all night, rumors about fingernails in the food, and he'd gotten lost on a hike once and had spent an hour walking around the woods in circles, freaked by every twig snap and strange shadow, panicked that he was never going to make it out alive.

Seneca's phone beeped. She pounced on it, hope on her face, but then she scowled. "Not from Viola, I'm guessing?" Maddox asked.

"No," Seneca mumbled. "*Or* from RedBird. But if anyone wants a fifty-percent-off card from Barnes and Noble, I'm your girl."

"RedBird will get in touch," Maddox assured her. Last night, in the room they all shared back in the Reeds Hotel in Avignon, Seneca had run down every lead they had on Brett . . . but she'd found very little. How could a person just dissipate into molecules? There had to be a trail of Brett *somewhere*.

On the other hand, Madison and Maddox had looked into Damien Dover and found a ton. They'd created a whole profile and timeline for Damien's disappearance. In Maddox's Google-stalking, he'd found out that the Dover family ran a place called Catskills Adventure; it sat at the mouth of a river, offered mountain bike and kayak rentals, and had ropes courses and a zip line that reminded him way too much of the one he'd nearly fallen off at Camp Spruce Creek. Now here they were. Two hundred miles north of Avignon. A whole different state. Tracking a missing kid that wasn't Aerin.

The parking lot was mostly empty, but the place opened at eight a.m., which meant the Dovers were probably already here, getting ready for the Saturday tourists. Maddox peered at the place's enormous wooden playground, giant water flume in which kids could pan for gold and other minerals, and retro ice cream stand. Had Sadie surreptitiously watched Damien here, biding her time until she could kidnap him?

"My heart goes out to the kid," Maddox had told Seneca last night, as they both lay on the king-size bed—though many hand widths apart, two remote, lonely islands. He didn't dare make a move until she said it was okay. He'd showed Seneca a recent picture of Damien. "I was just as skinny as he is when I was nine. Even had the same cowlick. And look! He's crazy for Legos, and his favorite video game is *Civilization*—I loved that game. And you know what? I bet he'd love that *What candy are you most like?* game." It was an inside joke from their web-chatting days—Seneca used to liken people in her life to brands of candy, which Maddox found adorable.

A slight smile appeared on Seneca's face. "Maddox, we're going to look into this case, okay? You don't have to try to win me over with Damien details."

"I just want you to want to look into it, too. I mean, just think—maybe looking into Damien will give us some insight into who Brett is. And don't forget that while searching for Chelsea was a distraction, we did find her in the end. What if we get Damien *and* Aerin back? Wouldn't that be a double win?"

"I know. I really do. It's just frustrating doing Brett's bidding, that's all." But then she placed her hand on Maddox's shoulder. "We're all on the same page, I promise."

Now Seneca pointed to the only building on the property, which bore the establishment's name and a sign that said *Check in for your epic saga here!* "Let's do this."

They walked toward the entrance. On the way, Maddox noticed a girl with dyed-pink hair and wearing an army surplus jacket sitting on a small hill between two pines. There was a huge camping backpack in her lap, and her hiking boots were held together by duct tape. He recognized her from some of the photos online, although her hair had been brown then.

He nudged Madison. "Is that Damien's sister, Freya?"

Madison paused, looking the girl up and down. "Yes, I think so."

Inside the building, big fans circulated the wood-smoke-scented air. An X Games pop-punk anthem played over the speakers, and signs listed the various services and rentals. Maddox noticed a man in a *Crocodile Dundee* hat and a red tee that said *Catskills Adventure* standing behind a counter. He had the same caterpillar eyebrows and tufty cinnamon-colored hair as the man in one of the video clips he'd watched, begging Damien's captor to bring his son home.

"Help you?" Mr. Dover asked the group, giving them a watery smile.

"Um, hi." Maddox stepped toward him. "We're from a group online that investigates cold cases and often comes up with insights the police missed. You're Mr. Dover, right? We heard about your son. We want to help."

The man's thin lips twitched. He glanced toward the snack bar. Just then, a woman Maddox recognized as Damien's mom appeared from a back kitchen. Her *Catskills Adventure* tee pulled across her ample stomach. Strands of graying hair had fallen out of her ponytail.

"These people want to talk about Damien," the man said to her in monotone.

Mrs. Dover went stiff. "No. If you want information, go to the police."

Maddox shifted his weight. "But we heard the police don't have any leads."

Mrs. Dover glanced helplessly at her husband. "I told you to keep people like this *out* of here, Harry."

Mr. Dover held up his hands. "I didn't tell them to come!"

Maddox noticed a flash at the window. The girl with the pink hair stood there, watching.

"Please go." Mrs. Dover's voice trembled as she turned back to them. *"Please."* She pointed to the door. At that exact moment, an eager family who looked as though they'd bought out the REI store stepped inside. They stared at Maddox and the Dover parents apprehensively, as if they'd just walked in on a robbery.

Maddox backed out of the building. The sun was too bright on the sidewalk. A waft of manure-scented mulch assaulted his nostrils. This wasn't a good start. Maybe Seneca was right—maybe they should just concentrate on Brett and only Brett.

But then he noticed a bolt of pink disappearing through the trees. *Freya.* "Hey!" he called. The girl didn't turn. "Hey!" He started after her, then glanced over his shoulder and motioned for the others to follow. "It's Damien's sister. Come on!"

His sneakers slipped on the dewy path. Just inside the canopy of trees, the world darkened. Maddox shivered in the sharp, sudden drop in temperature. Freya's pink hair flashed over a small rise in the trail, but when Maddox and the others made it over the hill, she was gone. He halted, looking around. Where the hell was she? The air was so silent and still. A shadow shifted to his right, and he jumped. Leaves rustled. Seneca cocked her head, an uneasy look on her face.

"This is the part in the movie where the aliens pop out and abduct us," Madison whispered.

As if on cue, Freya emerged from behind a tree. Everyone jumped. Madison let out a scream. "What part of *please leave* don't you people understand?" the girl yelled.

"It's okay," Maddox urged, his heart pounding in his ears. "We just want to talk to you. We want to help with your brother."

Freya stared at them, nostrils flaring like some kind of wild animal. After a beat, she took a few steps back down the trail, then darted to the left. Everyone followed. The trail opened into another clearing, and there the group saw a large tent. There was a little stone campfire in front of it, and from a clothesline hung a bunch of rusty bells and tin cans.

Freya noticed Maddox studying it. "That's to keep the bears from eating my food."

Madison made a freaked-out *eep*, but Maddox stood his ground. "Why won't you let us help you?"

Freya waved her hand dismissively. "The police thought they could help, too. But guess what? They didn't find shit." Her expression hardened. "Get out of here."

She was about to scramble into the tent, but then Seneca cried, "Wait."

Freya turned.

"I know how it feels to be left in the dust by the authorities—when my mother was killed, the cops acted like assholes, mishandling evidence, not following the right leads, basically dropping the ball left and right, and we never brought the killer to justice." Seneca paused a moment, letting Freya take this in. The girl's mouth twitched, but her eyes were still cold. "We're from Case Not Closed. It's a real site with real people who solve cases the police have abandoned. We really *do* get results."

Freya looked them up and down for a few long beats. Finally, she groaned. "God. *Fine,* okay?"

Seneca sank into one hip. "Are you going to actually talk, then?"

"Are you going to actually *help*?" Freya shot back.

"Tell us about what happened to your brother, and we'll see what we can do."

Freya flopped down outside the tent and motioned for the group to sit on a few logs strewn around the campfire. "One day Damien was here; the next day he wasn't," she droned. It sounded as though she'd given this speech many times. "They think it was our piano teacher, but I'm guessing that if you're such experts, you already know that."

"We do," Maddox said quietly. "Sadie Sage."

Freya wrinkled her nose. "It sounds like a fake name. That should have tipped me off."

"Did you know her?" Seneca asked.

"Uh, *yeah*. I took lessons from her, too. Maybe I should have seen this coming."

Maddox cocked his head, intrigued. "Why?"

"Well, she was . . . weird. *Really* into Halloween. Celebrated it all year round. She taught piano in this music facility a few towns over, and all the rooms were just generic classrooms with, like, instruments in them. But she decorated hers. It looked crazy. You'd be playing

Beethoven beneath a large gargoyle and a skeleton wearing a witch's hat. She had other weird stuff in there, too—a bunch of birdcages with no birds inside, tiny doll shoes all lined up on a windowsill, old surgical tools."

Madison's eyes widened. "What kind of tools?"

"Nothing harmful—they were behind glass, and nothing was sharp, but it was just . . . odd. Though when the cops first made the connection that Sadie had disappeared the same time Damien did, I was like, *Oh, they only suspect her because she's goth. They're just judgmental, narrow-minded old people.*"

"But maybe they were right?" Madison guessed.

Freya picked up a pinecone, peeled off its layers, and flicked them to the ground. "The cops told us that child predators often offer something tempting to kids, something they can't resist. Which made me remember." Her expression closed off, like she didn't want to go on.

"Remember what?" Maddox asked.

Something rustled in the underbrush nearby and a bird let out a lonely cry. "Sadie talked about how she wanted to take her students to Orlando to visit the theme parks," Freya said. "Damien was dying to go to Orlando, too—he used to watch all these YouTube videos about Universal Studios. He asked our parents if we could go, but it was too expensive. Maybe Sadie picked up on that. Maybe she surprised him with tickets."

Seneca frowned. "Would he have just *left* with her, though? Without asking?"

"I guess, because he's gone now, isn't he?" Freya looked like she was either going to burst into tears or punch one of them.

Maddox cocked his head. "Why do you think Sadie kidnapped

him? Did he fight with your parents a lot? Maybe that's Sadie's angle—she thought that by taking Damien away, she was 'saving' him from a bad situation?"

Freya rolled her eyes. "That is *such* a cop question."

Maddox felt a twinge, wondering if Thomas had rubbed off on him. He made a mental note to call the hospital soon to see if Thomas had woken up yet.

"I don't think she was trying to save him," Freya went on. "I think she took him for another reason."

"Which would be . . . what?" Seneca asked.

Freya pressed her lips together. "She really loved kids. Maybe wanted some of her own. And she seemed to *really* love my brother. I would catch her looking at him in this sort of marveling way, you know? Like she couldn't believe he existed."

Madison looked uncomfortable.

"It wasn't, like, *freaky*," Freya said quickly. "I didn't get a vibe that she was one of those teachers who want to sleep with their students. It was more of a spiritual thing. It's hard to explain."

There was a long pause. Somewhere above the trees, Maddox heard an airplane. The wind shifted, and he caught the scent of Seneca's coconut shampoo.

"I'm guessing she didn't take him to Orlando?" Seneca asked.

"Nope. They took a bus to New York City. I guess they could have gotten on another bus to Orlando, but the bus company has no record of it. Maybe that bitch used a fake ID or stole someone's car. Before the cops decided we weren't worth it, they scanned tons of surveillance images from Universal, Disney, Six Flags—any park we could think of. Nothing came up."

"Could they have stayed in New York City?" Maddox suggested.

Freya wrinkled her nose. "I hope not. Damien hates the city."

"It would be hard to hide someone in New York City," Seneca said. "There are so many surveillance cameras and cops. He might be somewhere more remote."

"Or he's dead." Freya's voice had a daring, I-don't-give-a-shit edge.

"I doubt it," Maddox said.

Seneca's head shot up. She shook her head ever so slightly. *No.*

But Freya was already turning to him, her expression one of begrudging hope. "Oh yeah? And how would *you* know?"

Maddox swallowed hard. He shouldn't have said that. It's not like Brett offered any proof. "I—I just meant that according to the profiling we've done, it doesn't *seem* like she's the type who'd kill him," he stammered. "It's of our opinion that she took him somewhere—but that he's okay."

Freya's sarcastic frown was back. "Because you're such the expert."

Seneca drummed on her knees. "The police reports say she didn't send any ransom notes."

Freya shook her head. "She never reached out to us."

"Is there anything they found out about Sadie that we could investigate ourselves?" Maddox asked. "Did she have friends we could talk to? People in the town who knew her well?"

"The cops told my parents that she had no friends."

"She never got any phone calls during your lessons?" he pressed. "You never saw her out in public with anybody?"

"I don't even remember her *having* a phone, and I never saw her out in town at all." Freya smirked. "Now do you see why the cops dropped the case? There's nothing to go on."

Maddox gritted his teeth. "There has to be. People don't just appear out of thin air. Sadie has to have a history. She has to have family, friends . . . from *somewhere*. The police could use that for leads."

"Nope." Freya smiled like she was about to get to a punch line. "Sadie's records go back just three years, when she moved here. Before that, she doesn't exist."

The world went still. When Maddox looked up, Seneca was staring at him, probably thinking what he was thinking—that sounded a hell of a lot like someone *else* they knew.

They asked Freya a few more questions, mostly about what Sadie Sage was like during piano lessons—*like a freaking piano teacher, what else?*—and whether kids ever took lessons in her house—*nope, and I have no clue where she lived, though I'm pretty sure the police know because I heard they searched her place and found it empty*. Finally, Maddox stood and stretched his arms over his head. "Thanks for talking to us."

Freya snorted. "It's not going to do any good."

Seneca's gaze lingered on the tent. "Are you sleeping here?"

Freya shrugged and avoided eye contact. "Maybe."

"What's wrong with home?"

She sniffed. "It's none of your business." And with that, she crawled into her tent and zipped up the flap. Fast, angry punk rock blasted through some speakers, though she stuck her head out once more and looked at Seneca. "Sorry about your mom or whatever."

On the walk back to the car, Maddox stepped in a puddle that soaked his shoes through. "She reminds me of Aerin when we first met her," Seneca said after a while. "Remember how combative she was? How closed-off? I'm surprised *she* wasn't sleeping in a tent in the woods."

"And what about Sadie Sage, huh?" Madison whispered. "Luring kids to Orlando? No records beyond three years ago? She obviously changed her identity. But why?"

"She's the female version of Brett," Seneca murmured as she climbed into the passenger seat. "She slips in and out of the public eye. She's a zillion steps ahead of everyone else. She has an endgame . . . but we don't know what it is. Just like we don't know what Brett's is."

Madison's eyes popped wide. "What if *she's* Brett's sister? Viola?"

Maddox twisted his mouth. "In the stories about her, it says people estimated her to be in her mid-forties when she took off with Damien. Not that we know *exactly* how old Brett is, but he doesn't look much older than twenty-five—that puts them twenty years apart."

"Let's not rule it out completely," Seneca said, looking disarmed . . . but also excited. "I never even *thought* of that, Madison."

"Well, whoever it is, we need to find her," Maddox said, feeling his stomach twist. "Because for all we know, this endgame—with Aerin—it's going to happen soon."

# SEVEN

**AERIN SLEPT FITFULLY** through the night, and in the morning, everything hurt: her stomach, her back, her eyeballs. She was dying for a Tylenol, but she didn't want to ingratiate herself to Brett and ask. In the wee hours before dawn, she lay on the bed, her wrists and ankles zip-tied, her eyes wide open in panic. She forced her brain to think about anything besides if she'd ever make it out of here alive.

She thought about kissing Thomas until the daydreaming became too painful. She thought about food because she had refused to eat anything Brett had given her—she'd rather die by starvation than let that asshole have the pleasure of killing her. She thought about her mom going through her daily routine: getting ready to pop in on the Scoops ice cream franchises to make sure everything was running smoothly. Going to yoga at Dexby Bikram. Making a Blue Apron meal for dinner. How could her mom not know she was imprisoned with a madman? Wasn't there some sort of ESP mom alarm that went off when your kid was in danger? Had Helena thought the same thing just before Brett killed her?

The only thing that calmed Aerin was a hallucination of Helena shortly before the sun came up. When she looked toward the door, she swore she saw Helena's flickering, ethereal figure, her blond hair cropped close, the white coat with the fur collar she'd worn the last day Aerin ever saw her zipped to her throat, a soothing smile on her face. Her sister walked toward her, eerily translucent, regally calm. *It's going to be okay,* she said. *I promise. You just need to find your way out.*

*How?* Aerin asked. But then Helena had popped like a soap bubble.

As the light filtered in, she started to investigate the space some more. There was a bureau against the far wall—could she tip it, somehow, and smash through the room's only window? But she probably wasn't strong enough, and she'd need use of both hands. The only time Brett let her out of the zip ties was when she needed to use the bathroom . . . and then he remained close, hovering like a prison guard.

She slithered off the bed, wriggled to the window, and lifted the heavy curtain. The glass was boarded up—so there was no getting out that way. Aerin pressed her ear to the window and listened for clues, footsteps, a train horn, *anything* that might give away where they were. Out of nowhere, there was a rumbling. She froze. It was a construction truck of some sort. It beeped to back up. Stopped, then beeped again.

That noise wasn't going to get her out of here, though. Aerin struggled back to the bed and flopped onto the mattress, exhausted. So maybe the bathroom was the answer—Brett let her close the door while she used it, and there was a tiny window near the ceiling that let in light and fresh air. Was there something Aerin could use to stand on to reach the window and climb out?

Suddenly, the door swung open. Aerin's body filled with dread.

"Rise and shine, sleepyhead." Plates clinked as Brett set them on the nightstand. "Made you an egg sandwich. It's just as yummy as that one we got from the food cart after that party in New York. Remember how awful you felt?"

Aerin pressed her head into her sweaty pillow, feeling a twinge of discomfort. Hungover after that party Brett had thrown at the Ritz-Carlton, she'd devoured the egg sandwich in practically one bite. Still. *Don't pretend like you know me,* she thought angrily.

But Brett was still talking. "Everyone was wrecked that morning." He chuckled lightly. "But I'll always remember that party. It was the best night of my life."

Aerin turned away. She knew where he was going. They'd almost kissed that night. He was trying to remind her.

The mattress springs squeaked as Brett sat down next to her. He undid her bound wrists and ankles, his fingers lingering on her skin. "Everything okay?"

His hand grazed her calf. An oily sensation spilled through her, and she felt her stomach contract. She didn't dare move, though. Reacting meant his touch affected her. She wanted him to understand that she felt *nothing* for him.

"I get it. You don't have to talk." Brett pulled his fingers away and leaned back. "But listen. If you eat, I'll tell you about my conversation with Seneca yesterday."

Aerin held her breath. *Good.* Seneca knew. That buoyed her spirits. Only, why was Brett communicating with Seneca directly? That seemed foolish on his part.

But no. She wouldn't ask. She wouldn't play by his rules.

"I mean, don't get your hopes up," Brett went on in a teasing voice. "Seneca knows we're together, but I told her that if she goes to the cops, she'll regret it."

Aerin's nose twitched. *Don't move. He's just trying to get a rise out of you.*

Then he patted the mattress. "By the way, is this comfy enough? I bought it special for you—a Serta pillow top. It's the same model your sister died on."

It felt like he'd stabbed a fireplace poker clean though her body. Unwittingly, Aerin's head shot up, and she stared at him, eyes wide. He held her gaze, amused. Her heart was beating in her throat. This guy could kill her so easily. He knew everything about her. He knew her weaknesses, her tells. What she needed to do, then, was be anything *other* than that girl, someone he wouldn't understand. But that was easier said than done.

The smell of almond butter was making Aerin woozy. She sat up, all at once wanting to get started on her escape plan immediately. "I want to take a shower."

Brett's eyes narrowed. "All of a sudden you want to take a shower?"

"Yes."

He looked her up and down. "You're clean enough. It hasn't even been twenty-four hours since you last took one."

A half smile shimmered onto his face, and Aerin felt an uneasy frisson. Maybe Brett was bluffing, or maybe he really did know the exact moment she'd taken a shower yesterday. It knocked her off her game, and it took everything inside her not to back down.

"I. Want. To. Take. A. Shower," she repeated.

"Fine." Brett held his hands up in surrender. "You have ten minutes."

Aerin dashed through the bathroom door and shut it tight. To her chagrin, the door didn't lock. She looked around for a surveillance camera but didn't see one.

She turned on the shower to drown out the sounds of her movements, then peered at the little window near the ceiling. It seemed to open by pressing up a small, metal handle in the casing. Using the toilet plunger, she poked at the lever until it creaked open an inch, filling her with joy. If she got up there, she could press it open farther and crawl out.

But how could she climb high enough? As the room filled with steam, Aerin opened the cabinet under the sink. The only items were bathroom spray and a package of toilet paper. Aerin pulled out the toilet paper, placed it on the ground next to the wall, then tried to stand on it, but it didn't support her weight or get her nearly high enough to reach the window.

Shit. *Shit.* Aerin grasped the sides of the sink and stared at her panicked reflection in the mirror. Then something on the counter caught her eye. It was a short brown hair. Definitely not hers—so, Brett's?

She stared at the hair for a moment, knowing it might be useful, somehow. Then she opened one drawer, and another, looking for some way to store it away. Finally, in the bottom drawer, she found a small case for contact lenses. She rinsed and dried it, carefully dropped the single hair inside, and tucked the case into her pocket.

There was a knock on the door. "Ten minutes are up!" Brett called from the other side.

Aerin froze. That was impossible; only three minutes had passed, max. She shoved the toilet paper back into the cabinet just as Brett burst into the room. He seemed confused about the open cabinet and running shower. Then his gaze darted to the little window—it was almost as if he *knew* what she was up to.

Aerin's heart sank. "I . . ." She fumbled for an excuse, but what excuse could she give?

Brett's eyes narrowed. She could practically feel the fury settling over him. As she moved to turn off the shower, he pounced on her, pushing her to the tiled floor. Aerin let out a yelp, but Brett clapped a hand over her mouth, his fingers squeezing roughly at her throat.

"You really think you're smarter than me?" Droplets of saliva hit her cheek, mixing with the swirling steam. "You should be bowing down to me, kissing my feet that I've been so kind to you, speaking to you nicely, making you food, *not killing you yet*. Because you think you know me, but you *don't* know me." He pounded hard on the floor, his fist mere inches from her body. "*You. Don't. Know. What. I'm. Capable. Of.* For instance, want to know where your lame little boyfriend is right now? The hospital."

Aerin's heart stilled. "What? Why?"

"Because I put him there. I can make those kind of things happen. You should know that by now. So you'd better adjust your attitude, or this is going to get pretty rough."

Aerin pinched her eyes shut. "I'm sorry," she said, her voice muffled. She could smell the bleach on the bathroom tiles. A faint breeze blew in from the open window, cooling her skin.

"What was that?"

"I—I'm sorry!"

Brett yanked her up, dragged her into the bedroom, threw her back on the bed, and bound her wrists and ankles with fresh zip ties. Then he pivoted, knocked the coffee and toast to the dingy floor, and marched out of the room, slamming the door hard.

Aerin collapsed back onto the mattress in a flurry of sobs. *Thomas,* she thought desperately. What had Brett done to him? Was he going to live? Had Brett hurt him *because of her*?

Anger flooded her, followed by desperation, followed by a humiliating pang of pain. Her fingers inspected her neck—it already felt tender, and she'd probably have bruises within hours.

But maybe Brett had a point: He *hadn't* killed her yet. Maybe she *should* be grateful about that. She had to find a way to prevent him from doing that for as long as she could—maybe that was the only way she'd *find her way out,* as Helena had said. Because what just happened? She couldn't bear it happening again.

Aerin shut her eyes, an answer suddenly occurring to her. It wasn't an answer she particularly liked, but it might be the only thing that would save her life.

# EIGHT

**"IT'S THE NEXT** left up here." Seneca gestured to the turnoff that was approaching. Maddox wrenched the Jeep's steering wheel, its tires careening over pitted road. Up ahead, a squat brown building sat alone in a parking lot. The only thing that indicated they were in the right place was the several police cars parked in the back with faded lettering reading *Catskill Police Department* printed on the side.

Maddox turned off the ignition, but no one moved to get out of the car. They were huddled around Maddox's cell phone, talking to Thomas at the hospital. "Don't check yourself out early," Seneca said into the speaker. "You haven't had your MRI yet."

"But I have to." Thomas's voice sounded thick and sleepy. "I have to help you find Aerin. I can't believe this is happening."

"We're on it, bro," Madison assured him. "We're going to find her. Right now, we just need for you to get better."

They hung up and sat in silence. It had been rough to call Thomas and break the news about all this, but Thomas deserved to know. Seneca still felt a little guilty, though. What kind of panicked, helpless thoughts were rushing through Thomas's mind? Did he feel afraid? If Brett had tried to hurt him once, he could do it again, especially now that Thomas was vulnerable and weak.

Which meant they needed to find Brett, and fast. And that meant finding Damien, too. Maddox was right—they had no other choice but to follow Brett's orders. And after talking to Freya, Seneca felt all in. The story about Damien's disappearance struck a chord, and she now felt for the kid, for his family, and angry at the useless police force who'd dropped the ball. And also, *could* Sadie be Viola? It was an interesting idea. On the other hand, would Brett point them toward a crime his sister committed? What was his endgame? What sort of bread crumbs was he dropping for them to follow?

Seneca rolled her shoulders back and pushed open the door to the Jeep. Silently, the three of them strode across the gravel to the front door of the police station. The lobby smelled like woodsmoke and looked like the inside of a hunting cabin, with its wood-paneled walls and exposed beams. There was a very old soda machine in the corner, buzzing away. A small table fan blew at an empty chair at the front desk.

"Hello?" Seneca called out.

A door to the back creaked open. A large woman in a T-shirt printed with two vicious-looking wolves ambled out, intently studying something on her phone. She held a two-liter bottle of Coke tucked under her other armpit and was humming what sounded like Taylor Swift's "Look What You Made Me Do." When she looked up and saw them, she jumped, then frowned. "Yes?"

Maddox stepped forward nervously. "Yes, hi. My name's Thomas Grove, and I'm from the Dexby, Connecticut, police department and have some family in the area. I was wondering if I could talk to the officer on duty?"

"I'm the officer on duty." The woman turned around a placard on the desk Seneca hadn't noticed and tapped it with a long fingernail. It read *Officer Lorna Gregg.*

"Oh, great," Maddox said, not missing a beat. "Any way I can access the records on the Damien Dover case? Interviews, any forensics, things like that?"

Officer Gregg twisted off the cap to the Coke bottle. It made a creepy hiss. "Can I see some credentials? You don't look like a cop. You look like a kid."

Maddox blushed. He made a show of riffling in his pockets for a badge. "If you call the station in Dexby, they can vouch for me, I swear. . . ."

"Just stop," Officer Gregg snapped icily. All signs of friendliness were gone. "You know it's a crime to impersonate an officer, right?"

Maddox stopped riffling through his pockets. Seneca swallowed hard. "We're really just trying to help," she jumped in. "Can you at least tell us where Sadie Sage lived?" The only thing they'd been able to find online was that Sadie Sage rented a property in Catskill. They'd called every rental agent in the area, but no one copped to being Sadie Sage's landlord. Only a fellow music teacher, Dahlia Quinn, gave them a hint: Sadie was always talking about how wherever she lived was "all her own"—she was the first person who'd ever rented it. Meaning she could put her mark on the place, the teacher surmised. But was it a brand-new place? Or undesirable, somehow?

The officer shook her head. "I can't give out those kind of details to the public. It's still an open investigation."

Seneca felt annoyance rising inside her. "Open investigation? We heard you let the case drop. I would think you'd want all the help you can get."

Officer Gregg shot her an annoyed look, then started busily flipping through some papers on her desk. "I'd advise you kids get out of town. And you"—she glowered at Maddox—"don't ever pretend you're an officer again. You're lucky I didn't put you in cuffs."

Maddox mumbled something under his breath and turned to leave, but Seneca stayed put. She wasn't done with this lady yet. "Why aren't you working harder to find Damien? Why are you in your office, swigging Coke, too lazy to even put on a uniform?"

Officer Gregg's eyes flashed. *"Seneca,"* Maddox whispered warningly.

But now that Seneca had gotten started, she couldn't stop. Damien deserved a better investigation. The whole family did. And yes, okay, maybe she was conflating this situation with her *own* family's experience—how the police didn't do much to find her mother's killer, either—but justice was justice. "What other crimes do you have to worry about up here?" She gestured to the mountains out the window. "Why didn't you call in reinforcements from other towns? Why didn't you have fund-raisers and bump this up to a national story? It was barely a blip on a website—and it's a *missing boy*. Someone's child. A family's life is *ruined*."

Maddox's nails dug into her arm. Okay, maybe she was becoming overwrought—but this cop needed to understand.

Officer Gregg rose to her feet. Her hand drifted to her waist; under her T-shirt was a holster holding a black handgun. "Threatening an officer is a crime, too, you know."

Seneca flinched but didn't back down. "Just let us check out her house. Give us ten minutes."

The officer pointed to the door. "Get out. Now."

"But—"

"Get out, or I'll slap you with a fine. You want that? And if I hear you're nosing around that place, I'll have you arrested for trespassing."

Seneca stared her down. The phone on the desk started to ring. Officer Gregg let it go, still watching them, her hand still on her belt. A lump formed in Seneca's throat. There was no winning with this woman. "Fine," she muttered, swiveling on her heel.

"*Now* what do we do?" Maddox muttered as he unlocked the Jeep.

Seneca peered through the smeared glass window of the station. Gregg had answered that phone call, and now she was propping her feet up on her desk, laughing like she didn't have a care in the world. As the woman switched the receiver to the other ear, Seneca thought of her own phone, tucked into her pocket. She pulled it out and checked it for the fiftieth time this morning. "*Still* no Viola," she muttered bitterly. "Maybe she *is* Sadie."

"And still no RedBird?" Maddox asked.

"I even sent her a second message through CNC, and nothing." No leads, *anywhere.*

They got in the Jeep and just sat there for a while. Maddox started to do arm stretches, and then waist twists, huffing through his nose as he pulled deeper into the stretch. "Will you *stop* that?" Seneca snapped finally.

"Sorry." Maddox let his arms fall to his side. "I have a lot of nervous energy."

"We could drive around, ask people if they know anything," Madison suggested from the back. "And also, the house has to got to be around here somewhere. Maybe we'll just run into it. Wouldn't it be the one covered in police tape?"

"It's not like we have any other plans," Maddox said, starting the engine.

They drove down the highway and into the little town. As Sadie Sage theoretically had to get supplies from somewhere, they stopped in at a small grocery store called Wink's and waved her picture to everyone from the cashiers to the guy running the deli counter to a derelict-looking preteen hanging out outside the shop. Everyone was sympathetic but standoffish—"Oh yes, that poor boy," an older woman bagging groceries said. "I think I saw that Sadie woman once, but I don't know much about her."

"You know, I don't have a clue where she lived," answered a man at the pharmacy—apparently Sadie stopped in to buy over-the-counter medications and sudoku puzzle books, but she never received any prescriptions that would have required her to give an address or phone number. "She didn't talk much. Really kept to herself."

They found the building where Sadie taught piano, an office complex that also housed several dentist's offices, a dry cleaner's, and a large outdoor fountain whose tiled bottom was littered with pennies. But the door to the music classrooms was locked tight, and there was no one around to let them in. Seneca wished she could look through the classroom Freya had described—it seemed full of her personality and maybe rich with a clue. Then they heard a *"Psst,"* behind them. A lithe, hippie-ish woman was hanging out the door to a yoga studio, staring them up and down as though she knew exactly what they were doing.

"We already went in there after-hours," the woman whispered, looking shadily back and forth to make sure no one was listening. "There's nothing left in that woman's office. *Nothing.*" Her eyes widened. "And for three years, I said *namaste* to her in the parking lot. I had no idea. . . ."

Everyone trudged back to the Jeep, feeling aimless. Seneca checked her phone *again*. Surprise surprise, no RedBird, no Viola.

"I'm really sorry, guys, but I'm starving," Madison admitted later, as they passed a hot dog shack on the side of the road. "Can we stop?"

Seneca wanted to keep going, but her stomach was growling, too. Maddox did a three-point turn and headed back. After they parked, Madison got in line for hot dogs, and Seneca sat on a bench and stared fixedly at the mountains. Maddox tentatively touched her shoulder, and she jumped.

"That stuff you said to Freya about the police screwing up your mom's case. I didn't realize it was that bad."

Seneca felt flushed. "Oh. Yeah."

"You want to talk about it?"

Across the gravel lot, a kid was flying a dragon-shaped kite. Or trying to, anyway—there was little wind, so he was just running with the thing and most of it was dragging on the ground. Part of Seneca *wanted* to tell Maddox everything she'd gone through. Like how it was almost criminal that the cops came up with absolutely nothing from the crime scene, and how that made her feel so powerless and lost.

But it also felt . . . well, *hard.* She'd built a wall in her brain between those soft, squishy, terrible feelings surrounding her mother and her semi-normal, semi-functioning self. Delving too deeply into the details would break down that wall, and what lay behind was pretty dark. Like how she'd ripped her mom's necklace off her body in the morgue. Like how she'd lie in bed some nights, holding her breath for as long as she could, trying to feel what her mom must have felt before she died. And then there were all the complicated emotions she had when Helena Kelly's story hit the news and took up all the available air space, pushing her mom's death to the bottom of the pile. And what about her feelings of satisfaction—or maybe relief—when Helena's case wasn't solved? It wasn't that she wanted Helena to have an unhappy ending.

She'd just selfishly wanted someone else out there to feel as miserable as she was. Did other people who had tragedies in their lives think this way . . . or was it just her?

The crunch of gravel interrupted her thoughts. Madison walked back balancing three hot dogs and sodas in a cardboard carrier. "I have news," she singsonged. "Sadie's house is at 101 Frontage Road. Only two miles away, but it's through this road in the forest that isn't marked."

Seneca blinked. "How'd you figure out *that*?"

"I flirted with the guy who works the hot dog stand, and when I asked him about Sadie Sage, he said he knew her address. And get this—the guy heard that when the cops went into the place, there was absolutely no furniture. She must have cleaned it out before she left."

"Huh." Seneca frowned.

"Why would she do that?" Maddox asked, reaching for his hot dog.

"Probably so the cops would have no leads on who she was," Seneca murmured. "No fingerprints, either, and no DNA."

"Where did all the stuff go? Did she get a dumpster? A moving van? No one's fessing up that they helped her?"

"Maybe she paid someone off." Madison plopped down on the bench next to them. "You never know."

"And no one saw her moving her stuff onto the lawn or into a van?" Seneca asked. "Not a single witness?"

"We'd know that if we had the police records." The bite Maddox took of his hot dog was so big that half the thing was already gone. "Maybe Thomas could pull some strings?"

Seneca considered this, but then shook her head. "We shouldn't bother Thomas unless we get really desperate." Of course, Thomas would be pissed off if he knew she'd said that, but she would rather he focus on getting better.

On the road, as if on cue, a huge moving truck rumbled past. Seneca stared at it for a while, its motor growling, its pure hulking size creating its own windstorm. Something shifted in her mind. "I bet Sadie dumped her stuff somewhere. It seems crazy that she'd carry her whole house on her back while on a kidnapping rampage."

"True," Madison said, wiping mustard off her face.

"Should we check out the house?" Maddox asked, standing.

"Definitely," Seneca said.

Madison tossed her napkin in the trash, then waved flirtatiously at a pudgy man in a ball cap who was handling the next customer. "Thanks again!" she trilled. "Bye-ee!"

The drive to Sadie's old place took no more than five minutes before they spotted a black mailbox at the side of the road marked *101.* A small, square, tidy brown house was nestled into the hillside. There wasn't a car in the driveway, there weren't any lights on inside, but shreds of yellow police tape were evident all over the property—snagged on tree branches, lying across the grass, even wound around a lightpost. This had to be it.

They parked on the road and walked slowly to the property. Maddox peered through the front window. "Hot Dog Guy wasn't lying. There's just a bunch of spiderwebs inside."

Seneca tried the doorknob, but it was locked. She checked the porch's floorboards for a hidden key, but there wasn't one. She spun around and stared out at the view, a 360-degree vista of trees, mountains, and clouds. They hadn't seen a single car as they'd driven up this road—so maybe there *hadn't* been any witnesses seeing Sadie pack up her things. But who would live here in the first place? Someone who wanted no contact with other humans. Someone who was starting over. Though starting over from *what*, Seneca still didn't know.

She stepped off the porch and padded around the side of the house, shining the flashlight into each window. An ancient clothesline drooped between two poles. A sectioned-off area that might have once been a garden was now overrun with weeds. Suddenly, Seneca's foot caught on something in the ground a few inches from the side of the house. She stumbled forward. After getting her balance, she turned around and looked at what she'd tripped over. At first glance, there was nothing special about the ground—no roots poking up, no piles of rocks. The spot did slope a little, though, almost as though the grass made a small shelf. And when she cautiously pressed the grass with her toe, the ground felt hollow and unsupported. Seneca dropped to her knees and pulled up hanks of grass. Just an inch down was . . . *wood*. She scraped away at more grass until she revealed part of what had to be a storm cellar door.

"Whoa." Maddox knelt down beside her.

Seneca brushed dirt of her hands. "I think this is some sort of storm shed. It probably leads to a basement. My grandma had a trapdoor like this."

After more digging, she found a partially rotted handle. The door creaked a little, huge roots ripping as they were torn from the earth, but finally the door budged open a few feet, revealing a set of small, dark steps.

"Hold this open for me," she told Maddox, then angled her body to squeeze through the crack and head down the stairs.

"Are you sure?" Maddox held the door obligingly, but he looked horrified. "You don't know what's down there. . . ."

Seneca stared into the abyss again. She had a feeling the cops didn't know this was here. *This could be her answer.*

"Whatever's down there had better watch out," she said. "I'm going in."

# NINE

MADDOX WAS COOL with horror movies. He could man up and watch chain-saw-wielding maniacs chase teenagers, or a flickering ghost girl traumatize people through the telephone lines. But when he saw his girlfriend do the classic horror movie thing—go down into a dark, musty, abandoned storm shed—he felt guilty for all the times he sat back, binged on popcorn, and watched the ax murderer chop the leading lady to pieces.

He scrambled after Seneca, clicking on his flashlight to light the way.

"Maddox!" Madison hissed above his head. "Don't leave me up here alone!"

"I'll only be a sec," he promised his sister. "Just keep a lookout, okay?"

"I'd rather not!" Madison screeched, but she made no move to follow them down.

The flashlight's beam bounced across spiderwebs, crumbling bricks, and motes of dust. An ancient hot water heater sat in the corner.

And as the light danced across the wall, he saw dark slashes of . . . *something.*

"Is that *blood*?" he cried, holding the light there.

Seneca crept closer, pointing her flashlight along the wall. "Just dirt, dude. Chill."

Maddox shuddered. It smelled nasty down here, sort of like a sewer line gone wrong. The air was close and claustrophobic. When he walked through a silky spiderweb, he let out a yelp and started pawing at the air. He glanced over his shoulder nervously at the small sliver of light shining from the stairs. What if Sadie Sage was still on the property and locked them in? What if this was a trap and *Brett* was here?

"Okay," he whispered. "There's nothing here."

"Wait. *Look.*"

The flashlight shone on a door. Seneca twisted the knob, and the door swung open to another set of rickety stairs—it must lead to the house proper. She started to climb, and Maddox scrambled after her. He had to admit he felt a little better about going aboveground again, even if it was into a building they'd been strictly forbidden to visit.

The first floor smelled like the mustiest, dingiest shower stall at his old summer camp. Light from the outside filtered in, but the layer of dust and grime on every surface was both impressive and disgusting. Not a stitch of furniture remained. Not a single item had been left behind in any of the kitchen drawers. Seneca shone her flashlight along the baseboards, searching for any kind of clue, but Maddox was pretty sure this was a dead end.

Seneca leaned against the counter and looked at him. "Let's think this through. Sadie Sage wants Damien for some reason. She puts together a plan to kidnap him. She has a place to take him. It's got to be a secure place, right? Somewhere private. She finds a window of time in which to take him. Shortly before she pulls the trigger, she packs up all her stuff, and maybe moves it, but probably dumps it." Her gaze did another sweep of the room. "I don't know what this place looked like before she left, but if it was anything like the way Freya described the room where she gave lessons—filled with weird clutter—I find it hard to believe she was able to methodically but hastily pack. I picture her throwing things into boxes quickly, getting everything out as fast as possible."

Maddox narrowed his eyes. He could tell where Seneca was going with this. "You think she accidentally left something behind?" He gestured around the empty room. "I don't know. She looks like a master packer to me. A poster woman for U-Haul. And wouldn't the police have found it?"

Seneca rolled her jaw. "Let's not give up quite yet." She started walking around the rooms again, opening closet doors, bending down to look into heating grates, feeling behind cabinets. "Years of living somewhere means a lot to accumulate and a lot that's forgotten. For a long time after my mom was killed, my dad didn't clean out her closet. When he finally did, he just shoved things in boxes to get it over with as soon as possible. A few days later, I went in there." She paused to peer behind the unplugged refrigerator. "The closet *seemed* empty, but there was this drawer in one of the built-in shelves that he'd missed. It was kind of stuck shut, which is probably why he thought it was empty, but I managed to get it open."

Maddox felt goose bumps. "W-was something inside?" he asked cautiously.

"Some old pictures. Stuff we'd totally forgotten about." She was down on her hands and knees now, feeling around behind a little door in the wall that led to a crawl space. Then she drew in a breath. When she backed up, she was holding an envelope. Maddox gawked. It was like she'd just performed a magic trick.

"See?" Seneca said softly, like she couldn't quite believe it herself. "It was stuck back there. I told you: People always forget things."

Maddox stepped closer. The plain envelope was yellowed from age and covered in dirt and cobwebs. Seneca moved to rip it open, but Maddox caught her hand. "Let's look at it in the light."

It was a bluff—mostly, he just wanted to get out of this place. Thankfully, Seneca agreed. The two of them left through the front door and found Madison running toward them with a look of relief. "Bingo," Seneca said, waving the envelope over her head.

They set the envelope on a nearby tree stump, and Seneca slowly undid the backing. A *snap* broke Maddox's concentration. He stood straight and alert, searching the sun-dappled woods. Was someone watching? He remembered Officer Gregg's threat that she'd arrest them if she caught them lurking around this place. That lady seemed like just the type who'd make good on her promise.

"Huh," Seneca said, staring at the contents of the envelope.

Two items lay on the stump. One was a book of tickets for a boat called the Tallyho Island Ferry; half the tickets had been ripped off. Then there was a photograph of a boy and girl about nine and twelve, respectively. They both had dark brown hair, big smiles, and they were holding ice cream cones. The color was fading. The sides of the photo curled from age.

"Damien?" Madison asked, pointing at the boy.

Seneca twisted her mouth. "It *kind of* looks like him . . . but also not really. And this envelope is so grimy, stuck down there for years—this picture has got to be pretty old."

Maddox peered closer. The two kids had similar noses and chins. Brother and sister? Cousins? They stood on a suburbanesque sidewalk, though it was impossible to tell where they were. They weren't near any identifiable landmarks, street signs, or mailboxes. They were wearing shorts and T-shirts, so it was probably summer. Or maybe they just lived in a warm climate.

Madison tapped the ferry tickets. "Anyone hear of Tallyho Island?"

"Nope," Seneca said. She typed in *Tallyho Island* into Google, then read aloud what she'd found on Wikipedia. *"Tallyho Island is a remote community accessible only by a ferry from New York City's outer borough of Staten Island. It has four hundred residents year-round, though it offers attractive dunes and parks for tourists on day trips."*

Madison riffled the edges of the remaining ferry tickets. "This has to be Sadie's stuff, guys—no one else ever lived in this place. And look: only a few tickets are ripped off. Meaning she used some of them to go to this Tallyho Island." She looked excited. "Maybe this was where she took Damien?"

"Meaning the reason no one could track Sadie and Damien after New York City is because they got on a ferry," Seneca said thoughtfully. "A lot of ferries still aren't very strict about people showing ID."

"I guess we know where we're going next." Maddox wrapped his arm around Seneca, and she let him. Even leaned into it. It finally felt like they were getting somewhere.

They climbed back into the car, which was beginning to feel stuffy after all the time they'd spent there. Seneca groaned as she clicked her seat belt. "I hate to bring things down, but there's someone we need to check in with."

"Oh shit," Maddox murmured. *Brett.*

But Madison perked up, intrigued. "Wait. We're calling him, right?" Seneca nodded. Madison smiled mysteriously. "I might have a way we can track him. It's something I read about this morning."

Seneca looked shocked. "Why didn't you tell us this before?"

"I can't make any promises," Madison warned as Maddox pulled away from the house. "But if you talk to him long enough, we just might be able to get somewhere."

# TEN

**IF BRETT HAD** to estimate how many miles he paced along the short hallway outside Aerin's room today, he'd have to say at least six or seven. When he wasn't talking to her or surfing online, he walked back and forth, back and forth, trying to figure out what to do, trying to calm himself, oscillating between perverse excitement at touching Aerin and annoyance that she hated it. There was the shame and guilt he felt over the fact that he was hurting her, and the billowing pride he felt because he was *totally overpowering her* and had the upper hand.

Up the hallway was *I like hurting Aerin.* Down the hallway was *I shouldn't hurt Aerin.* Up the hallway was *I love Aerin.* Down the hallway was *I hate Aerin.* Over and over and over, hour after hour after hour, flip-flop flip-flop, until it was time for him to prepare her food or answer another call from Seneca or make sure Aerin was sleeping or go inside her room and—Delight! Horror! Disgust! Ecstasy!—touch her again.

It was so freaking hot in here, so he walked to a window in his room and opened it. Then he peeked into her room. Aerin was sleeping again.

Her golden hair was splayed against the pillow. She didn't move even when the opening door squeaked. He watched her for a while, aware of his heavy breathing, and then shut it again, tamping down his desires. As much as he wanted to lie next to her, the anticipation was even more delicious than the actual act. He *would* lie next to her someday . . . and she would learn to like it. In his fantasies, that day would come when they were truly together, when she realized everything she needed to know about him, when she realized he was the one she should love.

Or that day would come when she was dead, and the only thing he'd nuzzle would be her corpse. It was quite remarkable, Brett noted, how wildly his mind could change.

His phone buzzed in his back pocket. He pulled it out and squinted at the screen, then smiled. Seneca was calling.

"Hello, darlin'," he purred. "What's new?"

As if he didn't know already. He'd slowly watched the pointer icon on the GPS tracker crawl to Catskill—first to Damien's parents' house, then to the police station, then to the middle of the woods. So they'd found the house.

"We dug up an old book of ferry tickets in Sadie Sage's place," Seneca said in a clipped voice.

Brett raised an eyebrow. *Impressive*. "Look at you," he said.

"The tickets are to a place called Tallyho Island, which is off of Staten Island. We're going to head there now."

"A ferry to *where*?" Brett asked.

"Tallyho Island," Seneca repeated. "Have you heard of it?"

Brett's gaze returned to the open window in his room. The curtains fluttered in the breeze. His heart stopped. What was he thinking? He might as well hang a neon sign over it for Aerin saying *Escape Here!* She'd already tried to leave once—she was going to try again.

He ran over and shut it fast. He couldn't believe he'd almost made such a crucial mistake. The first rule of kidnapping was to make sure there was no way for your prisoner to escape. Everyone knew that.

"Tallyho Island?" he scoffed, realizing they were waiting for his response. "It sounds like a fake name. Like I'm a knight going off to battle. *Tallyho!*" He said it in a British accent, but no one laughed. He glowered at the closed window. He needed to get a padlock on all the windows, actually. Why hadn't he thought of that before?

A new alert flashed on Brett's screen, this one from the security software he'd recently installed. *Warning. Someone is trying to access your location. Hang up and restart within thirty seconds or your security will be breached.*

Brett gripped the phone, seeing red. *Unbelievable.* "You really think it's going to be that easy?" he said in a low voice.

"Huh?" Seneca sounded caught off guard.

"You really think you're just going to find me through your phones? If you want a clue about where I am, Seneca, you should have just asked. Because guess what? You already *know* where I am. You've been here before."

"Wait. *I've* been there? Just me? What do you mean?"

Brett stabbed END, tossing the phone across the room. He felt so scattered, though it wasn't really because they were trying to access his location. He would have been insulted if they *hadn't* tried to do that. It was something else that was making him feel so antsy—something unexpected creeping up from his depths, laughing in his ear. The windows. Definitely the windows. How was it that he'd forgotten to secure the windows?

*My, my, my,* a voice inside him teased. *Is there actually something to put heartless, calculating Brett Grady off his game?*

*Hell no,* he told the voice, shaking off the feeling. He was in control and he was pleased—Seneca and the others were actually doing everything he wanted. He was still the mastermind here. And they were putty in his hands.

# ELEVEN

**"SHIT," SENECA WHISPERED,** whacking the passenger seat with her fist. "Shit, shit, *shit*."

Madison's phone was connected to hers through a USB cable, and it ran an app that could find the cell phone towers near where a caller was calling from as long as the phone call lasted at least two minutes. Seneca had tried to draw out the length of the call with Brett, and slowly, the little status bar on the app had begun to fill.

Until Brett figured it out. Would they *ever* get one up on him? Was this just a losing battle?

Seneca started fiddling angrily with the metal tab on top of the soda can she'd gotten from the hot dog stand, twisting it back and forth, back and forth. So close . . . and yet so far. The last thing Brett said to her swirled in her mind. *You know where I am. You've been here before.*

"What does he mean about me knowing where Brett is?" she murmured, more to herself than the rest of the car. "Is he back in Avignon? Did he take Aerin back to Dexby?" But Brett had said *You've been here before*—it was something specific to *her,* not the others. Annapolis, maybe? That was where she lived, after all. The University of Maryland? She'd done a semester of college there until her obsession with Case Not Closed got in the way of attending classes.

"Maybe he just said it to make you crazy." Madison popped a fresh piece of gum into her mouth. "Maybe it means nothing."

"But what if it's something? Should I go through every location I've ever been to in my entire life?"

"I agree with Madison," Maddox said as he put on his turn signal. "This is his way of distracting you from the case. You can't get obsessed with it."

"Who says I'm obsessed?"

Seneca wrenched the tab of her soda so vehemently it snapped off in her fingers. The exposed metal sliced into her skin, and a bubble of blood bloomed. She brought her finger to her mouth and sucked. Her blood tasted like metal, off-putting and unsavory. More blood trickled down her wrist.

"Are you okay?" Maddox cried worriedly. He reached over and opened his glove box. "I think I have a Band-Aid. . . ."

"I'm fine," Seneca snapped, her harshness surprising both of them. Then she curled into herself and stared pointedly out the window. She knew she was acting rash and overwrought. But she couldn't help it.

Maddox took the highway to New York City, then followed the bridges through the boroughs until they got to Staten Island. According to the website, the ferry for Tallyho Island departed from a port in the south. Once there, they found families sitting at picnic tables eating early dinners. A shredded flag bearing the crest of the state of New York whipped against a metal post. The ferry bobbed in the water, ready to go. Seneca kept sucking on her hurt finger, feeling unsettled.

Everyone climbed out of the car. Madison headed for the bathroom, and Maddox found a bench and sat down. He smiled at Seneca and patted the seat next to him. Reluctantly, she sat down and stared at the sparkles in the pavement. Why did it feel like she was about to be lectured?

"I'm sorry, okay?" she mumbled. "I'm sorry I'm acting so obsessive."

"I didn't say you were obsessive."

She lay her hands in her lap. Her thumb was pinkish, but at least it had stopped bleeding. "I can't stop thinking about him. It's like, if I don't get him, I'm going to lose my mind."

Maddox sighed. Then he turned to Seneca. She turned to him. Tentatively, he reached for her, pulled her close, and kissed her temple. Seneca stiffened. She knew he meant it to be comforting, but instead she felt claustrophobic . . . and guilty.

She pulled away, ducking her head. "Maddox, I don't think . . ."

Maddox twisted away. "I wasn't trying to . . ." He let his hands fall to his lap.

Seneca hugged her arms to her chest, her cheeks burning. What was wrong with her? He was just trying to make her feel better. And she *did* like Maddox. But at the same time, she wasn't sure she deserved the comfort or the pleasure of having a boyfriend. They needed to get Brett. They needed to save Aerin. She couldn't think of anything else. And suddenly, that Maddox *could* think of something else made her feel uncharitable.

She looked up at him. "We need to be serious about this. We need to focus. Not . . . you know."

Maddox blinked at her. "God, Seneca! Why do you keep saying I'm not focusing? Aerin's my friend, too. But if I think about how awful it is every second of the day, I'm going to go apeshit." He breathed out through his nose. "We just need to lighten up a little."

*"Lighten up."* Seneca felt a pinch of annoyance again. "Sorry if this is all too miserable for you to handle."

"That's not what I mean." His shoulders went limp, and he pressed the heels of his hands to his eyes. "Look, I can't turn off how I feel about you. I've wanted this for so long, and I know it's crappy timing . . . but it's still *there,* you know? It's hard." He glanced at Seneca, and though she wanted to respond, she just hunched her shoulders and stared at her lap. "I also want to *be there* for you. This is so stressful, and I can tell you're really feeling it. I wanted to do something. I thought kissing you might help. But if it's not, then maybe something else will distract you. How about you actually *talk* to me? Tell me what you're feeling? I know this is hard for you. I just want to know *how.*"

There was a big cloud over her head in the shape of a chomping alligator. Seneca let her gaze rest on it. How to explain to Maddox that she didn't *want* to feel better? That she wanted to sit with this pain, wallow in this anger, confront all the feelings, no matter how ugly, because that ugliness was going to push her forward and give her the courage to find what she needed to find?

She could feel a heat radiating from Maddox; his need for her felt palpable, like the leaves of a plant bending toward sunlight. But her sadness and anger and desperation tightened around her, forming a tourniquet, blocking all the blood to the emotional parts that needed human connection. She knew she was being brittle and unfair and, yeah, probably obsessive. But she couldn't help it.

A sharp horn sounded from the water. A blue-and-white ferryboat had arrived at the dock, bobbing in the waves. Madison strolled from a ticket machine with round-trip passes for everyone. Seneca looked at Maddox. "We'll talk about this later, okay?"

"Uh-huh," he said, giving her an unsatisfied smile.

She stood and took her place in line, and Maddox and Madison followed. Travelers queued up behind them. As the ticket taker began to accept passes, Brett's hint drifted into Seneca's mind once more. *You've been here before.*

She squinted at the boat looming over them. He must not mean Tallyho Island, then. She'd never been *there* before.

"First time on the island?"

A man in the line smiled amicably. He wore a Martha's Vineyard Black Dog T-shirt, had a pair of binoculars on a strap around his neck, and his nose was sunburned.

"Yep," Madison piped up. "First time."

"Hope you like it." He pointed at the phone in Maddox's hand. "But you know that's not going to work when we pull in, right?" He pointed out to sea. "Wireless signals are banned there. It's a quiet zone. Even if you did get service, which you probably won't, no one can call in, and you can't call out, unless it's to 9-1-1." His smile made his eyes crinkle. "Personally, I love it, but I could see how you young folks might get a little antsy without your Instagram and Snap-whatsit."

Seneca exchanged a spooked but intrigued glance with Maddox and Madison. Maybe they *would* find something at Tallyho Island. *No one can call in, and you can't call out.* The place sounded like a black hole, cut off from the world.

Seemed like the perfect locale to do very bad things.

# TWELVE

**AERIN WAS SO** exhausted from panic and worry and terror. And because she'd been too proud to eat all day, her stomach gnawed on its lining. She was thirsty, too, because Brett didn't allow her to just go into the en suite bathroom for a glass of water. Her throat felt like sandpaper. Her eyes were heavy, but whenever she closed them, she saw Brett looming over her, eyes wild, ready to kill her.

*It's okay,* she told herself. *I have a new plan*. She still wasn't fond of the plan, but it would hopefully keep her alive for as long as possible. Until Seneca found her. Until she could go home. Until she could go to Thomas's hospital bed and keep him alive by sheer will. She hadn't dared ask Brett exactly what he'd done to him, and her imagination had spiraled in crazy, irrational directions.

The door opened and Brett walked in. "Here," he said stiffly, dropping a tray to the nightstand. Not looking her in the eye, he cut the zip ties. "Five minutes."

"Thanks," Aerin said, grabbing a spoon and dipping it into the bowl of ramen he'd brought. This was part of the new plan: no more refusing the food. She needed to eat to keep her strength up if she was going to fight him at some point. She slurped the soup quickly, greedily, glancing at Brett for his reaction, but he wasn't looking at her. Since her botched escape, he'd become distant. This new Brett scared her even more than attentive, touchy-feely Brett. He was probably still smarting from her near escape, but he seemed distracted, too. What if he was tired of her? What if he somehow knew about the hair in her back pocket? What if he killed her?

She couldn't let that happen.

"Brett?" she called out, dropping the spoon back into the bowl.

Brett looked at her wearily. His hands were jammed into his pockets, and his jaw was taut.

"Can I still call you that?" Aerin asked. "I don't even know your real name." She shifted her legs around to face him. When she offered him a smile, Brett blinked, the confusion and mistrust obvious on his face.

"Brett's fine," he grumbled.

Aerin slurped. The ramen tasted delicious. In her old life, at school, she used to make fun of kids who microwaved ninety-nine-cent cups of ramen for lunch—it was the school's award-winning sushi bar or nothing for a girl like her. "So I've been wondering. How did you get my mom to buy that I was going to LA? It was you, right? Because I have no idea why she thought that otherwise."

Brett's eyes darted back and forth, like he was trying to work out if this was some sort of trap. "I hacked your e-mail. Wrote her a message as you."

"Wow. That's impressive."

Brett searched her face. Aerin could tell he wanted to enjoy the compliment, but he still wasn't sure.

She slurped up another bite of ramen. "So why LA?"

Brett stared toward the window. "I don't know. It's far away."

Aerin stretched out her long legs. For a moment, Brett resisted looking, but then he gave in and seemed to drink in every inch of her. "I guess you don't know me as well as you think. I can't stand LA. Want to know why?"

It took him a moment to answer. "Why?"

"My father took me there on a work trip when I was younger. We stayed on Hollywood Boulevard, and right in front of our hotel was this dude dressed up as Spider-Man who accosted me every single time I walked out into the sunshine. I hated that we kept getting stuck in traffic. I hated the scenery. And the air smelled weird."

Brett didn't crack a smile, but he hadn't left yet, either. "Tell me where I *should* have sent you."

She felt her soul lift from her body and examine this scene from above. *You are having a rational conversation with your kidnapper,* a voice in her head screamed. *What is* wrong *with you?*

"Well, a long time ago, my parents took me and Helena to Mallorca," Aerin said, ignoring the voice. "I was maybe seven or eight. It was beautiful. *That's* my go-to fantasy place."

"What did you like about it?" Brett asked, sitting down on the bed. *Yes,* Aerin thought, though she felt nervous, too. Brett was so close. He could reach out and squeeze her throat, pressing his fingers into those bruises that were still purple and painful.

She tried to keep her cool, taking a sip of water. "The house was open and breezy. We had this awesome pool that overlooked the sea. And it smelled so good there . . . nothing like the beaches here. At the end of the two weeks, I never wanted to come back." She moved a smidge closer to him. "Have you been to Spain?"

"I haven't been anywhere. I didn't take vacations as a kid."

"No? Why not?"

Brett shrugged. "It's a long story."

Aerin watched as he chewed the inside of his lip. He looked uncomfortable suddenly. She didn't want to lead him in an uncomfortable direction. "You had that beach house in Avignon before you visited us in Dexby, though. So you *learned* to like the beach."

"That's true. I got that place as an adult. I went there most summers."

"What did you do during the winter?"

"Oh, you know." He raised his gaze to her. His face was full of confidence again. Swagger, even. "This and that."

"Come on. Did you work on a cruise ship? Ski in Aspen?" *Kidnap people? Kill women?*

"Why don't you tell me more about this Mallorca trip you loved so much?" He cocked his head, and a taunting smile played on his lips. "Did you kiss a sexy Spaniard while you were there?"

"I was *seven*," Aerin reminded him. "I wasn't looking at boys. But even if I was, the brooding Spanish guy isn't my type."

This seemed to intrigue Brett. "Why is it your go-to place, then?"

Aerin looked away, then felt a surprising rush of honesty. No one had ever asked her that question. She'd actually never talked about Mallorca with anybody, not even Thomas. "It's just so . . . *different*," she admitted. "And I don't know anybody there. I feel like I could be anyone there. And best of all, my problems wouldn't follow me." She swallowed hard, recalling something. "A year ago, I stole my mom's credit card and bought a one-way plane ticket to Mallorca. I needed out of Dexby, *bad*."

"Why?"

Aerin pulled her knees to her chest and rolled her aching wrists. Five minutes had definitely passed, but she wasn't going to remind Brett to re-zip-tie her. "Well, my mom was getting on my case about not being enrolled in enough AP classes—it was all, *What are you going to do about college?* And it was Helena's birthday, but no one remembered. My dad was pissed because I hadn't visited him and his new girlfriend in the city, but meanwhile, she's only a few years older than me, which is disgusting." She shrugged. "Shit was hard, so I wanted to bolt. It's kind of what I do."

"So did you go?"

Aerin shut her eyes. "Nope. I chickened out. I just hid in my room instead. Didn't talk to anyone. Drank a bunch of Mike's Hard Lemonade by myself—same old, same old."

"What made you stay?"

Aerin pressed her lips together. She knew why. It was because she didn't want to put her parents through another daughter going missing. They might ignore her, they might not be there for her in ways she needed them to be, but she'd seen how Helena had damaged both of them. There was no way she could willingly do that to someone.

Brett's gaze fell to his lap, and a contemplative expression flashed across his face. "I understand wanting to hide, you know. I go through phases of being like that, too."

A strange jolt went through Aerin. There was something so fraught about his voice, so weak and small and utterly . . . *human*. For a moment, she wondered if she was seeing the real Brett.

Something beeped in the hall. Brett's head swiveled toward the door, and he stood. He leaned over her and redid the zip ties, but he seemed reluctant, even apologetic, and he made them just a teensy bit looser this time.

"It was nice talking," he said as he picked up her tray. "I told you I'm a nice guy once you get to know me."

"Yeah." Aerin managed a smile.

Only when he'd disappeared could she let all the coiled-up pressure in her body release. She fell back on the bed, not sure if she wanted to laugh or cry or kick something. *But at least he didn't hurt you,* she told herself. *Hell, he barely* touched *you.*

Mission accomplished.

# THIRTEEN

**TALLYHO ISLAND LOOKED** like a cross between a secluded island paradise and a zombie apocalypse wasteland. What Maddox could see of the landscape was cool—lots of waving reeds and dunes, water as far as the eye could see, a towering sky—but where the hell were all the people? The other passengers from the ferry disembarked and then got swallowed up in the mist, disappearing like ghosts. Maddox figured there had to be telephone poles, electrical towers, street signs—stuff that hinted at civilization—but it was way too foggy to tell. The little ticket booth at the end of the small parking lot looked spookily abandoned—he was almost ready for a limping zombie to burst out of it, drooling and half-crazy and infected with an island-borne disease.

"Wow," he mused to the group. "You leave New York City, and suddenly you're on another planet."

To their surprise, a man stepped out of the ticket booth. He was older, in a short-sleeved button-down shirt and a Mets ball cap pulled low over his forehead. Seneca stepped toward him. "Excuse me, sir, but have you seen this person?" She held up her phone, showing him the picture of Sadie Sage they now knew by heart.

The man's brown eyes narrowed. "Not sure. In the summer, a lot of people come and go from this island."

Maddox almost burst out laughing. *Seriously?* He peered at the desolation. *Where are they hiding?*

"But those are tourists, right?" Seneca pressed. "Like, just visiting for a day or two. I read about this island—there are no hotels here, right?"

"Yep." The ticket man nodded. "We've been approached by a few hotel chains, but we like this island locals-only."

"So has anyone new moved to the island in the past month or so?" Seneca asked.

He thought about this, then nodded. "Actually, yes. About a month ago, we had a huge load of stuff come over on the ferry. Some furniture. Some boxes."

Maddox's heart jumped. Maybe Sadie Sage *had* held on to her belongings. "Who did it belong to?"

"A woman. First new resident we've had in a while." He looked at the picture again. "That *could* be her . . . but I'm not sure. She keeps to herself. I haven't seen her since she moved."

"Was anyone with her?" Seneca asked. "A boy, maybe?"

The man chewed on his bottom lip. "You know, there might have been a kid. I wasn't paying much attention, though."

The hair on the back of Maddox's neck rose. He exchanged a loaded look with Seneca—was this Sadie and Damien?

The man looked at them pointedly. "Is there some sort of trouble here? We're a peaceful community. We don't want any commotion."

"Oh, it's nothing like that," Seneca assured him. Then she yanked the group toward the only road that was visible. "Thanks for all your help!" she called as she walked away.

When they were a safe distance from the ticket guy, Madison said in a whisper, "The new person on the island has to be Sadie, don't you think?"

"We have to figure out where she lives," Seneca said.

Maddox smiled. "I have an idea how. But we have to find people first."

They continued down the road. Maddox had to admit it felt good to walk, actually, after all those hours stuck in the car, and he started to jog ahead of the girls, raising his knees high, lengthening his stride. Air filled his lungs. His heart seemed to smile. He was definitely running tomorrow morning.

Occasionally, houses would rise up through the mist, ramshackle beaters that looked like they'd had their butts kicked from the weather. Huge, spooky, pterodactyl-size birds circled out at sea. Heavy gray clouds blotted out the sun. But then a little strip mall arose through the mist. Maddox jogged toward it. There was a small market, an ice cream shop, a place that sold bait and tackle, and a little store called Quilting Corner.

"Aha," Maddox said, spying a pretty blonde through the window at the ice cream shop. "Leave this to me."

The bells jingled as he opened the door. The small shop smelled like vanilla, waffle cones, and that horrible potpourri scent Maddox's mother loved. The girl at the counter wore a pink apron with the business's logo and a pointed hat in the shape of an ice cream swirl. She smiled at Maddox with interest. Time to turn on the charm.

"Hey," he said, sidling up to her and offering one of his signature, I'm-a-cute-track-star grins. "I like your hat."

"Oh my God." She touched it self-consciously. "This thing is awful. They make me wear it."

"Nah, it's cute." Maddox turned to the window. The others were watching him curiously, especially Seneca. "I'm just here for the day. This island is something, huh? Do you live here?"

The girl shook her head. "No way. I commute from Staten Island. I'd lose it if I lived here." She rolled her eyes.

"Right? I didn't realize the no-cell thing until I got on the ferry." Maddox gave her a commiserating smile. She giggled. He stuck out his hand. "I'm Maddox, by the way."

"Amberly."

"Amberly," Maddox repeated as they shook. "Sweet."

She giggled again. He'd forgotten how easy it was to flirt. Glancing over his shoulder, he saw Seneca shifting at the curb. It wasn't that Maddox wanted to make her jealous, exactly, but it wouldn't be such a bad thing for her to see that he could hold his own with girls. And okay, the strange argument they'd gotten into while waiting for the ferry still bugged him. Yes, yes, this was crappy timing . . . but couldn't they be together *and* solve this case? And how could she accuse him of not taking it seriously again and again? Just because he wasn't freaking out 24-7 didn't mean he didn't care about Aerin's safety. Honestly, he thought he was being more levelheaded than Seneca was. She'd been so impetuous lately, so unpredictable. If she just *talked* to him, maybe he'd get it. But she was doing the opposite of talking. She was pushing him away.

He leaned against the counter at Amberly again. "Do *any* kids live on this island?"

Amberly rinsed off an ice cream scoop in a small metal sink. "This one family used to, but they moved away. There's a baby and her mom that always come in, though."

"How about a nine-year-old? Someone said a boy just moved here."

She peered at a ceiling fan for a moment. "Oh yeah—maybe. I've only seen him once." She made a face. "He must be so lonely."

"Does he live by the water? A house by the beach wouldn't be too bad."

"Nah, I think he's over on Tweed Lane. It's okay. Sort of in the woods."

*Bingo.* "Any idea which house?"

Amberly smoothed her hands over her apron. "It's not a big street, but no."

Maddox pretended to check his phone. "Ugh. I signed up for some sort of scheduled hike that starts in two minutes." He rolled his eyes. "But maybe I'll see you again?" He tapped the glass case of ice cream tubs. "Save me a scoop of mint chip?"

Amberly's eyes twinkled. "You got it."

Maddox strolled out, his chest puffed triumphantly. Madison lingered at the curb, scowling at her phone. "Where's Seneca?" he asked, suddenly worried she'd taken this the wrong way. She had to know he was flirting just to get info, right?

"Over there." Madison pointed across the parking lot; Seneca was speaking to an older couple pushing a shopping cart. He watched as she thanked them, and strolled back toward the group.

"The new woman moved to a red house on Tweed Lane," Seneca reported. "It's a half mile up the road."

"Way to steal my thunder. I found that out, too." *Except not the red part,* he thought with chagrin.

Seneca gave Maddox an *uh-duh* look. "It wasn't that hard to figure out, Maddox. This woman is the only person who moved to the island in years. Of course all the locals know where she is." She gave his forearm a little pinch. "And also? Don't try to make me jealous by flirting with a girl in an ice cream hat ever again. You should know by now I don't fall for that crap."

"You got me," Maddox said, grateful for Seneca's levity. He bumped her hip. "And that's why I like you."

**TWEED LANE HAD** a crooked road sign and was surrounded by thick, dense woods. The first house they came upon was a small, battered-looking ranch with a bunch of howling dogs and a VW bus in the driveway. The second house was a colonial with two old people sitting on Adirondack chairs in the front yard. They waved to Maddox, and he was tempted to ask them where the single mom lived, but he didn't want to draw attention to the group in case crazy shit was about to go down.

*"Look,"* Madison whispered.

She pointed to a neat gravel driveway up ahead. Through the trees was a small, tidy red A-frame house. There was no car in the driveway, but a light was on in the window.

They crept toward the house. Their footfalls sounded like exploding bombs. Every time Maddox heard even a tiny *snap*, his stomach did a flip. He inched toward the glass and listened. Wouldn't a kid cooped up in a house be making some sort of sound?

Suddenly, a figure passed in and out of view through the second-floor window. Maddox's heart thumped. It was a child. He looked to be about Damien's age.

"Could that be . . . ?" he whispered, pointing.

The figure slipped out of view. Seneca stared at the window. Madison held her breath. They all waited for Damien to appear again. Maddox could hear his heart in his ears. He hadn't actually thought they'd get to this point. What were they going to do if it *was* him? They couldn't call Brett from here because of the no-cell signal. They could call 9-1-1, but what if that was against Brett's orders? They hadn't discussed what they'd do if they actually found who they were looking for.

Then they heard a new sound—and this one was much closer, right behind Maddox's head. It was a sharp, metallic noise of something clicking into place. Just before Maddox could wheel around and figure out what it was, he felt something heavy and hard press into his skull. He flinched, and his eyes slid to the right. He saw a sliver of red hair. The metal butt of a gun. A wild look in someone's eyes.

*"Freeze, assholes,"* a voice said. And Maddox did exactly that.

# FOURTEEN

**SENECA STARED AT** the gun. The woman holding it was tall and pointy-chinned, and though her hair was red, she could be Sadie Sage. She aimed the gun at them with the ease of someone who'd practiced using a weapon. Her nostrils flared in and out. As if on cue, the wind whipped through the trees. Branches cascaded from the sky, one narrowly missing Seneca's head.

"Get the hell off my property!" the woman roared. "Leave or I'll shoot, I swear!"

"Wait a minute!" Maddox's voice was steady. "Let's all just calm down. We know what you've done. People are looking for you. If we just go *calmly*, no one will get hurt."

The woman looked livid. "I'm not going *anywhere*."

She raised the gun higher. Seneca felt woozy. This was a terrible idea. Sadie Sage was a maniac. Of course she wasn't going to go quietly. Of course she was going to shoot anyone who tracked her down.

Seneca glanced toward the trees. Could they run for it? Maybe they could go back to the strip mall, find a phone, and call the cops. But what if Sadie chased them? What if she shot Damien hiding inside?

Was *this* Brett's endgame? Maybe he knew all along that Sadie was crazy and murderous. Maybe he wanted to lead them straight to her so she'd just kill them.

"He has a family," Maddox said, his eyes still trained on Sadie. "Please think of how scared he is. He just wants his mother back."

The woman waved the gun slightly. "*I'm* his mother. I'm *their* mother. What, did Gerald tell you I wasn't? What kind of bullshit is *that*?" She pointed the gun directly at him. "I'll kill you before I let you take them from me. I *swear*."

*Them?* Seneca blinked hard. Something about this didn't feel right.

Suddenly, the sliding glass door opened, and a small head poked out. "Mom?" The boy's face went sheet-white. "Mom! What are you doing?"

"Go away!" The woman's gaze was still trained on Seneca and the group. "Get back inside, Marcus!"

*Marcus?* Seneca dared to stare at him. The boy was nine or so, but he wasn't wearing glasses, and his hair was curly, not poker-straight, as Damien's was in the pictures. Actually, he looked nothing like Damien at all.

As she watched, two more kids appeared. The girl looked to be about seven. She held the hand of a towheaded toddler who was wearing a T-shirt and a diaper. Both kids stared at the scene with wide, watering eyes.

Seneca's eyes darted from the children to the woman. She could tell the others were registering this, too—Madison gasped, and Maddox took a small step backward. Suddenly, the boy shot out from the glass door and threw his arms around the woman's waist. She let out a wail, and the gun clattered to the ground. Madison scrambled for it, held it in her arms for a few scared seconds, and then tossed it across the driveway, where no one could reach it.

"Okay," she said, turning back to the group. "Let's all just chill."

But the woman wasn't listening. She and her son were a puddle of tears. The other kids came out too and whimpered at the woman's side. They clung to her desperately, their little nails digging into her back. "I don't want to go back, Mom," the oldest boy wailed.

"I know, honey," the woman murmured. "I know you don't. And I won't let that happen. I promise. Remember how I promised?"

Seneca's heart twisted. No kidnapped kid would hug his captor like this, would he? This couldn't be Damien. This didn't fit at all.

"Uh . . ." Maddox whispered, sensing the disconnect, too. The lump in Seneca's throat expanded. Whatever they'd walked into was bad, but it didn't feel like a kidnapping.

No one knew what to do while the woman and the kids calmed down. It felt rude to leave, but it also felt rude to stay. Seneca wished she could just dissolve and reappear somewhere else on the island, pretending this had never happened. Finally, the woman lifted her head and gave them a supplicating stare. "Well? What are you going to do?"

Seneca shut her eyes. "I'm so, so sorry. We're looking for a woman who kidnapped a child—just *one child*—from Upstate New York. We thought it might be you."

"I didn't kidnap any of them," the woman pleaded. All three kids watched them with big, scared eyes. "If Gerald's telling you that, he's lying."

"We don't even know Gerald, we swear," Maddox explained. "This was all a horrible case of mistaken identity. Gerald doesn't know you're here. We promise."

"And we won't tell a soul you're here," Madison piped up.

The woman studied them suspiciously, still clinging protectively to her kids. They were clearly all one another had. "For real?" she asked after a beat.

"For real," Seneca said. "Honest."

"We get it," Maddox said gently. "You're just protecting them. I'm guessing Gerald kept saying he was going to change, but he just kept doing the same things, over and over."

The woman's eyes were bloodshot, full of fury and shame. She didn't confirm what Maddox said, but she didn't deny it, either.

"Some people are just evil through and through." Maddox's voice quivered. "They will always be bad. They will always do bad things. Of course you had to leave." He looked around. "This place is safe, as far as we know. No one is going to hurt you."

Seneca watched Maddox, proud at how wise he sounded. The woman's throat bobbed as she swallowed. Saying nothing more, she grabbed her children's hands and pushed them through the screen door. "Get out of here. If I see you here in two minutes, I'm calling the cops."

They jogged down the driveway. Once on the road, Seneca suddenly broke down, letting out the terrified tears she'd been holding in. Maddox grabbed her and hugged her tight, and then Madison piled on, too. Never had she felt so close to death as what she'd just been through—and considering their run-ins with Brett, that was saying a lot. No one said anything for a long while.

Maybe this *was* getting too intense, just like Maddox said. And even worse, they'd followed a false lead. They'd found a scared, sad woman and her son who were obviously running from an abuser . . . not Sadie Sage.

After a while, Maddox cleared his throat and checked his watch.

"Unless we want to sleep on the beach, we need to get back. The last ferry leaves in a half hour."

The bell was ringing for the ferry when they reached the dock, and they had to rush to the gangplank before the boat pulled away. Once they were on board, Seneca fidgeted awkwardly, needing something to do with all of her excess energy. They'd wasted a whole afternoon on this island. They only had a few more days to figure this out, and they were no closer to reaching the answer. Every time they advanced, the target shifted, and suddenly they were far away again.

She reached to check her phone for a response from Viola, until she remembered there was no cell service here. Who could *live* in such a place? Then she pulled out the old ticket book they'd found in Sadie Sage's basement and glared at it. Was this even a clue? Maybe Sadie had just come here to do some sightseeing. Maybe she was into whale-watching tours or whatever.

The boat rocked back and forth as it pulled away from the shore. Overhead, the clouds were getting even darker, threatening rain. The tickets made a riffling sound as Seneca flipped through them. "Where'd you find those?" a voice said above her. "A flea market?"

The conductor stopped at their seats. It was the same man from the ticket booth, and he smiled with recognition. "Sorry?" she asked.

He pointed at the ticket book. "We haven't used old-school punch books since 2005. Everything's digital now." He stared at the ticket book fondly. "There wasn't much of anything on the island back then. It's only gotten touristy in the past seven or eight years." And then he moved to the next customers, two tourists wearing fanny packs speaking another language.

Seneca turned to Maddox. "I guess that means that if Sadie came here using the ticket book, it was prior to 2005."

"Yeah." Maddox made a face. "A zillion years ago. And I don't want to imagine what this place was like *before* it was touristy."

As the boat rocked and creaked, this new piece to the puzzle vibrated inside Seneca. Why was Sadie visiting an island before there were any tourist attractions? Did she know someone here? Or maybe she *had* lived here, long ago? But how would they find out if that was true? After all, she wouldn't have gone by Sadie Sage. She would have been someone else.

Something pinged in her mind. She looked at the group. "Sadie Sage used this ticket book almost fifteen years ago, back before she changed her identity. We haven't really thought about *why* she changed her identity, though. Maybe we should."

Madison shaped her hair into a ponytail. "People change their identities for all sorts of reasons. I bet that woman we just met changed *her* name so she could get away from Gerald."

"Yeah, but come on." Seneca held on to the rail to brace against a particularly bumpy wave. "An abused woman doesn't turn into a kidnapper. Sadie's like Brett. Isn't it more likely that she changed her identity to escape something bad that *she'd* done?"

Maddox nodded. "Yeah. I would think so, actually."

"So let's assume in her past life, she was doing bad things. Maybe she was doing some of those things *here*."

"Okay . . ."

Water droplets splashed the side of Seneca's cheek. She pulled the sleeves of her hoodie over her hands and shivered. The words Maddox had spoken swirled in her mind: *I'm guessing Gerald kept saying he was going to change, but he just kept doing the same things, over and over.* It had struck her, reminded her of something she'd heard before. Suddenly, she knew why: In the hospital, Chelsea had said that when the news story broke about Gabriel Wilton being a person of interest, Brett was barely fazed. *Maybe this wasn't the first time he'd done this,* Chelsea said.

Old habits died hard. What if Sadie Sage was in a toxic rut, too?

Goose bumps rose on Seneca's arms. "Maybe Damien isn't Sadie's first victim."

Maddox blinked. "You think?"

"It could fit. It could be why she changed her name a few years ago. It also could be why she was able to steal Damien without a trace—she's *good* at it. She's done it before."

"But how does that connect to Tallyho Island?" Madison asked. "Why did she come here? What was in it for her? Does it connect at all?"

Maddox scrunched up his nose. "Could she have *taken* a kid from here? The girl in the ice cream shop said that more kids *did* live here once. . . ."

Seneca nodded gravely. "Bingo."

But Maddox just shrugged. "That's interesting, but it doesn't help us find Sadie *now*."

"We don't know that." Seneca stared down at the dark, rippling water. "Another kidnapping could give us some information on Sadie's patterns. It's interesting that she saved the ticket book. Maybe she's holding on to old mementos of past crimes. That picture of those other kids could be a memento, too."

Seneca had never been so thrilled to get a cell signal when the boat pulled into shore. After quickly checking if Viola had written—nope, and nothing from RedBird, either—she typed *Kidnappings, Tallyho Island* into Google. The search page loaded, and an article caught her eye.

She let out a weak cry. "Here. A boy was kidnapped off the island in 2002."

Maddox leaned over the screen. *"Jackson Jones, age nine, went missing from his home on Tallyho Island, New York, on June 5, 2002,"* he read.

Seneca stopped in her tracks. "Wait. *Jackson?*"

Maddox looked confused. "What's significant about Jackson?"

The passengers behind her nudged Seneca to keep walking down the gangplank, but her legs felt wooden. Her heart was pounding, and her head felt scrambled. She took a breath. "Remember that shack in Jersey we thought Brett was hiding Chelsea in? The one Aerin and Thomas went to, though it ended up being a dead end?"

"Yeah . . ." Maddox narrowed his eyes.

"Aerin found a paper crane there. It had the name *Jackson* on the bottom."

"Meaning . . . ?" Madison sounded spooked.

"I don't know," Seneca said quietly. With shaking hands, she consulted Google again. *Jackson Jones,* she typed into the search box. *Kidnapped boy, Tallyho Island, 2002.*

Slightly different hits popped up. Seneca clicked on the first one. Jackson Jones had been nine years old when it happened. He had lived all his life on Tallyho Island. It was suspected that a woman named Elizabeth Ivy kidnapped him. She'd been his piano teacher—Jackson had traveled to see her on the mainland for a lesson and had never come back.

*Piano,* just like Damien. And he looked a lot like Damien: In a picture, he had similar brown hair, the same sort of nondescript features, round, Harry Potter glasses, and an impish but unremarkable smile. In fact, he looked like that boy in the photo they'd found in Sadie's basement. The one that looked like Damien . . . but also didn't.

Hands shaking, Madison pointed to a line at the bottom of the story. "Look at Jackson's middle name."

Seneca looked at her phone. But even a split second before her eyes took in the name, she knew what it was going to be. The photograph they'd found in Sadie's basement sizzled in her brain. She pictured that young, scrappy-looking boy, the generic smile on his face. When she aged those features forward, when she took a few mental leaps, the answer was right there.

*Brett.*

She grabbed her phone and dialed the scrambled number at the top of her call list.

"Your real name is Jackson Brett Jones," Seneca whispered when Brett answered. "Sadie Sage kidnapped you, too."

# FIFTEEN

**BRETT HAD BEEN** expecting the call—once Seneca had zeroed in on Tallyho Island, the pieces were going to fall into place. She was a smart girl. And thanks to the internet, all the info was there for anyone to find.

But it still was hard to hear her throw his past back in his face. Sure, he wanted this group to know who he really was—this was part of the plan, and he'd wanted *them* to get at the truth versus just vomiting it up from the start. But it was also unnerving. For as long as he could remember, he always controlled his identity, shifted his story. Never before had he had to tell what was real.

"Yes," he said after a pause. "I'm Jackson Brett Jones. You get an A-plus, Seneca. A gold star."

"You grew up on Tallyho Island. You knew Sadie Sage. She taught you piano. And then she took you. *This* is why you want us to solve Damien's case. His kidnapper is *your* kidnapper."

"Except she didn't go by Sadie back then," Brett muttered. "She went by Elizabeth Ivy. Didn't you read the story?"

"Was that your paper crane we found in that shack in Jersey?" Maddox burst in. "The one that said *Jackson* on the bottom? Is that where she was holding you?"

Brett laughed. "Oh, no. I planted the crane there. Just as a funny little inside joke with myself. I gave a crane to Helena, too." He chuckled to himself. "Remember that one? It said *Hi* on it?" He could hear Seneca sucking in a breath. "I literally meant *Hi,* but all of you thought it stood for *Harris Ingram*. It was a smart deduction, though. I wasn't going to burst your bubble—and besides, it led to Harris's arrest."

"But you planted that *Jackson* crane deliberately," Seneca said. "You wanted us to figure this out."

Brett leaned his head against the wall. "Sure. We're friends, aren't we? And friends tell other friends about their pasts."

There was a long pause. Brett could tell everyone was taking in what he'd said. It was kind of mind-blowing, if you thought about it. He felt proud that he'd been able to keep such a secret, and he also felt kind of proud of them for figuring it out.

"Sadie was keeping a picture of you in her house, too," Seneca added. "We found it with the Tallyho tickets."

"Huh," Brett said blandly, though in truth it made his skin crawl to think she still had a picture of him in her possession. When had she even *taken* a picture? *He* didn't remember any cameras. Then again, he'd suppressed so much from that time. . . .

"How long did she keep you?" Maddox asked after a beat.

"Six years." It was so chilling to say it out loud. He'd never told a soul. "From when I was nine to when I was fifteen and could finally overpower her."

"God," Maddox murmured. His voice cracked a little. "That . . . *sucks*."

"Yeah, well." Brett paced up and down the hall. "We all can't have picture-perfect lives."

"No one deserves that, though. How did it happen? Do you remember? Because if it were me, I would have blocked that out."

The memories buzzed around Brett like flies circling a rancid piece of meat. He hadn't planned on telling them more than the basics, but Maddox was being so cool about it, like he actually cared. "We were buddies. She gave me piano lessons, sometimes on the island, sometimes at her studio on the mainland. My parents thought she was great—I was homeschooled, so I didn't get a lot of interaction with people, and they were happy I'd made a connection. Then, one afternoon, she said she would take me to a Harry Potter convention in the city. I was obsessed with the books. But on the way, she turned on me. Said my parents didn't want me anymore. Said they were putting me into foster care." He swallowed. "I freaked out. And she goes, *They say you're a terrible, worthless drain.* She said that unless I went with her, I was going to be turned over to the state and sent to live with people I didn't know."

"There's no way that would have happened," Seneca pointed out.

Brett breathed forcefully through his nose. "I was nine years old. How was I supposed to know that? So I got in her car. And that was the end of my life."

"Where did you go?" Maddox asked.

Brett stared out the window at the squirrels in the tree in the front yard. They were flitting around one another strangely, almost like they were getting ready to have sex. "This house near the ocean. I was never allowed to go out. *Never.* Or, well, sometimes she put me in the shed *behind* the house. But I was locked in." The words were coming out in a gush, like blood. "The first time she shut me in there was a few months into my time with her. I'd tried to escape. I'd slipped out the front door when she was taking out the trash, and two doors down I saw a car in the driveway. I banged on the door, and this woman opened it, holding a little girl. I told her what was happening. I was crying so hard and I couldn't get my words out straight. I figured she'd call the police right then and there, but guess what she did instead?"

"What?" Seneca said breathlessly.

Brett cackled joylessly. "She *walked me back home.* Apparently Elizabeth had introduced herself to this woman already. Charmed her. Said she had a son who had behavioral issues—me. Elizabeth grabbed my arm tightly. She was so thankful to the woman for returning me. The two of them were just hugging and being sweet to one another, and meanwhile, I was like, *You have got to be fucking kidding me.* And then, of course, the moment that woman left, Elizabeth tossed me into the shed. For *days.* With only water. Do you know how demoralizing that is?"

"God," Maddox murmured.

"Why didn't you scream for help?" Seneca asked.

"I didn't think that would do any good. Elizabeth had already woven a tale that I was a troubled kid. People would probably just think I was having a meltdown."

"But how did this woman that walked you home not recognize you or Elizabeth from the news?" Seneca cried.

Brett sniffed. "Elizabeth changed her hair color, lost some weight. As for me . . ." He trailed off. He'd asked himself that question so many times. "She shaved my head. I lost weight, too. I didn't think I looked *that* different, but people only see what they want to see. This woman down the street wanted to trust that Elizabeth was a good mommy. She didn't want to believe that anything could go wrong in a happy little beach town."

He was breathing hard now, his head swimming, his heart

pounding. Just telling the story made him feel like he was back there in that beach shed, quivering with fear, begging that bitch to let him out. And just talking to the group in particular, unsettling as it was, felt *right*. There were so many parts of this story, so many separate, angry vendettas he waged, but they were all beginning to congeal, forming a neat, perfect little endgame. They had to know this for his game to continue.

"How much longer was it until you escaped?" Maddox asked.

Brett blinked, regained his composure, and let a few seconds of reverent, expectant silence pass. Once he got over the fact that he was regurgitating the shittiest moments in his life, this was really something. They didn't even care about Aerin in this moment. They were solely focused on *him*. It felt like they cared about him again. How carefully they were listening! How *captivated* they were! They wanted to drink him up like a sugary soda, needing more and more and more, and that gave him renewed strength.

He took a breath. "Years. I had to get strong enough to overtake her."

"Why didn't you go to the cops after you escaped?" Seneca asked. "There aren't any stories about the kidnapping having a happy ending. Just that you disappeared."

"When I did finally escape, I went back to my house on the island . . . only to find out my parents were both dead. I didn't get to say goodbye to them. What were the cops going to do about that? How were they going to help me?"

"What about your sister?" Seneca asked. "Where was she when all this happened?"

"Who?"

"Viola," Seneca said. "We know you have a sister, Brett. So where was she?"

Brett felt another shiver of the past and the present meshing together in ways he didn't like. "Let's leave Viola out of this."

Seneca made a noise under her breath like she didn't appreciate that answer, but then she pressed on. "You could have told the police about Elizabeth, though. You could have given them information to catch her. Unless you didn't want *them* to catch her. Is that it? You wanted to catch her *yourself*?"

Brett rolled his eyes. Did she really think her conclusions were so earth-shattering? "When I saw that story about Damien, when I saw that the kidnapper was a freaking piano teacher and saw a picture of her, I was like, *There she is*. So yeah. I've been waiting for her to strike again. I've been waiting to *find her*."

"But, Brett," Maddox said, "don't you see the irony? You went through a horrific experience as a prisoner, but now you're putting Aerin through the same thing. We'll still help you if you give her back. We promise. A woman like this deserves to go to prison."

Brett's heart twisted at the tenderness in his old buddy's voice. *Could* he do that? *Could* he send Aerin back to them? *Could* he just rely on them to help, even without a bargaining chip?

He shut his eyes tight. *No*. That wasn't the plan. "We have an agreement. You hit a dead end at Tallyho Island. You found one of her *old* victims—me. But that tells us nothing about where she is now, and you'd better get on that before it's too late."

Seneca let out a note of protest. "But, Brett—"

"No *buts*!" Rage flooded him. "You're running out of time. Aerin's family is going to be looking for her soon, so find Elizabeth or Sadie or whatever she goes by now, or you'll never see Aerin again. We'll be on a plane out of here so fast. She'll never see her family. She'll never see *anyone*. Or maybe I'll burn her up, just like I did to her boyfriend. So if you really want to fuck with me, go for it, but if you don't, you have until Monday night."

He stabbed at END and dropped to the floor, trying to hold back the hot, angry demons from slithering through the locked grate in his brain. But when he turned, he noticed he'd left the door to Aerin's room open. Aerin was sitting upright on the bed, her mouth dropped open, her hands trembling in her lap.

She'd heard everything.

# SIXTEEN

**AERIN COULDN'T MOVE.** If Brett were to touch her right now, she felt like she would disintegrate to dust. Crumple to bones.

*Or maybe I'll burn her up, just like I did to her boyfriend.*

She despised him. She wanted to turn away from him and scream, *Fine, then I won't be nice anymore, either.* But she knew that would only push him to actually do the things he threatened. Only sympathy would keep his rage at bay. Not that she felt particularly sympathetic for him. The world was a mess. Bad things happened to good people. But on the other hand? Most of those people didn't transform into monsters.

As Brett watched her, the mortified expression on his face began to shift into irritation. *Think,* a little voice inside Aerin pushed. *What would a friend say right now? What does he want you to do?* She tried to remember what she'd wanted people to say to her after Helena disappeared. Few people actually said the right thing. It was always pleas to talk about her feelings, or weird platitudes about Helena's fate being in God's hands, or her personal favorite, that the universe only gave people what they could handle.

"That totally sucks," she finally said, quietly, hoping she didn't sound as sarcastic as she felt.

Brett looked away fast. His jaw tightened, but then the air seemed to go out of him. He slid down until he was sitting on the carpet just inside her door.

"She really locked you in a shed?"

He shrugged one shoulder.

"Come on," Aerin mustered. "You can talk to me about it."

He gave her a strange look. "I know you don't want to be nice to me. I know you heard what I did to that dude of yours."

Aerin felt a ripple of dread go through her. *That dude.* She wanted to claw his eyes out. Smash in his skull. He'd *burned* Thomas? How?

It took every ounce of willpower to give him a kind, sympathetic smile and let the comment go. Because he *did* want her sympathy, she could tell. He *did* want to talk about this with her. "When you were in the house, was it just you and her?" she asked. "Were you all alone?"

"Not totally alone."

Aerin raised an eyebrow, then waited for Brett to expound upon that. He didn't. "Your kidnapper's name was Elizabeth, right?" she went on.

"That's what I called her."

"Was she always so awful?"

Brett shuffled his feet, making patterns in the carpet fibers. But then he turned to her. Actually *looked* at her. His expression was crushing. He looked so young, maybe even younger than she was, and so very lost. "No. Sometimes, she acted like a . . . *mom.*" He squirmed at the word. "She knew how scared I was, so she sang me lullabies to sleep, even though I was much too old for that sort of thing. And we worked on reading together. Math. She was smart. And when she was in a good mood, she let me watch TV. Never the news or anything—because the news might have been about me, and she was very intent on making me believe that *nobody* cared where I'd gone. So we watched cartoons. Nature shows. *MythBusters!*"

"That doesn't sound so bad. I watch nature shows when I'm stressed, too."

Brett laughed mirthlessly. "The flip side was that she hit me. Threatened me. Verbally abused me. And then there was the shed. Every time she shut me in there, I lost all concept of time. When she finally let me out, I felt like a vampire. The sun was too bright. I was too weak to talk. I was also too keyed-up to sleep."

Aerin felt a pull in her chest. "You really didn't go to the police because you wanted to get Elizabeth for yourself?"

Brett's eyes were coal black and haunted. "I wanted to see my parents, but when I got there, I found out they both had died." He looked away, pressing his lips together. "And then afterward . . . I don't know. I still believed a lot of the things Elizabeth told me—I was worthless, I was a bad person. I worried that if I went to the cops, I'd somehow be in trouble."

"For what?"

"I don't know. My head was a mess." Brett squeezed his kneecaps. "I was also afraid of doing anything too public. I escaped from Elizabeth. I'm sure she was furious. I had this horrible feeling that if she ever found me, she'd kill me."

Aerin chewed hard on her bottom lip. Ironic: It was the same way she felt about *him.* But as Brett sat there on the carpet, he looked so placid and harmless—and almost handsome. Aerin swallowed hard, astonished her brain could conjure up such tenderness for someone she hated so much. But people were people, weren't they? Everyone was vulnerable. Everyone was scared. Even maniacs.

Aerin awkwardly pushed herself to standing and shuffled to him in the doorway, covering his hand with hers. "I'm really sorry. I understand how hard it must be to move on."

Brett glanced at her cagily. She'd taken a huge risk, leaving her bed. But then he lowered his head again. Breathed in and out. Let her stay there. "Yeah right," he grumbled.

"No, seriously!" She pointed at herself. "Do you think *I've* moved on since I lost my sister? Hell no! I'm still swirling in that pain! I've basically pressed pause on my life because I don't think I deserve to be happy because she's . . . you know." She peeked at him. It was beyond bizarre that she was having this very conversation with the person who'd *killed her sister in the first place*, but she knew Brett needed her to connect. That her survival depended on it. "So I know a thing about being stuck in the past."

"Yeah, well." Brett shrugged. "It's very hard to forget."

"Exactly."

They fell silent. Carefully, she peeked down the hall. There were two doors at the end of the corridor, then a railing that led to a set of steps to a first floor. They seemed to be in a house . . . a rather *nice* house, actually, with pretty wood baseboards and a stained-glass window above the stairway. This wasn't a house that was in the middle of nowhere. She could intuit it in her bones. Down those steps would be a front door that would spit Aerin back into civilization.

But she didn't run. She stayed put next to Brett, needing him to trust her. Because if he trusted her, maybe eventually he'd lower his guard again, this time for real. She would plan her escape, one that actually had a chance of working.

The AC ticked on. Shadows shifted on the other side of that stained-glass window. Aerin considered everything she'd just told Brett. She'd never really thought about how *stuck* she was since Helena vanished . . . but it was totally true. Did it make sense, though? Would *Helena* want her to be in pause like this? Wouldn't her sister want her to move on with her life, do great things, try and be happy?

She looked at Brett, wishing she could tell him this. He was the poster child for how dwelling on the past had done absolutely nothing good. Couldn't he just try and let it go? Couldn't he just try and change? But she knew that wasn't what he wanted to hear, and right now, it was more about stroking his ego than telling the truth.

"I totally get why you want revenge," she said. "That bitch deserves to be locked up forever. She shouldn't be allowed to walk the streets. She'll just keep doing terrible things again and again."

Brett nodded at her. "Yeah. You're so right."

Little did he know, though, that there was more Aerin wanted to say. More that was spiraling around in her head, poignant and humming. *She deserves being locked up forever . . . and you do, too.*

# SEVENTEEN

**AFTER CLIMBING OFF** the ferry, the group grabbed a booth at a diner near the dock. It was past six, and the place was crowded and smelled heavily of french-fry grease. Seneca stared at the thick, stained laminated menu the waitress had handed her as soon as they sat down, but the words swam before her eyes, meaningless. Hot, uncomfortable pressure was building inside her, ready to explode.

"I just can't believe it," Madison was saying into the phone as the waitress delivered their drinks. They were on the phone with Thomas in the hospital, eager to relay him the news. "The guy grew up in darkness. *Literally.*"

"It explains a lot." Thomas sounded groggy but better than when they'd spoken to him earlier. "We had to do this whole course at the police academy about the psychology of killers and kidnappers. Most of them had really messed-up pasts."

Madison fiddled with her straw wrapper. "Messed-up is putting it lightly. A nine-year-old kid, stolen from his parents and locked in a freaking *shed*? It sounds like a horror movie."

"You gotta sympathize with the guy." Maddox poured sugar into his coffee. "To be honest, I'd probably want to kill Elizabeth, too."

A scream exploded inside Seneca. *Sympathize with the guy?* She couldn't believe what was coming out of their mouths. It was like they'd been brainwashed.

"Elizabeth Ivy, Sadie Sage, it seems like there's a pattern," Madison mused. "Were they part of a song, or maybe characters on *Sesame Street*?"

"Let's hope not," Maddox said. "A demonic woman using cute little *Sesame Street* characters as her aliases?" He shuddered. "Her victims must be living a nightmare."

That was it. Seneca slammed her water glass on the table, liquid spilling over the side. Everyone looked up in alarm. "Oh, so now we feel bad for Brett, is that it?"

Maddox shook his head. "I was thinking about *Sadie*. If she did that stuff to Brett, she's probably doing it to Damien, too."

"Yeah, but you care about him now." Seneca's voice was shaking. "Admit it. You feel *bad* for the guy. That's why you said we'd help him with finding Sadie even after he gave Aerin back. You actually want to help him."

Maddox held up his hands in a *whoa* gesture. "I said that because I thought it would keep Brett talking, Seneca. *And* like maybe he'd see what he was doing and return Aerin to us. This doesn't mean I like Brett. I'm just processing this new side of him."

Seneca was seeing stars. "There is no *new side* to Brett, and there's no reason to process his feelings! This is still the man who killed Aerin's sister and my mother and is now *holding our friend captive*!" She narrowed her eyes. "Are you next going to tell me that if we have the chance to capture Brett, you're going to let him go? Because the poor guy has been through enough already?"

"Seneca, that's not—"

Seneca waved her hand to stop him. "You can't let anything Brett tells you interfere with who he is and what he's done. If you feel like you can't handle that, maybe that's something we should discuss."

Madison touched her arm. "Hey. You know I want Aerin back more than anything. That's not what we're saying. We still know Brett's awful. We're just talking, okay? Trying to understand."

The waitress reappeared, ready to take their orders. All of a sudden, Seneca felt claustrophobic in the sticky vinyl booth. She stood, wriggled around Madison, and headed for the door. "I'm not hungry anymore."

Outside, the sky was gloomy. Across the street, in a vacant lot, a bunch of wild turkeys pecked and clucked. Seneca wandered out of the parking lot and into a neighboring empty playground, plopping down on one of the swings. She knew she should be happy that they'd finally figured out who Brett was and what he was all about. And she wasn't totally heartless—his story *was* sad. It tugged at her, too.

But that bothered her. She didn't want there to be meaning to Brett's actions. She would have been happier if Brett had chosen the Damien case at random, not because it was connected to his dark, tragic past. She didn't want to feel anything for Brett except blind, vengeful hatred; she didn't want to imagine him as a scared little kid, not unlike Damien, actually, locked up by a madwoman. He had done unspeakable things, and that was what she needed to focus on. Sure, he could blame his actions on a horrific past . . . but a lot of other people went through awful things and didn't grow up to be murderers. Why didn't Maddox understand that? Why was he trying to be so *objective*?

The door to the diner jingled, and Seneca looked over. Madison walked across the lawn and dropped into one of the swings next to her.

"In case you were wondering, Thomas's MRI was clean. He doesn't have a concussion. His burns aren't that serious, either. He'll probably be able to get out in a few days."

Seneca gripped the rusty swing's chains. She'd actually forgotten Thomas was still on the phone, hearing her outburst. "And are you also out here to tell me I was out of line with Maddox?"

Madison started to swing higher, her untied shoelace flapping. The swings were the type that groaned at the slightest movement. "Nah. He's okay. He understands where you're coming from."

"Does he, though?"

Madison gave her a look. "Uh, *yeah,* Seneca. Believe it or not, Maddox and Brett aren't BFFs. He still understands the guy's a psychopath."

Seneca swallowed hard. *But I want him to be as angry as I am,* she thought to herself. *I want all of you to feel exactly how I feel.*

"But for what it's worth?" Madison said. "I'm going through some frustrating stuff, too."

Seneca gave her a quizzical look. Madison, frustrated? She seemed so straightforward, so well adjusted. "What do you mean?"

Madison dug her toe into the mulch to stop swinging. "It's kind of stupid. I've tried to tell my cheerleading teammates I'm doing important stuff, and that's why I'm not at summer practice. But just now I got a text where they're like, *You're not dedicated. Maybe you don't have the heart to be captain.*" She rolled her eyes. "I know it barely compares to the stuff you're going through, but it still sucks."

"Oh. That does suck." Seneca breathed out. A plane soared across the sky. She watched it until it disappeared behind a highway overpass. It hadn't occurred to her that all of them were giving something up to be here. It also made her feel bad because, although she'd been by Madison's side all week, leaning on her, utilizing her, she didn't feel like she actually knew her well. That should change.

Maybe her whole attitude should change. There was no use squabbling with the others. It was probably what Brett wanted: for them to splinter, with some of them siding with his plight, and others—like her—hardening even further . . . and lose sight of their goal.

Well. She wasn't going to fall prey to Brett's schemes. They were running out of time.

She straightened up. "We need to make this worth your while, then. Imagine the looks on those cheerleading bitches' faces when they find out you solved a major cold case—*and* saved Aerin."

Madison tossed her ponytail over her shoulder. "I'll be the Wonder Woman of the team."

"Totally." Seneca gripped the swing's chains hard. "That thing Brett said about keeping Viola out of this was interesting. Maybe she *isn't* part of this scheme—or at least not Sadie."

"I think you're right."

"If only we could reach her. Maybe Brett wants to leave her out of this because she knows where he's hiding out."

"Still nothing from RedBird?"

Seneca pulled out her phone for the millionth time, expecting the same result, but to her surprise, there was a PDF from RedBird in her inbox. She let out a happy cry. The PDF was a record of all of the phone calls made from the number attached to Brett-as-Gabriel's condo in Avignon over the past month.

"Whoa," Seneca whispered, showing Madison after she opened the file. Her eyes boggled at the long list.

"Huh. It seems like it's all businesses." Madison pointed to line after line of 1-800 numbers. She dialed the first number on the list, and when someone answered, she burst out laughing. "It's a psychic hotline!"

"I just got the weather forecast for Alaska," Seneca said, puzzled.

They called customer service lines for Lowes, Amtrak trains, and several numbers that were now disconnected or didn't have weekend customer service support. Why on earth would Brett call these numbers? "Maybe Viola works at one of these places?" Seneca wondered aloud. "Maybe that's how Brett reaches her?"

"Usually when you call a 1-800 number, you get a random person," Madison said.

"Did you guys notice there are wild turkeys across the street?"

Seneca looked up. Maddox stood over them, his hands shoved into his pockets. She cut her gaze away, feeling sheepish at her outburst in the diner. It seemed easier just to brush over what happened than acknowledge it, though. "We finally got the call list for Brett's phone line in the condo." She showed him the PDF. "One of these numbers has to be Viola's. We're thinking maybe she works at one of these businesses."

"I'll help," Maddox said. His hand brushed Seneca's wrist as he leaned in to check the screen, but he quickly pulled away. He was being careful with her. He probably thought she was going to blow up again.

Maddox chose the next number on the list. "Yes, can I speak to Viola Jones?" She waited, frowning, then hung up. "No Viola Jones there."

They went down the list with this tactic in mind, but there were no Viola Joneses working any of the help desks. Frustrated, Seneca called yet another toll-free line. When she heard the woman's voice on the other end, her heart dropped to her feet. "*Hello. Thank you for calling Addams and Stern LLC in Annapolis, Maryland.*"

The phone fell from her hand and thudded onto the mulched ground. "What?" Maddox asked, his head swinging up. "What is it?"

Seneca could barely swallow. "It-it's my mother."

She picked up the phone again. Her mother was still talking. *"Press one for directions, press two for attorney Christopher Addams . . ."* It was the law office where Collette used to work as a paralegal. How did she not know her mother was still on this answering machine? Even more bizarre, why had the office kept her voice on the outgoing message? *How did Brett know?*

Wooziness swept over her. She pressed her head between her knees and took deep breaths. Brett probably knew they'd access his phone records. This was just another *fuck you,* reminding her of what he'd done, how much power he had. But she couldn't help thinking about a barrage of questions. Why, why, *why* had Brett chosen her mother in the first place? She just couldn't buy that she hadn't paid him enough attention at Starbucks—it had to be *more* than that. But what? Would she ever know?

Without knowing quite how she got there, she was suddenly in Maddox's arms. He held her tight, stroking her hair, whispering to her that it was going to be okay. He'd taken her phone from her, too, and had hung it up. After another tight squeeze, he held her at arm's length and gave her a firm, almost stern look. "He's a demon, Seneca. You can't let him beat you."

Seneca nodded and tried to breathe. That's all Brett was doing. She had to use the anger to fuel her to find Viola and get Brett.

With that, Seneca, Madison, and Maddox called more of the 1-800 numbers, asking again and again for Viola Jones. *No, no, no.* But then, when someone at the help desk of an organic dog food company answered, he said, "We don't have a Viola *Jones*, sorry." After Seneca hung up with her, she started to think. Did the office have a Viola by a different last name?

"We're assuming that Viola has the same last name as Brett," she told the others. "But maybe she changed it. Maybe she got married."

"That dog place is the only company that seemed to have a Viola, *period*," said Madison, who had been working from the bottom of the list up. She tapped her phone and typed the 1-800 number into Google. Seneca watched as some hits came up for a company called Frieda's Raw and Organic Pet Meal Plans. The company was based in Brooklyn, New York, and when Madison clicked on *Meet the Staff*, there was, indeed, a Viola on the payroll. Viola Nevins was the head of customer support and ran a newsletter called the *Dog Blog*.

Seneca chewed on her bottom lip. "Could this be her?"

"All we can do is try," Maddox said.

"But it's Saturday. What are the odds she'll be in?"

Maddox shrugged. "Maybe the universe will be on our side with this one."

They dialed the 1-800 number again. This time, a man answered in a chipper voice, asking, "How can I make your day even more puptastic?" Seneca rolled her eyes and asked for Viola Nevins, and *voilà,* she was put on hold to the tune of "Who Let the Dogs Out?" She suddenly felt nervous. Was she about to talk to Brett's *sister*? What if she was as crazy as Brett?

"Hello?" A voice broke through. "This is Viola. How can I help?"

"Um . . ." Seneca couldn't believe Viola had answered. She swallowed the lump in her throat. "It's Seneca Frazier. I sent you an e-mail. We know your brother, Brett. I mean Jackson Brett Jones."

There was an awkward pause. "I'm in the middle of something right now."

Seneca's skin prickled. It *was* the right Viola. There was no way Seneca was letting go of her now that she had her. "Look, he's done something awful. Something related to his kidnapping. We need your help."

There was another long beat of silence. "What did he do?" Viola asked quietly.

Seneca raised an eyebrow at Madison, wondering if they could trust her. "We'll tell you if you talk to us. You know him better than anyone. We can meet you where you live. We'll come anywhere. *Please.*"

The other end of the line was filled with the sounds of ringing phones and soft murmurs. Seneca stared at crabgrass sprouting out of the sidewalk. One of the turkeys in the vacant lot let out a mean-sounding gobble. *Please,* she willed in her mind. *Please let something in this case go right.*

Finally, Viola sighed. "All right. Grand Central Station tomorrow, under the clock, three p.m. But for the record, Jackson isn't my brother. We're not technically related at all."

# EIGHTEEN

**ON SUNDAY AT** 3:00 p.m., Maddox shifted uncomfortably under the big clock at the center of the terminal in Grand Central Station. He listened to the echoing sounds of footsteps, announcements over the PA, and chatter as people rushed to catch their trains. He'd been to this station plenty of times before—Grand Central was the place in NYC where you caught Metro North to Dexby. He'd had his first kiss here, actually, down one of the corridors, with Esme Richards from track.

But he'd never associate Grand Central with kissing Esme again. Now he'd forever associate it with a murderer's "sister."

He kept craning his neck, searching for Viola Nevins, though that was a joke—he had no idea what Viola Nevins looked like. He couldn't even look for someone who resembled Brett, because, as Viola had so mysteriously told Seneca, she and Brett weren't related.

So who *was* she, then?

Seneca, stood next to him, smelling deliciously like coffee, picking at the Band-Aid on her finger. Maddox smiled at her, and she smiled back. At least she was smiling at him again. The immature part of him wanted to bring up how hurt he felt that she'd accused him of siding with the enemy or whatever, but he held his tongue. He was so tired of the swings in their already-fragile relationship—one minute, Seneca was joking with him, the next, she was a stress ball again, taking her frustration out on him. But he knew better than to bring it up. She might accuse him of *not taking this seriously* again.

"Are you Seneca?"

Everyone spun around. A tall, skinny woman in her late twenties stood a few feet away. Her eyes looked tired. She was in a black blazer and jeans, an outfit Maddox's mom wore when she was going to Back to School night. She had chin-length brown hair and high cheekbones and looked nothing like Brett, but there was something familiar about her, something that tickled the edges of Maddox's brain.

Seneca stepped forward. "Viola?"

Viola nodded, then glanced around the station. "Let's find somewhere private."

She peered around the busy terminal and the same corridor where Maddox had gotten up the guts to kiss Esme. She marched toward a trashy, nearly empty gift shop called I Heart NYC. It was full of bug-eyed Beanie Boos, Empire State Building snow globes, and T-shirts that had dumb phrases on them like *I got bageled in NYC*. Viola marched past racks of gum and Statue of Liberty–printed socks, stopping next to a rack filled with self-help paperbacks. She appraised everyone, her arms crossed tightly over her chest like a shield.

"Thanks for meeting us," Seneca said. "I'll get right to it. Jackson kidnapped our friend, Aerin Kelly. We've been communicating with him, and the only way he'll give her back is if we find the woman who kidnapped *him*, who's currently holding another child hostage."

For a few moments, all Viola could do was stare. "No. He would never kidnap someone. That's impossible."

"Actually, he's done way worse than that," Madison muttered.

"No. *No.*" Viola's face was starting to turn red. She peered at her watch and then at her phone, suddenly seeming desperate. "You've spoken to him recently? Maybe I could talk to him. This has to be a misunderstanding. He wouldn't have done that."

Maddox was about to explain, but Seneca spoke first. "Actually, he made us promise to leave you out of it. If you got on the phone, he might get angry we went against his wishes."

Viola blinked hard. "His *wishes*?" she spat angrily. She looked around at the group. "Is this some kind of joke? He would never, *ever* do this stuff. He's a good, sweet guy."

"Then why are we speaking in private?" Seneca put her hands on her hips. "Why did you not want to speak at *all*? You sensed something was off about him, didn't you?"

Viola shook her head. "I didn't want to talk to you about him because what happened to Jackson isn't my story to tell."

"You mean his kidnapping?" Maddox asked, narrowing his eyes. "Why?"

"You wouldn't understand." Viola shifted her purse higher onto her arm and started for the station again. "This was a mistake."

"Wait!" Seneca lightly grabbed her arm. "Viola. *Please.* Hear us out."

Viola turned back impatiently. The hurt and disbelief was all over her face. *She has absolutely no idea who Brett really is,* Maddox thought. He wondered what sort of person Brett pretended to be around her. A nice guy, obviously. A hapless victim. The unassuming dude they'd met in Dexby. Someone who wouldn't hurt a fly.

Seneca cleared her throat. "We're doing this to save a life. When you said Jackson wasn't your brother, what did you mean? We got the sense that you were family."

Viola looked away. "It's . . . complicated."

"Were you good friends? Did you grow up on Tallyho Island, too?"

"No, I grew up in New Jersey." Viola stared into a refrigerator containing bottles of water and soda. Her shoulders were hunched up to her ears.

"So where did you two meet, then?" Madison asked. "After he was kidnapped? Before?"

Viola's jaw twitched. All of a sudden, Maddox realized why she looked familiar. There was something about her face that reminded him of the girl in the picture they'd found at Sadie Sage's house in Upstate New York. He'd been thinking about that picture a lot. If Brett was the boy in the photo, then who was the girl? Could it be Viola? But that would mean . . .

Seneca's eyes flashed with the same realization. "Wait. Were you kidnapped *with* Jackson?"

Viola's gaze dropped. Tons of emotions washed over her face. Holy shit, Maddox realized. They were *right.*

"I was eleven," Viola said in a small, halting voice. "The woman—Jackson knew her as Elizabeth, but I knew her as Heather Peony—she was my math tutor. I saw her every week. She was really friendly. Made me friendship bracelets. Finally explained fractions to me in a way that made sense. That fall, she pulled up to me when I was riding my bike in this park near my house. Said she had newborn puppies at her house—did I want to see?" Viola shook her head ruefully. "Oldest trick in the book. But like I said, I knew her. It wasn't, like, stranger danger."

"And she took you to the same house where Jackson was held?" Seneca asked.

Viola nodded. "He came about three months, give or take, after I did. While she went to get him, she left me in this dark, locked room with food and water. I was so scared. There was no way out."

"Jackson told us you were near the ocean," Maddox said.

"Yes, I realized that after we escaped. But she never let us out of the house except when she put us in the shed if we misbehaved."

Maddox felt his stomach lurch.

"I was happy when Jackson got there," Viola admitted. "We leaned on each other. And we *became* like brother and sister. We were all we had."

Everyone fell silent. Maddox's gaze drifted to a shadow in the corner—a grisly man in a janitor's uniform was staring at them, his eyes blank and hollow. He felt his throat constrict. The janitor looked away in a blink and continued to sweep the floor.

"What was it like, living that way for so many years?" Madison asked quietly.

A shadow fell over Viola's face. "I . . . I can't talk about it. I've been through so much therapy to put it behind me, and there are some things I just can't get into."

"Was it all bad?" Maddox asked.

"Not all of it. That's what I always forget. Sometimes it almost felt *normal* . . . we had meals, watched TV, she taught us school lessons. But the bad times . . . they were really bad. And it was all just so twisted." She fiddled nervously with her hair.

"Can you talk about when you escaped?" Seneca asked. "And can you talk about why Jackson's part of this story isn't yours to tell?"

Viola twisted her hands together.

"Please," Seneca urged. "It would really help."

Viola took a deep breath. "We picked the lock to the back door while she was asleep. She woke up, though, just as we were leaving. We had to fight her off. But we did, and then we broke out of the house and ran. Our plan was to go straight to the police station—I ran to the next block and stopped and asked someone where it was. I grabbed Jackson's arm to pull him with me, but he stepped away. Said he didn't want to go to the cops. And he begged me not to tell them that he'd even been kidnapped."

"Oh." Seneca rubbed her chin. "Why?"

"I don't know. Even later, when we got back in touch, he didn't explain. I immediately went to the cops and reported what had happened. I didn't mention Jackson. The cops went to the house where we were held, but Elizabeth had already fled the scene—she had to have known what we were planning on doing. I thought the police would find evidence that Jackson had been there with me—clothes, DNA, something—but Elizabeth had cleared the place top to bottom."

"How could she have done that so quickly?" Maddox asked.

"It wasn't so hard, I guess. She didn't let us in many rooms. And she was constantly making us clean up, wipe stuff down, scour the sinks. We were getting rid of our evidence." Viola hands were clenched. "The cops asked me over and over what happened. They even mentioned the other boy who'd gone missing in the area, from Tallyho—they probably wondered if the two cases were related. But I kept Jackson's promise and didn't tell. It was the least I could do for him."

"And then your parents came for you?" Seneca asked.

Viola smiled weakly. "They couldn't believe I was alive. *No one* could. But it took so long to get back to normal." She pressed a shaky hand to her cheek. "After going through that, you're sort of *never* normal."

Maddox nodded. He couldn't even imagine.

"Were you interviewed a lot?" Seneca asked.

Viola shrugged. "*People* wanted to do a story on me, but my parents thought it would be too traumatic. I was in a few smaller papers, but mostly my parents kept the media away."

Maddox felt confused. Why hadn't they found those stories? But then, they weren't searching for a Viola with a different last name. They also weren't looking for a kidnapped girl.

Viola went on. "And then, when I got older, especially after I met my husband, we talked about me going to the press to tell what had happened, but I decided against it. Why dredge up the past?"

Seneca sank into one hip. "Jackson mentioned he went to find his parents, but they'd passed away."

"That's right. He called me when he found out. Before we escaped, I gave him my parents' phone number and told him to come live with my family, but he said no. He didn't want to be a burden."

"Huh," Maddox murmured. *Was* that why Brett didn't want to stay with them . . . or was he already too far gone by then? After all, he couldn't carry out crazy, violent deeds when living under his "sister's" roof. "Do you know where he lived instead?" Maddox asked.

"I don't. I was really worried about him. I called him a lot, but the numbers he gave me were often disconnected. He was the one who got in touch with me about two years later. He said he was living in Arizona. I asked him what he'd been up to, but he wouldn't tell me. He just wanted to talk about Elizabeth, nonstop. It made me uncomfortable.

I'd already started therapy then, so I was trying to put it behind me." She flicked a keychain shaped like a double-decker NYC tourist bus. "He was obsessed with her."

In the main terminal, an announcement sounded for a train going to Dexby, of all places. Maddox felt a nostalgic tug. He looked at Viola again. "It doesn't sound so crazy, then, that he'd kidnap someone and demand that the only way she's safely returned is if we find the woman who stole his life, does it?"

Viola's eyes dropped to the floor. "But he's a good person."

Everyone fell silent. Maybe back then he was.

Seneca cleared her throat. "This is going to be hard to hear, but Jackson . . . well, he's done some other terrible things beyond kidnapping our friend. He also murdered my mother. And my friend's sister."

The blood drained from Viola's face. "No. That's insane."

"He did. I swear."

Viola's eyes were wide. She shook her head faintly. "No."

"Viola, he wrote us a letter." Seneca stared at her hard. "I can show it to you. He confessed, more or less."

Viola's mouth hung open. "Wh-when did he do this?"

"Five years ago."

Viola took a moment to respond. "B-but that's impossible. Jackson and I were in touch five years ago. He didn't act . . . He wasn't seeming . . . There's no way!"

Maddox touched her arm. "Jackson is an incredible actor. It took us a while to figure out who he really was."

"Are there any places he likes to return to? Does he own another house somewhere?" Seneca asked.

"We need to find our friend," Madison urged. "We're afraid he's going to hurt her."

Viola's eyes darted. "I—I can't think of anywhere. He was always moving around. I can't think of anywhere he stayed for more than a few months—except that condo in Avignon."

"There's no way he's going back there," Maddox muttered.

Seneca frowned. "How did he *afford* that condo, anyway? Did you give him the money?"

"Nope. But Jackson always had nice cars, nice stuff. It's not from his parents' inheritance, or even anything he could have found in their house—he was always telling me they didn't have much. He said he had a good job, something in tech, something that he was able to do from home." She bit her lip and looked around nervously. "Jackson *was* really smart. Elizabeth always used to praise him when we did school stuff. But something told me he was lying. Like maybe . . ." She stared down at the floor. "Maybe he was getting the money illegally."

Maddox thought of the sweet BMW Brett had shown up with the first time they'd met at the CNC meet-up in Jersey. Brett had also stayed at the nicest hotel in Dexby *and* threw a kick-ass party at the Ritz in New York City. Never once had he mentioned a job—in fact, when they'd first met him, he said he was the grandson of Vera Grady, the famous fashion designer, and suggested she'd left him a lot of cash when she died. Which obviously wasn't true.

"And what about your kidnapper?" Madison asked. "The cops never had any leads on where she went after you guys escaped?"

Viola shook her head. "They couldn't find her. They looked everywhere. Asked everyone who lived in that town. A *lot* of people knew her—and they were stunned."

Seneca squinted. "And no one *else* said they remembered Brett kidnapped with you? No other neighbors who met Elizabeth?"

Viola shook her head. "We *never* went out. People never saw us.

She kept the windows pulled tightly closed. Jackson got out once—he banged on someone's door down the street, begged her to take him in, but the family brought him back to the house, and that was that. I'm pretty sure it was a tourist. The police mostly just talked to locals." Then her Apple Watch beeped, and she peered at it. "Oh. I need to get going. My dog's stuck in his crate at home."

"Hold on," Seneca cried. "Just a few more questions. Where was Elizabeth holding you? Do you remember the house?"

"The Jersey Shore. Not really far from the city, in a town called Halcyon."

"Do you know the street address?"

"I only know it by sight. It was near the ocean. Nothing special, really. Just a house."

Seneca licked her lips. "I know this is a lot to ask, but could you take us there?"

Viola's eyes grew large. "I don't think—"

"Please," Maddox interrupted. "That house might give us a clue about where she's hiding Damien."

Viola kept shaking her head. "But this happened years ago. And the police searched everything that was there. It's not like she left anything behind."

"You never know," Madison pointed out.

Just outside the gift shop, a cop walking an enormous, drug-sniffing German shepherd passed by. Maddox could feel the rumble of a train under his feet.

Viola looked tormented. "My husband's expecting me at home. Sunday is his only day off."

Seneca took her hand. "Look. There's a child being put through hell right now, just like you were. Our friend is in that situation, too. So if you help us, you'll save two people—*and* put your kidnapper behind bars. Jackson needs help. He's sick. We have to stop him before he hurts someone else. We only have one more day to figure all this out. And if we don't, he'll kill Aerin."

Viola's big brown eyes blinked and blinked. The pale green light from a lotto machine on the counter flashed across her face. Maddox hated what they were asking her to do, but he could also tell that she was a good person. How could she *not* help?

Viola lowered her head so that the group could see her jagged part. Her shoulders heaved. "I guess I could have a neighbor look in on my dog. Let's go before I change my mind."

# NINETEEN

**EVERYONE PILED INTO** the Jeep. Viola pulled her car out of a garage near Grand Central and drove separately, though she remained in sight ahead of them so they wouldn't get separated.

The drive was frustrating. Traffic in New York was never good, and it took forever to get through the tunnel. The sun was sinking lower in the sky, indicating that Sunday was slipping away. They only had Monday left. Twenty-four little hours.

Seneca wished Viola was in the car with them; she wanted to grill her for details—dates, times, places she and Brett had gotten together five years before, cross-referencing them with Helena's and her mom's deaths. But maybe it was better to give her some space. They were lucky Viola had even agreed to bring them to the place she'd been imprisoned.

"Sadie Sage, Elizabeth Ivy, Heather Peony," Madison kept murmuring. "It sounds like a rhyme. What do those names mean?" She tapped Google on her phone and did a search. Seneca peered over her shoulder as the results came up. The first results were for baby names. Sadie Sage was a clothing brand, and there was an Elizabeth Ivy who took photos of newborns and weddings, but there was no clear link between the three of them.

They took an exit for Halcyon and wove through quaint, all-American streets, which glimmered in the setting sun. A sign pointed toward a boardwalk; another showed the way to a lighthouse. A brass band was playing in a gazebo in a little square. Seneca felt a tug inside her. This place seemed far too pleasant to be a site for all the darkness Viola and Brett endured here.

Viola's Toyota turned on a street called Philadelphia, and Maddox did the same. Viola slowed once passing through a second stop sign; Seneca wondered if they were getting close. Suddenly, Viola stopped short, her brake lights flashing. Maddox slammed the brakes, too. Seneca craned her neck out the window. Most of the houses on the street were lovely, with well-manicured, grassy lawns, cheerful awnings, and spotless front porches. There was a pretty white one on the corner with a porch swing and a widow's walk. There was a quaint blue one down the street with a pinwheel in the yard. Only a small, spare house wedged between two large brick wonders, practically forgotten, looked different than the rest. Its siding was painted a faded red. The awnings on the top window were rotting away. The only sign of life was a large, well-preserved set of wind chimes hanging from the eaves over the front porch; they clanged together noisily in a gust of wind. There was a big tree in the front yard that had a perfect square burned into the bark. Seneca stared at it a moment, something flickering in her mind.

But then she turned to Viola, who stood at the curb with her hands in her pockets, staring at the place with a blank expression. She pointed to a bulldozer and front loader parked in an empty lot several doors down. "Those trucks should knock this down next."

Seneca looked up and down the wide avenue. Two blocks away,

she could see a barrier blocking vehicles from entering the beach; a sun-dappled ocean loomed beyond. There was a strange energy about the place, something familiar to the cracks in the sidewalk, the light dancing off the roofs.

"Can we go inside?" Madison asked Viola.

Viola shrugged. "We came all the way here. But if I can't handle it, I'm leaving, okay?"

Seneca walked up the front steps. The porch groaned under her weight. When she tried the doorknob, it turned easily. Inside, the walls were scrawled with graffiti and the floor littered with trash. Seneca recoiled at the sour smell and covered her nose. It seemed like this was where kids came to party.

Viola stared at the two front rooms, dim in the evening light. She pointed at a spot in the kitchen. "That's where the table was. We'd do 'school' there." Then she pointed at an empty room that probably once held a couch and chairs. "We weren't allowed in there. It used to have a door. Actually, I never saw most of these rooms. She only let us in the kitchen, the bathroom, and a bedroom." Her expression changed when she peered down a set of stairs that led to a dark, moldy-smelling basement, though when Seneca checked it out, it was totally bare save for some beer bottles and cigarette butts. "That's where she locked me when she went to kidnap Jackson."

"Really?" Seneca asked. "Jackson told us she locked him in the shed."

Viola looked away. "Yes, that was her special place for him." She said it in such a dark voice that Seneca felt a shiver.

Seneca, Maddox, and Madison looked inside drawers in the kitchen and medicine cabinets in the bathroom. They peered under sinks and lifted the lid of the washing machine. They felt their way up the stairs to find three empty rooms; the closets bore no secret messages, the marks in the wood floors told no tales.

Viola shifted from foot to foot. "It's weird to see this place with so much light. She had every shade drawn at all times. She never wanted anybody to see us or for us to see anybody."

Seneca stared at the bannister. It was eerie to think that Brett's hands had touched it, too. She'd hoped something of Brett would have lingered here—a smell, a change in the air temperature, even just a feeling. But this was a dingy, trashed house, nothing else.

She found Viola in the kitchen again, peering into the backyard. "It's gone," she chanted, as though in a trance.

"What's gone?" Madison asked, pausing while inspecting an empty pantry.

"The shed. See that little square of grass? That's where it was."

Seneca squinted, but all she saw was a patch of mostly dead grass. It was hard to believe something so horrible had happened in such a mundane-looking space.

Viola turned to her. "There's nothing in here, is there? Nothing you can use?"

Seneca shook her head. "Not really. I'm sorry for dragging you here."

Viola ran her finger along the kitchen countertop. It brought up a layer of dust. "I have dreams about this place almost every night. Terrible dreams that I'm back and I'll never be able to escape. But seeing the place again . . . it kind of takes the terror out of it. It's just a house. It's still standing. And *I'm* still standing."

"You're very brave."

Viola sniffed. "Some days, anyway."

Seneca picked at a loose strip of laminate on one of the drawers, a question forming in her mind. "Can you tell me anything else about Jackson?"

Viola placed her palms flat on the counter. "He crawled into my bed at night, hugged me close. Eventually, Elizabeth figured out that we relied on each other too much, and she separated us by a curtain. She tried to tell me things that would make me hate him—like that she caught him looking at me while I took a shower, and how he hated that I was his pretend sister—but I didn't believe her. I knew she was just trying to drive a wedge between us."

The mental image of that filled Seneca with a bottomless sadness. "Why do you think you turned out okay and he didn't?"

Viola shrugged. "Maybe because I had a family to go back to."

After Maddox and Madison had thoroughly scoured the house, they slipped out the front door and stepped down the creaky porch. As Seneca was inspecting a crack in a basement window, she heard footsteps behind her.

"I'm not going to say that being here in the very place where Brett was held prisoner makes me feel for the guy, even though I sort of do," Maddox said. "But I understand your point. We shouldn't feel for him."

Seneca sighed. "Maybe I was wrong." She told him what Viola had just said about Brett—how much he relied on Viola while they were trapped in the house, how he might have taken a turn for the worse because he had no family to go back to. "It's too bad he didn't live with Viola and her parents after they were released. It might have helped him to have people who cared about him around."

"Totally," Maddox said softly. "Family is everything." He glanced meaningfully toward Madison, who was lifting up the mailbox's small brass lid. Of course there was nothing inside.

The only sounds were the melodic *clang*s from the wind chimes.

They seemed to strike a chord in Seneca's mind—an old, nostalgic feeling of summer. She heard voices and tensed, but it was just two little kids in that vacant lot with the big trucks. The kids were using the huge dirt pile as a slide.

Suddenly, she remembered something. She reached into her messenger bag and pulled out the limp, folded photograph she'd found in Sadie Sage's—or Elizabeth Ivy's, or Heather Peony's—crawl space in Catskill.

"Viola?" she called out. Viola was unlocking her car at the curb. Seneca walked toward her. "Here. Take this."

Viola opened the door to her car so that the interior light could illuminate the photograph. After a moment of staring at it, she made a face. "Who are these people?"

"I-isn't it you? And Jackson? We found it among Elizabeth's things when we searched her place in New York."

Viola gave the photo back. "This isn't me. It isn't him, either."

As Seneca looked closer, she realized that Viola was right. This girl had green eyes, and Viola's were brown. She had a mole on her chin, and Viola didn't.

Viola studied the photo, then looked away. "I have to go," she said quietly. "I've spent too much time here already. Will you keep me posted, though?" Her face was so full of concern. "If you find Jackson? And about your friend?"

"Of course," Seneca said.

The good-byes were awkward; Seneca wasn't sure whether to hug her or shake hands, so she settled on a heartfelt wave. As Viola was getting into the car, she stuck her head out the window. Her eyes darted back and forth like she was considering saying something. Finally, she blurted, "She didn't call me Viola, by the way. She called me Julia."

"Julia?" Seneca repeated. "Why?"

Viola shrugged. "She said she liked the name. She called Jackson Alex." With a sad smile, she pulled away.

Everyone stared at one another. "Why would she call them by other names?" Seneca whispered.

Maddox looked baffled. "Because she was crazy?"

Another few beats passed. The wind ruffled the edges of Seneca's hair. Something inside the house they'd just toured moaned, and Madison grimaced. "Maybe it's just me, but can we move away from this house?" Madison suggested. "Maybe walk to the beach? This place is giving me the creeps."

"Sure," Seneca said absently, and they turned in that direction. There was a small path and wooden bridge leading over the dunes, and soon enough they were on the sand. The beach was more crowded than Seneca would have expected: A bunch of people were taking in the last dregs of the sunset, a dogged man was still swiping with his metal detector, and a bunch of teenagers were chasing each other near the shore. She inhaled the sharp, salty smell and let her body relax. There was something about even being at the beach that calmed her just a little, even with all of the questions swirling in her brain.

She puzzled over what Viola had just said, and then, in the dying light, she stared hard at the picture Viola hadn't wanted. Two kids, a boy and a girl, stood on a sidewalk. They were smiling. *Happy*. That should have been her first clue—she doubted Brett and Viola would have ever smiled for Elizabeth. So who were these two? What did they mean to the kidnapper?

Maddox stepped farther down the beach. Madison started to climb an abandoned lifeguard stand. But Seneca stayed put. On a hunch, she pulled out her phone and typed in *Viola Andrews*, which had been Viola's maiden name. Sure enough, a few stories about Viola's disappearance and her return appeared. The details matched up to what Viola had told them: She'd gone missing from her neighborhood and no one had seen what happened, but unlike Damien's story, where Sadie Sage the piano teacher was missing, too, no one seemed to connect that Heather the math tutor had skipped town. It was only after Viola escaped and she explained who'd taken her did the police dig up some intel on Heather Peony, as Sadie went by then. The images of Heather were grainy, slightly out of focus, but she had the same sharp nose and pointed chin as Elizabeth Ivy *and* Sadie Sage.

Seneca kept looking at the woman's nose. The little girl in the photo they'd found in Catskill had the very same nose. And come to think of it, the boy in the photo had Sadie's eyebrows, arched high and expressive. They were the only two things that really stood out about either kid—otherwise, they were nondescript-looking, as nondescript as Brett was. Which was probably why Seneca had mistaken Brett for the boy in the photo in the first place.

Slowly, her mind latched onto a shocking idea. Could it *be*?

*Family is everything,* Maddox had just said. And then she thought about what Freya had told them in the woods about Sadie: *She really loved kids. Maybe wanted some of her own.*

"Maddox, Madison," Seneca called out. Both of them turned quickly, their eyes wide and alert. They ran back to her, perhaps seeing the shock on her face.

She showed them the picture of the kids, and then a picture of Sadie, pointing out their shared features, their similar genetic traits. "The kids in this picture," she started, her voice catching and tight, "could they be our kidnapper's biological children?"

# TWENTY

**"SAY *WHAT?*" MADDOX** stared at Seneca in horror.

Seneca clutched the picture so hard that the edges crinkled. Not far away, a wave crashed. A car passed on the beach road playing loud hip-hop. A bird—or maybe a bat—soared silently over their heads, giving him a shiver.

"Could they be the real kids of Elizabeth-Sadie-Heather-whatever-her-name-is?" Seneca repeated. "They look just like her."

"Let's see if there's any record of her having kids." Madison's fingers flew on her phone.

"And maybe their names are Julia and Alex," Seneca said.

Maddox looked at her, surprised. "You mean the names Elizabeth called Viola and Brett?"

"It's just a thought."

Maddox stared at the rising moon over the ocean. Was it possible?

Madison sank down until she was sitting in the sand. "Okay, I'm not finding anything about Sadie Sage or Elizabeth Ivy having children of her own named Julia and Alex, though I suppose it might not be in any records. If Elizabeth went by another name when she had the kids, that's what would be on their birth certificates."

"Keep looking," Seneca advised. She held up the photo. "Maybe we can reverse-search this image. Maybe it's on Facebook or something."

They uploaded the image on TinEye, but there were no results. "I'm not surprised," Madison said. "This photo looks over fifteen years old. We weren't taking millions of pictures of ourselves and our kids like we do now. Did cell phones even have cameras back then?"

The wind was whipping Seneca's hair into her face, but she didn't seem to notice. "Okay, so Sadie Sage had kids. And maybe their names *were* Julia and Alex. If this photo was taken more than fifteen years ago, those kids would be in their twenties now. Are we thinking maybe *they* know where Sadie's hiding?"

"Maybe," Maddox said, not having considered that. "So how could we find them? They might be able to tell us a lot."

"It won't be easy going on first names only," Seneca grumbled. She sat down on the curb and rubbed her temples. "What does all this *mean*?"

Everyone kept clicking on their phones as the sun sank over the horizon. Social media sites, chat rooms, news channels—but they didn't know what to search for, exactly. It wasn't like Julia and Alex were going to do some tell-all on the *Today* show as the children of a crazy kidnapper mother. And because their names were fairly common, they couldn't pin down surefire matches that lived in Catskill or northern Jersey, which Viola was pretty sure was Heather's home base when she gave piano lessons to Brett.

Stuck, they trudged back onto the street and tried Thomas at the hospital. He was awake, and Seneca filled him in on the details of what they'd discovered. "There's something you guys haven't considered," Thomas said. "Julia and Alex might be twenty-whatever years old *now,* but they were kids when Brett and Viola were captured. So where were they when all that was happening?"

"Living with their father, maybe?" Madison suggested. "Mom and Dad didn't get along?"

"That's possible," Thomas said. "A lot of kidnappers are non-custodial parents. They feel powerless that the court awarded the other parent their children, so they grab the kids and run."

Seneca narrowed her eyes. "Yeah, but then why didn't Sadie just steal her *real* kids? Why did she take kids that just *looked* like her real kids?"

"Maybe they had a restraining order?" Madison suggested.

Thomas sniffed. "She wouldn't have cared about a restraining order. People in her mind-set rarely do."

Seneca paused next to an overfilled trash can. "Maybe we're not thinking about this the right way. It just doesn't make sense that Sadie would take other kids instead of her own. And not just one time, either, but at least twice. And if she called Brett and Viola Alex and Julia because they were her kids' names—is she calling Damien Alex, too? What does that suggest? Why would someone do that?"

Everyone was quiet. Maddox stared blankly at the stars that were beginning to emerge. Then Madison breathed in. "Maybe something else happened to her kids that makes her feel powerless? Like, not a bitter divorce . . . but something tragic, maybe?"

Maddox felt a chill. "I was thinking the same thing," Thomas's voice crackled. "Say Sadie's kids were in an accident . . . or they were killed. Maybe it was something she can't forgive herself for, or something that was out of her control. When she sees a kid that *looks* like her own kids, strong emotions are triggered inside her. She snaps. She has to have those kids, whoever they are, to make up for her kids who were taken away. It's like a sickness. And so she kidnaps the look-alikes. Again and again."

"And she calls them Alex and Julia," Seneca said, thinking this through. "And she plays house. Feeds them, teaches them, but never lets them out of her sight. And she punishes them if they step out of line. Try to escape."

Madison stared at her phone but didn't seem to know what to google. "Search for something like *horrific accidents, children*," Seneca instructed. "Or maybe a double murder? If we get a hit, this could give us Sadie's real name. Which could be *huge*."

"It would have to be before 2002." Thomas's voice crackled with phone static. "Because that's when Brett was taken, and you'd figure the tragedy would kick off the pattern."

"And Brett was nine, right?" Seneca asked, her eyes on her screen. "Viola was eleven. Damien is also nine. Maybe there's something significant about those ages. Maybe that's how old her kids were when it happened."

More phone searches. The first items to fill Maddox's Google results were a lot of accidental deaths of tweens from the "choking game," kids playing with their parents' guns and mistakenly shooting one another, and a freak accident involving an eleven-year-old and a pit bull. He scrolled and scrolled, not finding anything that matched.

After forty-five minutes, fatigue was starting to set in. Madison rubbed her eyes. Thomas had to get off the phone because a doctor had come in the room. "Guys, maybe this is a dead end," Maddox said. "Maybe Sadie just really liked the names Julia and Alex. And maybe those kids in the picture are just . . . nobody."

Seneca groaned. "But I feel like we're *this close* to figuring out her real name."

They were back at where they'd parked by now, in front of the house where Brett had been trapped for six long years. Suddenly, a light snapped on in the house across the street, and Maddox turned. Two people passed by the front picture window. Did they see Maddox and the others? They probably looked nuts, standing in front of this derelict building, all on their phones. Still, Maddox opened a new tab, wondering what else he could look for. He'd already typed in *murdered children, horrific car accidents, beach drownings, shark attacks*, and other freak incidents that might drive a mother mad. What else was there?

He looked up again, beyond frustrated. The window across the street was dark again, but the couple had lit a candle, easily visible on the mantel. Maddox watched its hot orange tip flicker and dance. New lights snapped on upstairs, and he saw the couple move through a bedroom. Did they remember that candle was still lit downstairs? He could just imagine his OCD mom watching this play out: She was a nutcase when it came to leaving candles burning unattended. *Those always lead to house fires,* she said again and again.

*Fire*. His fingers flew, typing in a new search using some of the same details. "Oh my God," he whispered once the results came up. Just change a few words, and suddenly a whole new world was revealed.

He showed Seneca the story he'd found. *Family members identify nine-year-old boy and eleven-year-old girl as victims of devastating house fire in peaceful ocean town of Lorelei, New Jersey.* The story was dated 2001.

"Whoa," Seneca said in a haunted voice.

The page took a moment to load. Maddox's eyes scanned the text, his heart speeding up with every word. A single mother, Candace Lord, an eleven-year-old girl named Julia, and a nine-year-old boy, Alex, were on a family vacation when their rental property caught on fire. Candace was out on the deck at the time; her children were sleeping. By the time the fire department arrived, the house had burned almost to the ground; the children didn't survive. Faulty wiring was suspected.

The story talked about the school the children attended, somewhere in the middle of New Jersey, and that their father, a Richard Quigley—Candace had never changed her name when she married—had passed away from a sudden heart attack just six months before. Candace's parents, Dawn and William, lived in a town called West Prune, an hour away from the vacation spot. There were a few sentences on funeral services and three pictures with the story. Two were the latest school pictures of Alex and Julia Quigley—and after a quick check of the photo in Seneca's hand, they were indeed the same kids. The third photo was of a puffy-eyed woman. As Maddox leaned in to look at her closer, the hairs on the back of his neck stood on end. There was something about the shape of her eyebrows and her nose that made him suddenly sure.

"Sadie," he whispered.

"Could this incident have made her snap?" Madison whispered. "And is this why she feels the need to kidnap other children and keep them under lock and key? She couldn't save her kids, so some twisted part of her brain now thinks she can heal if she just keeps kids safe inside."

"She can't accept that her kids are gone," Seneca suggested. "It's obviously why she picks kids that look like Alex and Julia—she wants to get as close to her old family as she can. It seems like she even wanted to choose kids who had the same interest as hers—Brett and Viola both played piano like Alex and Julia, and so does Damien."

"It's why she taught piano lessons and became a math tutor," Maddox said. "She was trolling for more kids. It's also why she took students from all over the place—so she could find the perfect victims. The closest matches to Alex and Julia."

"She has a pattern, just like Brett has a pattern," Seneca whispered.

Everyone took a moment to let it sink in. An ice cream truck rumbled past, a saccharine, tinkling song leaking out its speakers. Maddox turned back to the group, a terrible feeling washing over him. "Except there's something we haven't thought of."

"What?" Madison blinked hard, her voice edgy with fear.

"If she's trying to create her perfect family, she chooses a replacement Alex and a Julia. Brett was Alex. Viola was Julia. But in her latest kidnapping, we only have an Alex."

Seneca looked sick. "You're right."

Madison nodded, which was fine—Maddox wasn't even sure he wanted to say the words out loud. It might not just be a boy trapped in this deranged woman's lair. There might be a kidnapped girl, too.

# TWENTY-ONE

**BRETT STARED OUT** the window into the darkening night. He could hear as cars passed and voices called. Most of the voices he recognized. He knew every inch of this street. Every flower bed, every bush. He knew every neighbor—who was friendly, who wasn't, who was nosy, and who didn't give a shit. He knew, too, when new people so much as stepped onto the street. It was like the street was *part* of him, a piece of his soul.

The phone rang, and he checked the screen. Seneca again. Wasn't she an A-plus student!

"Yes?" he drawled. He peeked again at her GPS marker on his screen. His stomach turned a little; it was obvious where she was. But he couldn't let that get to him. So she was finding it all out, turning over every stone. This was part of the process. He had to be cool with it.

Except, well, he *wasn't*.

"Elizabeth Ivy's real name was Candace Lord." Seneca's words came out in a rush. "She had two children who were eleven and nine, and they died in a brutal house fire. She began kidnapping kids who looked similar."

Brett nodded. "Yes. That's right."

There was a pause. "What do you mean *that's right*?"

"I already knew that."

He could just picture Seneca's mouth falling open. "Then why didn't you *tell* us?"

"I wanted to give you a day to see if you could figure it out by yourself. And you did, so bravo."

"But we wasted a day! We could have been much farther ahead by now!"

The walls in this place were sloppily plastered, with big bumps here and there and huge, mountainous swirls. Brett ran his fingers along the ridges hypnotically. It wasn't exactly like he was trying to bog them down with busywork. Seneca was welcome to think it was game playing, but this was strategy. He knew how leads worked. If he spoon-fed them everything he knew, they wouldn't look for new clues or come to their own conclusions. They'd just be following his lead, and possibly get stuck where he did. If they wasted a day, so be it. It was worth the fresh look. The endgame was the woman who took him, and he'd do anything to find her.

And there was the issue of Aerin, too. Brett inhaled; he could smell the soap she'd used to shower, even from the hall. He wasn't sure if he wanted to give her up. Because once he did, he'd never see her again.

"Did Elizabeth *tell* you her children died?" Maddox jumped in.

Brett moved away from the window now and began pacing down the hall. The carpet was worn from all the circles he'd done. "Never explicitly, no. But I figured it out. And after I escaped, I found out her real name and what happened to them. I even visited her parents to try and figure it all out."

"What did they say?" Madison asked.

Brett slid down the wall outside Aerin's room and thought of walking up to the Lords' house all those years ago. It had been a hot, dusty day. He'd already begun to sweat profusely on the doorstep, and he'd felt sick to his stomach.

"I knocked on their door. They lived in this huge house. Didn't tell them who I was or anything. I'm sure they wouldn't have believed me. People had heard of a girl being kidnapped, but it was by a woman named Elizabeth Ivy, not their daughter. So I said I was selling magazine subscriptions. I had a booklet, forms for them to fill out."

"What were they like?" Thomas asked.

When Brett closed his eyes, he could still picture the Lords' craggy faces, the mother's unattractive gray hair, the father's potbelly. The house smelled like potpourri. A cat wound around his legs, leaving tiny, sticky hairs. He'd wanted to throw that cat across the room, make it yowl. He'd wanted to knock down all the pictures of Candace as a young girl that sat on the grand piano, smash the glass. He'd wanted to jump on the coffee table and tell those people exactly who their daughter was . . . but he'd been weak then. The fury was still curled up inside him, sleeping; he didn't know how to use it yet. So he'd just sat on the couch, drinking the coffee they offered, tongue-tied with his fake magazine booklet on his lap.

"They invited me in," he said. "I gave my spiel. Tried to make conversation. Asked if they had any pets, and then any kids. They mentioned a daughter." His throat felt prickly as he remembered the hatred he'd felt when they'd said the word *daughter* so lovingly. "I asked where she was. But they clammed up. Wouldn't tell me a damn thing." Okay, so actually *he'd* been the one to clam up. He'd walked into that house and it was like any house, with furniture and rugs and an air freshener and coffee brewing in the kitchen. When he sat on the couch, he'd noticed a small watercolor of an owl hanging on one of the walls, and he'd done a double take. The same picture had hung on the wall at *his* house, the one Candace had stolen him from. It seemed unbelievable that his life could have intersected with hers in any way, but there it was, that stupid owl on a branch, its big eyes unblinking. And then he'd gotten to thinking about that owl painting and the rest of his parents' belongings: their couches, their blankets, their books, the things that made it a home. Who knew what had happened to all of it. He hadn't even checked. He'd suddenly gotten so choked up, and his heart started beating too fast.

But he didn't need to tell them that. If they didn't understand that he wasn't clearheaded when it came to hunting down his own kidnapper, he wasn't going to spell it out.

"Do you think they know what she's up to?" Seneca asked incredulously.

"I got the sense that they just hadn't seen her in a long time. That's it."

"They didn't mention the kids and the fire?"

Brett sniffed. *We didn't even get that far.* "They kicked me out pretty quickly. The father was pissed. Said they didn't have any money for what I was selling—which was bullshit, because their house was pretty dope. And that was it. I couldn't find anything else about her. I asked about her around where the parents lived, but no one knew a thing." He stood, his legs feeling stiff, his nerves jangling. "So there you are. Now we're all on the same page. Though I'm not going to say a word about how you involved Viola in this, which you should consider a gift. You disobeyed me."

Seneca sucked in a breath. "How did you know we talked to Viola?"

Brett ignored her. "Do it again, and I won't be so friendly. Got it?"

And with that, he stabbed at the END button and slid the phone languidly across the carpet, sending it bumping softly against the far wall.

He pressed the heels of his hands to his eyes. Images of the cramped, dark house where he'd been imprisoned danced into his mind. He could practically feel the place's shadow looming over him, and now that Viola had been dragged into the fold, he was bombarded with memories of her, too—soft, kind, but as scared as he was. And that shed—he could *smell* that shed's rot, feel those invisible bugs crawling over him, hear his own voice as it sobbed quietly, relentlessly. He'd never been sure she was going to let him out. Every time she stuck him in there, he was always half-afraid she'd leave him there to die.

So Elizabeth had lost kids of her own in a fire and it had unleashed a poison inside her. It didn't mean she had to transfer that poison to other people. It didn't mean she had to leak it into *him*.

Brett sometimes wondered who he might be if he hadn't gone with Elizabeth that day. If only there had been a tear in the fabric of the space-time continuum; if only he'd stayed at school a little longer and hung out on the playground with his friends. She wouldn't have been able to get to him, wouldn't have told him her lies.

There would have been video games. Christmas mornings. Amusement parks, school plays, first girlfriends. There wouldn't have been shouting and cold, dark nights in a shed. He wouldn't have been mutated and ruined. He probably would have graduated high school, gone to college. Maybe Alternate Jackson had a job by now, a girlfriend, a normal life.

It was as unfathomable as living on Saturn. As breathing in helium instead of air.

A small, dirty moan escaped from his lips. It was from a shameful part of him, a regretful part, maybe the part that still existed from before all this, the part that sometimes slithered its way out of the cracks and looked at him, horrified, at what he'd become. He stared at his hands, suddenly not recognizing them. *Oh my God,* a voice rang out in his head. *Oh my God, who am I?*

"Brett?"

Aerin was calling out from the other side of her locked door. Slowly, he twisted the knob. Dim gray light spilled from inside the room; it was only then that he realized he'd been sitting in absolute darkness, not unlike the deep black nothingness he'd wallowed in when Elizabeth had trapped him in the shed. Aerin sat cross-legged on her bed, staring at him with her big, beautiful blue eyes with such kindness it almost hurt.

"A-are you okay?"

For a moment, Brett had no idea what to say. When had someone last asked him that question? Years? *Decades?*

"Come on," she said with an uncertain laugh. "Let's try this new thing where we actually talk about our shit instead of shoving it under the rug."

He wasn't sure he deserved Aerin's kindness. He wasn't sure he deserved anything. He thought unearthing Elizabeth would be so much easier than this. He thought by this point he was immune to feeling. It would be so much simpler that way.

"I'm not okay," he admitted. "Not at all."

# TWENTY-TWO

**AT 7:00 A.M.** the next day, Maddox leaned against his Jeep in the parking lot of a roadside Motel 6 and stretched his calves. He'd run seven miles this morning, and even though he'd had to wake up at 5:00 to do so, even though he had to jog down a creepy stretch of highway with barely any shoulder, it had felt delicious, cleansing, and necessary.

He spied Seneca across the parking lot, coming out of the lobby. She walked over to him, wordlessly handing him a cup of coffee she must have grabbed from the check-in desk. "Thanks," he said, and took a long sip. So did Seneca. The coffee tasted tinny, just the way Seneca hated it, but she didn't seem to notice. Her eyes were bloodshot. Her hair was wild around her face, uncombed.

Maddox cleared his throat. "Tough time sleeping?"

She looked at him blearily. "Didn't *you*?"

Maddox nodded. "I only got a couple of hours. Running sort of cleared my head, though."

Seneca opened her mouth, looking like she was going to say something snarky about his addiction to exercise, but then wilted. "I wish I had something like running."

"You can always come with me. I'd go slow, just for you." He gave her a little wink, expecting her to jab back with something like, *Hey, who says I'm slow?* But Seneca just stared into her coffee cup.

She looked so miserable. It was weird, not knowing the right thing to say to her anymore. He wanted to tell her he understood. He wanted to tell her how panicked he felt, too—they had mere *hours* left to find Aerin, and things weren't looking good. He also wanted to say he wished she'd talk to him more, open up. But the words felt jammed in his throat. How was it that they'd felt so connected just two days ago, and now they were like strangers?

He shoved his hands into his pockets. "Maybe you can sleep on our way to the Lords'?" he suggested, but by the look Seneca gave him, he had a feeling she was up for good.

He went back into the room and showered, and then Madison roused from sleep, had coffee, and they were ready to go. No one said much as they climbed into the Jeep and Maddox started the motor. "What's the Lords' address again?" Maddox asked aloud.

Seneca read it off. Maddox typed it into the GPS on his phone. The sun blazed in his eyes as he made a left onto the parkway. Was it crazy they were going to the same place Brett had already tried? Did they really think they'd get farther than he did? It was possible—for one thing, Brett was so much younger when he questioned the couple, and he was still emotionally scarred from all that had happened. But still, Maddox wasn't sure.

"Take the next exit," Madison recited, reading the GPS app on Maddox's phone. They were going west. In the articles about the fire involving Candace's children, Candace's parents were listed as living in a town called West Prune, New Jersey; twenty years later, 411.com said they were still there, though it seemed that they'd moved from a house to an apartment building called the West Prune Arms.

The drive took them forever, through miles and miles of cow country; they went long stretches without seeing another vehicle—which felt, in Maddox's opinion, like an eerie, dystopian nightmare. Seneca lifted the hair off her neck again and again, complaining of the humidity. Madison shifted uncomfortably in the backseat, staring at the endless empty fields and generic billboards out the window. Maddox couldn't find a single station on the radio he liked and settled on a country station, even though he hated the singer's twang.

Finally, they arrived in West Prune, which looked like it had been a lovely place once, but was now filled with boarded-up storefronts and an abundance of mini-marts, Dunkin' Donuts, and sketchy-looking people loitering on the street corners. Seneca pointed to a building in the distance. "I think that's it."

The West Prune Arms apartment building was very prison chic. It had a flat brick exterior, and some of the windows were boarded, and others had dripping air conditioners dangling out. A scraggly haired woman sat on the stoop, muttering to herself. A very loud fight emanated from an open window on one of the upper floors.

"Cheerful," Madison said sarcastically, hugging her chest.

Maddox wrinkled his nose. "Didn't Brett say they lived in a nice house? I would have thought the apartment they moved to would be similar."

As they started up the sidewalk, Seneca faced the group. "We should tell the truth to these people—as best we can, anyway. A kid's life is in danger. We're running out of time."

Maddox's green eyes narrowed. "Do we tell them their daughter is a kidnapper?"

"I'm not sure. I think we need to feel out if they have any idea where Candace is and what she's up to. Brett said they wouldn't tell him anything about her—which means that maybe they were hiding something, or maybe they just didn't know. I think we should start out just saying we're following a lead on a cold case and need to talk to her."

"That sounds good," Maddox said, and everyone stepped out.

The door to the lobby wasn't locked, so they pushed straight in, passed a bank of mailboxes, and peered at the resident list on the wall. It said that the Lords lived in apartment 4G. The elevator had a printed sign that said *Broken* over the doors, so they hiked up four flights of stairs, the heat rising and becoming more claustrophobic with each level. They walked down stained carpeting until they found apartment 4G. Inside, Maddox heard someone talking—a radio, or maybe TV. Next to him, Seneca drew in a breath. Maddox tried to understand what she was feeling. How weird was it that he was in the building that housed the parents of the woman who set forth a terrible chain reaction? Of course she'd tossed and turned all night. So many pieces to her personal puzzle were coming together, and little of it was good.

He reached forward to ring the doorbell, but no sound came. It must have not been working. Madison reached out and rapped strongly on the door, then stepped back and squared her shoulders.

Nothing happened.

Maddox knocked next. The radio droned on. He peered out a window; it looked into an airshaft. A black cat strode lazily toward a garbage can. It was almost comical, seeing such an unlucky symbol right then.

Finally Madison reached out with her fist. "Hello?" she said impatiently. "Is anyone here?" Midway through her third knock, they heard a cough behind them. A gray-haired woman with purplish circles under her eyes and a tangle of lines around her mouth appeared at the top of the stairs, two CVS bags slung over her wrists. Maddox jumped back, his heart in his throat.

"Oh!" Madison squeaked, straightening up. "Are you, um, Mrs. Lord?"

The woman blinked laboriously, as though she were a windup toy in the final stages of winding down. "Yes," she said in a watery voice. She looked at the group with confusion, like she'd never seen quite so many people in the hallway at once.

Seneca took a breath. "Yes, hi. We're a group of investigators looking into cold cases, and we're following a lead about your daughter, Candace. Do you have any idea where she is? We really need to speak with her."

Mrs. Lord's lips parted. The color slowly drained from her face, revealing blue veins at her temples.

A tall, craggy man with big hands, bushy hair, and a beer belly that folded over the waist of his postal service uniform appeared on the landing. He rushed to Mrs. Lord, and she sort of melted into him, burying her head into his chest.

"What's going on here?" the man—Mr. Lord, presumably—demanded to the group. "Who are you?" He gestured to the apartment. "There's no point in robbing us. We don't have anything."

"It's nothing like that, sir." Seneca cleared her throat. "We have some questions about your daughter."

The man slowly relaxed, though he didn't look pleased. "*What* kind of questions?" he asked slowly after a beat.

"We're investigators," Seneca said. "We need to track Candace down."

Mr. Lord shrugged and started to unlock the door. "Well, *we* have no idea where she is. Haven't for years."

He bustled inside and made a motion for his wife to follow, but she stayed put on the hall carpet. "Wait. I want to know what this is all about."

Mr. Lord looked annoyed, but he shrugged, rolled his eyes, and opened the door wider to let everyone inside. Maddox peeked into the room before going in. A gray cat, thankfully not black, lay on a leather couch, and a white one perched on the pass-through counter to the kitchen. There was a grand piano taking up all the room in a dining area. The Lords' furniture was old, but some of it was made of leather or heavy wood.

"You work for the post office?" Seneca asked Mr. Lord politely, gesturing to his uniform.

Mr. Lord looked at her as though she had three heads. "Uh, *yes*," he said sharply. "Though I have no idea what that has to do with anything."

"It doesn't." Seneca had a serene smile. "I was just curious."

"Please tell us about Candace," Mrs. Lord said impatiently. She had barely crossed the threshold of the apartment and was clasping her hands so tightly her knuckles bulged. "Has she done something? Is she in trouble? Do you know where she is?"

"Actually, we were hoping *you* could help with that," Maddox said. "When did you see her last?"

"We already told you." Mr. Lord set down the shopping bags on the kitchen island, which was visible across the living room. "It was over ten years ago."

"Did something happen that made her leave?" Seneca asked.

Mrs. Lord blinked quickly. "Well, there was . . . an accident. She was very upset."

Seneca nodded solemnly. "A house fire, was it? In her vacation home? It killed her children?"

Mrs. Lord looked surprised. "Yes! How did you know that?"

"Because they *internet-stalked* us," Mr. Lord snapped. He glowered at the group suspiciously. "That's what kids do these days."

"Can you tell us about her mental state after that fire?" Seneca directed the question at Mrs. Lord.

The woman's gaze fell to the carpet—which, Maddox noticed, was filled with cat hair and something gritty, maybe litter. "She lost her kids, and it broke her."

"I'm sure," Seneca said sympathetically. "So she was behaving strangely? Did she do anything . . . alarming?"

Mr. Lord slammed a can of soup on the counter. "That's none of your business."

Mrs. Lord looked at him helplessly. "Can I just tell them the thing at the grocery store?"

He shook his head faintly. "That's *private*, Dawn."

Mrs. Lord's mouth tilted downward. Maddox thought of how Brett had said he'd gotten nowhere with this couple—he was beginning to see why.

"Please," Seneca urged. "If you just tell us a little bit, it might link to something that's happening now. We might be able to *find* her for you."

Candace's mother lifted her head hopefully. A few more looks passed between the couple, and then she turned back to Seneca. Her throat rose and fell as she swallowed. "She tried to get two kids from town to come home with her from the grocery store." The words came out in a rush. "She didn't *mean it*. But for a little while, it was like she couldn't . . ." She trailed off, casting a guilty look toward Mr. Lord, who now had his face covered with his hands. "It was like she didn't understand they really weren't her kids. Does that help? Where do you think she is now? And what's this case you're following?"

"After that grocery store incident, did she leave right away?" Seneca asked, ignoring her questions.

"Yes," Mr. Lord answered. "And she never came back." His voice cracked, and Maddox suddenly realized how hard this was for him, too. He just showed it differently.

The screams from the upper floor got louder. A car alarm started to blare outside.

Seneca hitched forward a little. "Do you have any idea where she might have gone? Do you have family in other parts of the country, maybe? Or did she have friends out of town? Or anywhere she loved to visit?"

Mrs. Lord's eyes flicked back and forth. "I can't think of anything. We looked for her. We looked a long time. But she never turned up anywhere we thought she'd be."

The hallway was silent again. *Another dead end,* Maddox was beginning to think.

He let his gaze wander into the apartment, noticing a photo in a silver frame. It showed Candace, her husband, and her children, Alex and Julia, standing on a windswept beach. The kids looked young—five and seven, maybe, with gap-toothed smiles and pudgy bellies—they had no idea what was in store for them in a few short years. The whole family was barefoot, the waves lapping at their feet. Candace grinned blissfully. Her husband had his arm around her. It was a perfectly crystallized moment of pure joy. Maddox understood why the Lords had kept it. Why not remember the good times? Why not stare at that photo and try to pretend, even for a split second, that the present was just as uncomplicated and sweet?

Suddenly, something hit him. He pointed at the photo. "Where was that taken?"

Mrs. Lord peered at it, a rueful smile appearing across her lips. "Lorelei Beach."

Madison let out a little gasp. "Isn't that where the fire was?"

"They went there every year. It was their tradition. Well, until the fire, obviously. She never went back—and believe me, we checked."

Mr. Lord blew air out of his cheeks. "Okay. You've asked your questions. Now you should go. Leave us be."

"Wait," Seneca said. "Candace didn't grow up here, right?"

Mrs. Lord shook her head. "We had a house outside town." She gave her husband a sidelong glance. "But we had to sell it."

"Do you have any of her things? Anything she kept from when she was young . . . or when the kids were still alive?"

Mr. Lord's nostrils twitched. Mrs. Lord looked unsure, too. Seneca took a breath. "*Please.* It might help. You never know. There might be a clue in there that tells us where she ran to . . . and where she is now."

The only sound was a ticking clock somewhere in the apartment. Finally, Mrs. Lord's shoulders lowered. "Down the hall, on the left. It's a craft room, but I have a box of her things in the closet. It's marked with her name."

They could hear her husband grumbling at her as they hurried down the hall, which smelled like a mix of mustiness and cat fur. Unable to hold in his theory for any longer, Maddox grabbed Seneca's arm. "What if it's not just that Candace is trying to take kids that look like hers? What if she's also trying to re-create that beach vacation where it all went wrong?"

Seneca stared at him, her eyes wide. "Think about it," Maddox continued. "Brett and Viola were held at a beach house—not quite in Lorelei, but pretty close. What if Damien's *also* at a beach house?"

Seneca sank into one hip. "But how is she *paying* for that stuff? And what, are we supposed to search *every* beach house in New Jersey?"

"I don't know, but . . ." Maddox suddenly felt a presence behind him and looked up. Mr. Lord lurked at the end of the hall. Maddox shot him an apologetic smile. "We'll only be a second, I promise."

They found the crafts room. A twin bed was pushed against the wall, and there were bins full of girly craft accessories and a rolling cart marked *Scrapbooking*.

Seneca pulled on a creaky closest door and peered inside. The place was packed with boxes emblazoned with *As Seen on TV* logos, though the images on the boxes were very faded. On a top shelf was indeed a cardboard box marked with Candace's name. Maddox reached up to pull it down.

Inside the box were a few old T-shirts and photographs. Seneca sifted through blue ribbons for swimming competitions and an award for the *Biggest Pumpkin at the West Prune Fall Festival*. "It's just crap," she muttered. She got the whole way to the bottom, then lifted out several cloth-bound journals. The spines cracked as they opened, and the paper smelled old. Maddox felt a flutter of guilt—it felt intrusive to read someone's old diary. On the other hand . . .

But there wasn't writing in the journals. Instead, each page was filled with drawings of haunted-looking girls. One had long bangs and a pert nose and blackness where her eyes should be. Another had a furrowed brow and angry eyes and no mouth. A third was a skeleton from the neck down, only her face whole and alive. Page after page, these girls repeated: the same darkness, the same speechlessness, the same girl trapped between the dead and the living. One of the drawings was dated almost forty years ago, when Candace was a teenager. A shiver ran down Maddox's spine. They were so *eerie.*

Seneca shuddered. "Whoa."

Madison turned the next page. It was a drawing, once again, of the girl without eyes. "Oh my *God.*" She pointed to a small scribble at the bottom corner. "Look at her name."

Maddox leaned in. Clear as day, Candace had written *Sadie Sage.*

Seneca flipped a few pages ahead to a picture of the girl without a mouth. "I don't believe it," she murmured. Candace had named her *Heather Peony.* The skeletal girl was named *Bethany Rose.*

"Did she make these characters up?" Madison whispered.

"She at least made up the names." Seneca sounded certain. Maddox agreed. They'd scoured Google for ways those names could link and hadn't come up with anything.

They flipped ahead a few more pages, but they were blank. At the back of the journal, however, a few dried rose petals fell out and fluttered to the carpet. As Seneca reached down to pick them up, Maddox flipped to the page they'd marked. There was a new drawing of a tall, thin girl with wild, flowing hair and wearing a billowing gown and high heels. Half her face looked chewed up by insects. Maddox backed up, unsettled. The girl's empty eyes were sucking him in.

"God," everyone whispered in unison, blinking at the drawing. And then, with a shaky hand, Seneca pointed at the name Candace had given this new character.

*Elizabeth Ivy.*

# TWENTY-THREE

**IT WASN'T UNTIL** after they'd said awkward good-byes to the Lords and were back in the Jeep that anyone spoke—maybe even *breathed*. Seneca gave Madison a thrilled, astonished smile. "Did we just figure out where Candace's aliases came from?"

"When I was younger, I used to draw characters like that," Maddox said as he buckled his seat belt. "I mean, not like *that,* exactly—mine were ninjas, and I wasn't as good of an artist, but you get the gist. I had names for them, too. They were almost like imaginary friends."

"I guess Candace had some imaginary friends, too. That carried over into her adult life. It's like she *became* those creepy drawings after her kids died." It felt good to have figured this out. It got them closer to figuring out what made Candace tick, and it was also something Brett missed. But would it get them close *enough*?

Seneca checked her watch. It was almost ten thirty. Brett hadn't specifically said *when* their clock ran out on Monday, but they had mere hours left to figure this out.

"But what about that skeleton character?" Madison shifted in the backseat. "Bethany Rose? Do you think Candace was her at one point?"

"Or maybe that's who Candace is now," Seneca suggested.

Maddox steered the vehicle down another street; a giant flea market was taking place in a parking lot. "Maybe there's a way to track her under that name. A lease application, registration with the DMV . . ."

*"Bethany Rose,"* Madison repeated, tapping on her phone. "There's one in Albuquerque. A bunch in England." She looked up, a skeptical expression on her face. "Maybe?"

"There's no way she could have transported Damien all the way to England," Seneca said. "I'll message MizMaizie." Her fingers flew on the CNC site. As an ex-cop, MizMaizie, as was her handle on the website, still had the log-in codes to run plate numbers and look up driver's licenses faster and cheaper than a regular online search. Seneca requested what they were looking for, supplying Bethany Rose's name. She guessed Candace was probably somewhere on the east coast—replicating a dreamy beach vacation elsewhere wouldn't give it the same vibe.

As she waited for MizMaizie to reply, she stared out the window at the bland landscape. Something nagged at her, something she couldn't put her finger on. She was jazzed about the lead they'd found about Candace's aliases, but it felt like there was something at the Lords' house she'd missed.

Her phone pinged. MizMaizie had found an image of an Ohio driver's license of a woman named Bethany Rose. The stats said she was fifty-one, which seemed about right, and she had dishwater-blond hair and the same turned-down eyes, as Seneca had seen in the news photograph of the woman who called herself Sadie Sage. "This could be her," she said, showing the image to Maddox. He glanced at it briefly. An exit was up ahead, directing them east toward several shore towns listed in large white letters.

"Am I taking this?" Maddox asked. But no one answered.

"Should we call that address?" Madison asked, still looking at the screen.

The license listed an address for Bethany Rose at 108 Court Street, Apartment 5J, in Dayton. A quick Google search brought up an image of the nondescript six-story building along with the name of the company that managed the renters. Madison was already calling the 1-800 number. "Yes, I'm calling about a particular unit?" she asked. "It's 5J. Is it rented right now? No?" She raised her eyebrows at Seneca, though Seneca wasn't particularly surprised. Of course the woman who now went by Bethany Rose didn't live there. She probably never had.

"I doubt she took Damien to Ohio just to get a new name and license, you know?" Seneca said after Madison hung up. "She probably has a whole cache of fake IDs at the ready."

"It's not like it's hard to get a forged ID, either," Madison said. "All you need is a social security card—and for fifty bucks, you can buy that all over the internet. A birth certificate can be forged, too. Our girl's probably a pro at it."

Maddox gave his sister a surprised look. "How do you know this stuff?"

She glared at him. "You're not the only good detective in the family."

Seneca started a new text to MizMaizie. "I'm going to ask if Bethany Rose got any traffic violations under that license ID. If she did, we'd find out where she's driving these days, and that could link us to where she's hiding." But soon enough, MizMaizie wrote back that Bethany Rose got a gold star for safe driving. "Damn it," Seneca whispered. "Why can't we just find something *real*?"

"We'll figure out something," Maddox said.

She looked at him. "When? Tomorrow? That'll be too late!"

"If only we knew what social security number she was using with this license," Madison said after a while.

"Why?" Maddox asked. "It's probably fake."

"Yeah, but maybe she used it to open some credit cards. That would make it easy to trace her."

Maddox made a face as he steered onto the highway. "Would a kidnapper really use credit cards? And how would she pay the cards *off*? I can't see a kidnapper holding down a nine-to-five job. Does she play online poker or something? Does she have some sort of work-from-home business we don't know about?"

"She'd have to pay taxes on that," Seneca said. Her dad was an accountant; she knew more than most almost-nineteen-year-olds about the way taxes worked. "That would put her in the system, which would make her easier to find." She shook her head. "I bet she isn't using a social security number except to get that driver's license. Which means she probably isn't using credit cards, either. Though that still doesn't answer our question of how she's paying for everything. Even if she's only using cash, she has to *earn* it. How was she doing that if she was keeping an eye on her kidnapped kids all the time? This would make more sense if she asked for a ransom."

"Maybe she makes money the same way Brett does," Maddox suggested.

"And that would be . . . what?" Seneca asked.

"I don't know. Maybe she taught him some sort of scam."

Seneca pinched the skin between her eyes. "Maybe? We could call Viola back, perhaps?"

They tried that, but Viola didn't answer.

Miles ticked on the odometer. At every intersection, Maddox asked, "Uh, where am I going?" to which no one had the answer. The theory about Elizabeth re-creating the beach vacation again and again was a good one, but what were they going to do, check every beach town up and down the coast? And what if Elizabeth chose to mix it up? What if she, as Sadie, took Damien to the mountains, or to a lake?

As they got onto the highway, driving aimlessly toward the shore but with no true destination in mind, Madison cleared her throat. "Not everyone works, you know."

Seneca turned to her. "Sorry?"

"I was thinking about what you said about Sadie working. Not everyone works, though. When I want money, I just go to my parents."

Maddox groaned. "Not helpful, Mad."

Seneca tapped her lip. "Are you saying she's getting it from her parents?"

"I don't know. Maybe."

Maddox made a face. "Uh, you don't remember that apartment we were just in? The Lords are broke."

"And they didn't seem to know anything," Seneca added. "Are they that good of liars?"

Out the window, they passed a McDonald's, a Best Buy, a giant Walmart. A thought struck Seneca hard. "Actually, could that be *why* the Lords have nothing to give?"

"Meaning?" Maddox asked.

"Some of the things in their apartment didn't make sense—the solidness and size of their furniture, that piano in the corner, and they *did* own a nice house, years before. Those are all indicators that the Lords *had* money . . . but they don't anymore. And yet Dad's a postman, which is a decent, steady job."

"What are you saying, they're secretly wiring her money?" Maddox asked.

"That's exactly what I'm saying." Seneca looked at him, something pinging in her brain. "I need you to turn the car around."

Maddox looked shocked. "Wait, what?"

"We need to go back to the Lords'. I need to talk to them again. *Now.*"

"Are you sure that's a good idea?" Madison asked.

Seneca had no idea if it was a good idea or not, but she knew she had to try. Forty-five minutes later, Maddox was pulling back up to the West Prune Arms. She gazed at the building warily. If she was wrong about this, they would have wasted precious hours. It was past noon by now. They were running out of time.

She jumped out of the Jeep before it was fully stopped and hurried back through the busted security door to the lobby. Took the stairs two at a time. Mr. Lord answered her knocks. When he saw it was Seneca, his mouth flattened into an angry line. "I don't have anything else to tell you," he said tightly.

"You love her more than anything, don't you?" Seneca interrupted.

Mr. Lord went very still. "Excuse me?"

"No matter what she does, no matter how sick she is—you're her dad. You want to make sure she's okay. You know where she is. You've known all along. You just wanted to help her."

A shutter seemed to close down Mr. Lord's face, revealing nothing. "I have no idea what you're talking about."

"Bill?" Mrs. Lord called from the background. "What's going on?"

He glanced over his shoulder. "Everything is fine, Dawn."

"How did you get money to her?" Seneca persisted. "Was it through a secret credit card? Envelopes of cash?"

"What is she talking about, Bill?" Mrs. Lord sounded woozy.

"She's not making any sense."

Seneca stared the man down. If she just grilled him a little longer, she'd have him. "You know the postal system. You know secret ways you can get her money that won't raise any flags. It's why you have no money now. It's why you had to move out of your house."

Mrs. Lord stared at him. "But you told me it was because of salary cuts."

"I don't know who you are," Mr. Lord said, rubbing his face. "But you're picking on the wrong person. I have no idea what you're talking about. I could call the police." But when he took his hand away from his eyes, she could see there was fear in his expression. Her heart started to leap. He *did* know. All she had to do was push him a little further.

"You know where she is, Mr. Lord. I know you know. But your daughter has done something awful with that secret money you've been sending her. She's been kidnapping children. Kids she's trying to make into *her* kids . . . except it never works. Do you know that, too? Have you suspected, and maybe you don't want to admit it to yourself?"

Mr. Lord's eyes widened. He blinked hard at her but didn't say anything.

"They're scared. Lonely. She hurts them. She's *sick*. Some of those kids have escaped, and one has gone on to be a toxic person. He killed my mother . . . and it's all because of your daughter and the money you've been sending her." Seneca took a breath, the magnitude of the moment swirling around her. The nightmare had started here, with this family. If not for Candace, Brett wouldn't have been kidnapped and warped. Aerin's sister would be fine. *Aerin* would be fine. Seneca's mother would be fine.

Then she took a breath and pinned them with her gaze. "So if you think it's okay to hide this, if you think this isn't doing any harm, keeping your sick, sad daughter afloat, you're wrong."

The rage had disappeared from Mr. Lord's expression, replaced by something resembling horror . . . and maybe shame. He slowly licked his lips. Seneca's heart banged in her chest. What was he going to do now? What if *he* tried to hurt her? What if he had the ability to snap, just like his daughter did?

And yet she still didn't think she'd hooked him yet. She had to keep going. "Right now, your daughter is holding another boy hostage. *This* boy." She pulled out her phone and called up the picture of Damien. "He's nine and he loves Disney and he has a family that's desperate to get him back. And her old captive, the one who killed my mother, he's now kidnapped my dear friend. Time is of the essence, Mr. Lord. In just days, both these victims could be dead. I'm not going to report her or you to the police, but I do want information. *Please.*" Seneca pressed her hands together in prayer. "Undo all of this evil by just *telling* me, okay?"

The world seemed to still. Mr. Lord kept his head down, staring at the floor. His shoulders heaved up and down—maybe in anger, but maybe in sadness. Mrs. Lord breathed quietly behind him, her teeth biting down on her closed fist. "It can't be true," she whispered. "Bill, is this true?"

Finally, the man lifted his head. His mouth was gummy and amorphous, and when he first spoke, his voice had a bleating, honking tone, trying very hard to hold in a sob. "I didn't want her living on the streets."

*"What?"* Mrs. Lord cried. She blinked at him, dumbstruck. "What did you do?"

"When did you last send her money?" Seneca asked quietly, careful not to show her elation that she'd managed to crack through his tough exterior to the truth.

He swallowed hard. "A few weeks ago."

"A few *weeks*?" Mrs. Lord repeated.

"And where did you send it?" Seneca asked, ignoring his wife. They were so close. *So close.*

Mr. Lord shook his head. His mouth clamped shut, like a vault. Then his wife grabbed him by the arm and swung him around with great force, making him face her. "You tell them!" she screamed. "If this is true—if she's kidnapping children—you tell them right *now*!"

She started to shake his shoulders. The man's head rattled on his neck, and his arms hung at his sides, boneless. After a moment, Mrs. Lord collapsed against him, sobbing, wailing, pounding his chest. He pushed her away with a grunt and then faced the group, giving them a withering stare. He opened his mouth several times before actually getting out the words. "A PO Box. In Breezy Sea, New Jersey."

Seneca's mouth dropped open. Behind her, she could feel Madison shift and hear Maddox gasp. It made so much sense. Of course Candace Lord—aka Sadie Sage, aka Elizabeth Ivy, aka Bethany Rose, maybe—was hiding in a town called *Breezy Sea*. Even the name conjured up lapping waves, calling seagulls, mini-golf. Seneca could practically smell the sunscreen and the waffle cones.

And then she realized something else. She thought of the roads they'd just driven on, all the turns Maddox wanted to take, all the mile markers. A sign for the Breezy Sea exit shimmered into her mind, and she stood up straighter, energized. They were close. *Really* close. Breezy Sea was only one parkway exit away.

# TWENTY-FOUR

**AS THE HOT** sun made a long, slanting shadow out the window, Brett's phone rang. He looked up at Aerin, who was sitting on the bed across from him, watching a rerun of *Friends* on TV. He'd wheeled in the TV this morning, and he liked how pleased Aerin had been to receive it. He also liked how she moved aside to let him watch Monica and Rachel and Ross banter back and forth in their big apartment in New York City. Not like he gave a shit about Monica and Rachel and Ross—he'd never seen the show before this, and he didn't really find it that interesting. What he liked most was sitting next to Aerin's warm, sweet-smelling body and watching her laugh. He wanted this time to last forever. Sometimes, he considered adjusting things so that it would.

The phone rang.

Brett frowned. Aerin looked up, intrigued. Talk about shattering a moment. Then again, these were Seneca's last few hours of fact finding. Of course she was scurrying around, trying to put all the pieces together. He hoped she'd found something useful.

"We found the town where she's hiding him," Seneca said the moment Brett pressed the green ANSWER button.

Brett moved away from the window. "You got all that from the Lords?"

There was a pause. "How did you know we went to the Lords?" Seneca's voice sounded strange.

Brett's skin prickled. *Shit.* He knew they'd gone to the Lords because he'd watched Seneca's phone travel there on the GPS tracker. But he didn't want *her* to know that. "Because it was the only lead," he said haughtily. "And clearly, you got more out of them than I did. Good job. So where are you going now?"

"No way I'm telling you that yet. Not until you give us Aerin."

Brett let out a scoff. "I'm not giving you Aerin until you tell me."

"Make a trade, and we'll do just that."

"Tell me, and I'll make a trade," Brett countered.

He could feel Aerin watching him, so he padded out of the room, careful to lock her door, and entered his own room, clicking on his laptop. After typing in his password on the GPS app, a map swam into view. The pointer moved quickly across the state of New Jersey, heading straight toward the shore.

"If you can help us with something, we'll give you your information faster," Maddox broke in. "When you were with Elizabeth, were there any specific patterns you remembered? Times of day she went out. Stuff she brought back for you guys. Logos on grocery bags, brands of food she liked to get, that sort of thing?"

Brett watched the pointer steadily moving toward the blue expanse of ocean. It was soothing, really. Like watching an aquarium. "We always had fresh bread," he said. "She was crazy about bakeries. And she liked farmers' markets, too. Summer fruit, like peaches. And soft pretzels twisted to look like billy clubs."

"Okay," Seneca said. "That's good. Thanks."

Brett sniffed. "Don't I get a reward for my efforts?"

"Give us Aerin, and you'll get it all." And then Seneca hung up.

Brett glared out the small window in his little room. High above the rooftops, someone was flying a drone. It was a cheap one, probably purchased at the local souvenir shop. It looked so innocent, flying up there. So cheerful and uncomplicated. He wished his eyes were laser beams, burning it, smashing it apart, bringing it back to earth. Ruining a child's day.

He consulted the screen again. The little pointer icon was now going across a bridge that seemed to lead to a specific beach town. Brett leaned forward until his nose was nearly touching the monitor. He hit the maximize button, widening out the map to get a look at more of the land. That bridge led to only one little town. *Breezy Sea.*

Go-time, then. The GPS was portable. He could track them in the car. He wasn't wasting any time letting them get to Elizabeth first.

He closed the laptop, then marched into Aerin's room. Aerin sat up on the bed. "What did Seneca say?"

Brett ignored her, heading into the bathroom. A toilet wand and some cleaner were stashed in the cabinet. He took them out and began cleaning, mentally running over how he'd have to bag the wand when he was done and deposit it in a garbage can somewhere random and far away so no one would connect it to this place. Not that he was really worried about someone raiding here, scouring for Aerin's DNA evidence. He had the deed to this place; there was no reason to raid here unless the police were given a reason. Still, it was good to be careful.

"Brett." Now Aerin was standing in the doorway, watching as he peeled several of Aerin's long blond hairs from the tub drain. "Talk to me. What are you doing?"

Brett turned and looked at her. Backlit by the tiny sliver of sun he allowed through the blinds, she looked angelic, divine. Her blue eyes gleamed. The gauzy blouse he'd bought for her floated delicately across her thin midsection, and her shorts showed off the length and curve of her thighs. The scales had tipped, and now Brett loved Aerin more than he hated her, which made what he was going to do so much more difficult.

"I'm going to have to make a decision soon," he said evenly, trying to stare at her without emotion. "It's not going to be an easy one."

Aerin's brow furrowed. "Meaning?"

He dropped the toilet wand into a plastic bag along with a bunch of paper towels and a hairbrush containing a few ice-blond strands, then washed his hands and dried them on his jeans. "It means come on," he said to Aerin, taking her hand. "We're going."

"Going where?"

Something in Brett's face must have given him away, because she stepped away from him. The corners of her mouth twisted downward. Brett grabbed a towel from the rack and lunged for her, looping it around her head to cover her eyes. Aerin let out a yelp, but he clapped his hand over her mouth.

"Don't scream," he said into her ear. But his tone was gentle. Even a little regretful. "This will all be over soon."

# TWENTY-FIVE

**BREEZY SEA LOOKED** like the other beach towns they'd visited—bustling and touristy with quaint, residential sections, and of course with the ubiquitous ocean looming large to the east. As they drove over the bridge, Seneca's nerves jumped and snapped. They were close. *So* close. But it was almost 4:00 p.m.; the drive had taken longer than they expected. Brett had wanted answers by Monday *evening,* but did that mean by 6:00 p.m. . . . or by midnight?

There was another problem, too: According to the map, Breezy Sea was big. Without help, finding the woman who perhaps now went by Bethany Rose and her captive, Damien Dover, would be like finding a needle in a haystack.

"Where are you now?" Thomas said, speaking to them on speakerphone from his hospital bed. The doctors wanted to keep him for one more day, but Seneca could tell he felt out of his mind that he couldn't be here.

"Just found the post office," Maddox told him, swinging into its parking lot so abruptly the Jeep's tires screeched. If Mr. Lord was sending Candace cash through a PO box, a postal worker might have noticed her accessing it . . . *and* even know where she lived. But as they drove up to the parking lot, it was ominously empty. Seneca leapt out and ran to the door, staring at a hand-printed sign that had been taped there: *No AC,* it read. *Closed until Thursday. All PO box mail diverted to USPS at 104 Ocean Bright Road in Ocean City.*

"No," Seneca cried. *"No!"*

"What's happening?" Thomas asked.

"It's closed," Maddox told him. Thomas groaned.

No one knew what to do. Seneca could literally *feel* time slipping away.

Then Madison pointed across the street. *Darnell and Daughters Bakery,* read quaint letters on a window. "Fresh bread, right?"

They hurried across the street. The bakery smelled sweet and doughy and was crowded with beachgoers hoping for a late-afternoon snack. A red *Please Take a Number* dispenser greeted them as soon as they walked in, but Seneca brushed past it to the counter.

"Have you seen this woman?" she demanded, showing Sadie's picture to the first person behind the counter who looked her way.

The girl shook her head. Seneca showed the picture to another employee; when she didn't know, she showed it to several people in line. No one found Sadie familiar.

"Are you *sure*?" Seneca pressed. "Someone who looked like this wasn't in here for fresh bread? She might have different hair now. She might be thinner, or heavier."

The first employee they'd asked shrugged. "Maybe," she ventured. "The thing is, a *lot* of people come in here. Especially in the summer."

Back on the street, they paced around like animals trapped in cages. "Maybe the toy store?" Madison suggested, pointing.

Maddox shook his head. "Brett and Viola never mentioned her buying them toys."

"What about there?" Madison pointed at a farmers' market across the street. "Didn't Brett say something about fresh peaches?"

They entered the town square. Farmers had set up carts of fresh beans, corn, tomatoes, watermelon, and, yes, peaches, though the place had a droopy feel about it—the farmers had likely sat in the hot sun all day and were ready to get home. The group split up and showed the image of Candace to everyone who'd listen, but again, no luck. Only one woman perked up and said, "Haven't I seen her on *Nancy Grace*?" But she hadn't seen her in Breezy Sea.

By the time the cheese vendor, the organic beef farmer, and yet another watermelon grower had said no, Seneca's panic was at a fever pitch.

They filled Thomas in on their lack of progress. "We have to *think* instead of randomly trying places," he said. "There has to be evidence of her somewhere."

"Do you mind if I grab a water in there?" Maddox asked, pointing to a Wawa mini-mart a few storefronts away.

Seneca glared at him. "We don't have *time* to get water!"

"Fine, you want me to faint?" he countered testily. "We should all eat something."

They hung up with Thomas, promising to update him when they had news. Inside Wawa, the air-conditioning was cranked to near-frigid temperatures. Seneca drifted around the store senselessly. *Think, think, think,* she ordered her brain. Candace had to be traceable. How was she feeding Damien? What if he needed medicine? Where did she get stuff to clean the house? *Did* she clean the house?

Still feeling breathless, she moved toward Maddox, who was

waiting to pay for a bottle of Gatorade at the register. The checkout person seemed to be new, puzzling over his register and slowly ringing up the person at the front of the line. As he squinted yet again at the keypad, Seneca turned away, certain she might scream. Her gaze scanned the other items on the counter: packs of gum, local chocolate, and then something that turned on a light in her brain. It was a strangely shaped pretzel. She felt a jolt.

*"A pretzel shaped like a billy club,"* she murmured.

Maddox looked up. "What did you say?"

But Seneca was already pulling out her phone and calling up the picture of Candace Lord on Google. "Have you seen this woman?" she asked the cashier, startling him away from his intense inspection of his keypad.

"Who?" the cashier asked, squinting at the photo.

"She goes by Bethany. Have you seen her come in here?"

The worker shook his head. "Nope. Don't think so."

But maybe that made sense: This guy was new. Seneca strode to the deli counter, interrupting a guy as he constructed a turkey sandwich. "Have you seen this woman?" she asked him, showing him the picture through the glass.

"Don't think so," the deli guy said, barely looking up.

"Did you even *look* at the picture, dude?" Seneca snapped. She waved it in his face.

The Wawa employee dropped the knife he was holding with a clatter. His eyes were sharp, annoyed. "I said I haven't *seen* her."

Seneca peered at Maddox desperately. "Candace bought pretzels here. I'm almost positive. This is our *last chance*!"

"I've seen that lady."

The voice came from another customer in line. Seneca, Maddox, and Madison spun to the left slowly. The person who'd spoken was a tall man in a *Rip Curl* T-shirt and board shorts. He looked in his thirties, maybe, and a little boy held his hand.

"You have?" she heard herself say faintly.

The man's gaze bounced from the picture of Seneca's phone to Seneca's face again. "She's staying down the street from my family on Sea Tern Lane. It's about a mile down the road. We're only a block from the ocean." He cocked his head. "Why are you looking for her?"

Seneca glanced at the little boy by his side, desperately wanting to say, *Don't worry about it. Just keep your kid far, far away from her.* But she just shrugged and muttered something about it being personal.

She thanked the man and left Wawa. It took every remaining shred of composure she had left to walk with an even pace and keep her expression neutral. Only after the activity in the store went back to normal, only after everyone stopped staring at her, even that man with his son, did she break into a run, the others close behind. They had to get to that house. *Now.*

# TWENTY-SIX

**BLINDFOLDED, AERIN FELT** Brett pushing her from behind down a corridor. After a flight of steps, a door swung open, maybe the door she'd seen from her room, the same door she'd hoped to run out of when Brett was sleeping. A sharp, pungent sting of gasoline assaulted her nostrils. The floor felt hard and unforgiving—was she in a garage?

Brett's hands clamped down on her shoulders, steering her to the left. Her feet stumbled beneath her, and she wheeled her hands out in front of her, catching nothing. Brett threw a hand around her waist with a grunt. *"Walk,"* he groaned into her ear. After another step, her hip bumped something hard and metal. With a beep, she heard the sound of something popping and releasing—the trunk of a car.

"No," Aerin whispered, suddenly understanding what was coming next. She glanced over her shoulder to where she perceived Brett was standing. "Please, no. Let me sit next to you. I'll still be blindfolded. I won't say a word. Just don't put me in the trunk. *Please.*"

"Stop talking," Brett said calmly but sternly.

"Where are we going?" Maybe if she just kept him talking, he'd forget about what he was going to do with her. “Are we coming back here?” Brett hadn’t packed anything—not of hers, and not of his. She knew he was working on a laptop in another room. He wouldn’t just abandon something like that.

Brett’s fingers dug into Aerin’s shoulder. “I might,” he said. “But I’m not sure about you.” And just like that, he pushed her forward.

Aerin’s chin hit first. She felt Brett maneuvering her from behind, folding in her butt and her legs. He grabbed her wrists and tied them together behind her back. “Please,” Aerin kept gasping. “Please, Brett. I thought we were friends. Why are you doing this?”

Brett didn’t answer. The trunk slammed hard. Moments later, she heard the *thud* of the driver’s door closing and the car starting up. Then there was the telltale groan of a garage door opening.

Her body trembled with fear, but she tried to hold on to hope. While he was obsessively cleaning that bathroom, wiping away any trace of her skin and hair and saliva, she’d slowly, calmly bitten off a few fingernails and dropped them under the bed. And then she’d pulled out a few long hairs and stuffed them under the mattress. Also, she stuffed the contact case with Brett’s lone hair inside into her pocket. *I’ll show you DNA evidence,* she’d thought angrily. It had made her feel powerful at the time, but now it felt like too little, too late. And also? All those things she’d said to Brett. All those times she’d let him sit close to her, *touch* her. Hell, she’d even felt sorry for the guy—she’d even empathized with him! And this was how he repaid her? He was just going to kill her anyway?

Her body bounced as the vehicle began to roll. She was crunched in such an awkward position—her legs were bent, her back was curled, her head was turned to the side. It was dark in the trunk, too, and it seemed like the oxygen was slowly being sucked away. She was too afraid to even cry. Now, even more so than when she'd been trapped in that room, she realized how much she was going to lose . . . and how badly she wanted to live. If she got out of here, she was ready to change. Try. *Thrive.* Or at least give it a shot in a way she hadn't in years. And she thought of the relationships she'd let go—with her mom, her dad, her friends, all because she was too angry and closed off and defensive. What she'd give to have time back with them, to say she was sorry, to do things over. Her family would never know that she'd always loved them, deep down—because, like an idiot, she'd never *said* those things. She'd always just pushed and pushed and pushed away.

And *Thomas.* Her heart clenched. Would she ever see Thomas again?

*Please, Helena,* she prayed, though she didn't feel her sister's presence in the slightest. *Please help me get out of this. I'll do things differently from now on. I'll try to be a better, kinder, more open person. I'll try to be happy, too. I promise.*

She could hear sounds coming from the front seat. Brett had turned on the radio. A Metallica song came on, and he began to hum to himself. *"Off to never-never land . . ."* he sang off-key.

"Brett," Aerin called out. She wriggled around the trunk, finally touching the small pass-through door that led to the backseat—her mom had one in her car, too. She pressed against it, hoping it would fall open, but it was jammed. "Please. You don't have to do this."

Brett changed the station. NPR news blared out. He changed it again. Something country. He paused on that for a moment, but then there was static once more.

"Are you really going to kill me?" Aerin asked.

A weepy song from the '70s. A ballad with lots of violins.

"Brett?" Aerin pounded on the door "Talk to me! I know you can hear me!"

The car took several more turns. She could feel they were on a highway for a while, cruising steadily, but then the car jolted to the left, sending her body rolling against the side of the trunk.

"Brett, please," Aerin said wearily. Oxygen was definitely seeping from this space; she was beginning to feel light-headed and spotty. Maybe this was Brett's plan, then—drive around until she suffocated. "Please don't kill me," she wheezed. "I'll do anything you ask."

Did she mean that? She didn't know. But she did know she didn't want to die yet. The desire to live burned strongly inside her, brighter than it ever had.

After what felt like hours, the car jolted to a stop. The engine died, and Brett's door opened. There were footsteps coming her way, and her heart lifted. She braced herself, readying her eyes for the light and heat of the sun. But then, confusingly, the footsteps seemed to fade. Aerin's ears strained for more sounds . . . but there were none.

"Brett!" she screamed, kicking on the underside of the trunk's hood. "Come on, Brett! Not funny! Let me out!"

Cars swished by. Occasionally, she heard a roaring airplane. "Help!" she screamed more. She kicked until her knuckles were raw. But it did no good except to make her bleed and deplete her lungs of more precious air. As she struggled for oxygen, a new, crueler reality began to take shape in her mind. Brett wasn't coming back. He had left her here. And it was somewhere no one would hear her scream.

This was how it was going to end.

# TWENTY-SEVEN

**TEN MINUTES LATER,** Maddox and the others did laps around a packed beach parking lot near Sea Tern Lane and finally found a space. The sidewalks were eerily devoid of people, and it didn't look like anyone was in any of the vacation homes, either—on a sweltering day like today, you'd be crazy not to be camped out by the water. A radio played something cheerful in the distance. The boardwalk loomed over the dunes, its Ferris wheel slowly turning, a loud screech of an arcade game blaring through the air.

From their view, three streets jutted out from the avenue that ran perpendicular to the ocean: Sea Tern, Sea Glass Road, and First Street. Sea Tern seemed to be only a block long before it came to a T at a park, so they had a decent view of each house. Which one was Candace hiding in?

"Okay," Maddox said as he unbuckled his seat belt. "What's our plan? Get eyes on Candace? Then call Brett?"

"Not unless he gives us Aerin," Madison said.

"Right."

"Is anyone else uncomfortable with the idea of just telling Brett where Candace is even after we get Aerin?" Seneca drummed her fingers on her phone case. "We're basically giving him the okay to murder someone. It makes us accessories to the crime."

Maddox looked uneasy. "Could we call the police once we find the house?"

"I feel like Brett would have already thought of that. I wonder if he has something else up his sleeve. Whatever he wants to do with Candace, he doesn't want *us*—or the cops—around to witness it. And what about the kid? I hate the idea of Damien being caught in some sort of cross fire."

"Is there a way *we* can go in and grab Damien before shit goes down?" Madison asked, then shook her head. "Actually, forget I suggested that. That sounds insane."

They called Thomas to update him, running through the options. "I think you should worry about getting Aerin back first," he said. "Then, once she's with you, call the cops."

Suddenly, the other line bleated. Maddox's stomach lurched when he saw the number on the screen: *Brett.*

"Thomas, we'll call you back," Seneca said nervously. She switched to Brett's call. "What?" she answered sharply, putting the call on speaker.

"Well?" Brett asked.

"Well what?" Seneca countered.

"Do you have something to tell me yet?"

"No."

"You're lying," Brett spat. "I know you know. You've stopped. You *know,* and you're not letting me in on it—and that's not our agreement."

"Dude, we're not sure about anything yet." Maddox felt annoyed at Brett's hurry-up mentality. *Just let us do our job, dude. The day isn't over yet.*

"If you're lying, all bets are off. You know that, right?"

Maddox turned to Seneca, expecting her to freak out, but she'd gone silent, her eyes wide, her lips pursed. It was her Thinking Face. She barely registered when Brett hung up.

Maddox touched her arm. "What is it?"

Seneca's brow furrowed. "There was something weird about Brett's voice, don't you think? He sounded less clear than usual—more like he did when he called us the very first time. There was a lot of whooshing. I think he's in a car."

"Okay . . ."

"So where is he driving to? Where's Aerin? And did you hear how he said *you've stopped*? How does he know we're not moving?" She looked up, startled. "Do you think he can *see* us? Do you think he's tracking us somehow?"

Maddox's skin started to crawl. It had definitely been weird that Brett had so confidently guessed that they'd been at the Lords'. He'd guessed that they'd spoken to Viola before they'd volunteered the information, too. *Was* he tracking them?

He turned to Madison. "Could Brett do that?"

Madison twisted her mouth. "He could triangulate us during a phone call in the same way we tried to triangulate him. There's also software on the darkweb that puts a bug on someone else's phone they've been in contact with, so they can follow them at all times. But that's illegal and full of viruses. I wouldn't touch it with a ten-foot pole."

"Yeah, but *Brett* would," Seneca said. She looked down in dismay. "Brett's been contacting *my phone*. Meaning I'm the one he's tracking." She quickly turned her phone off and put it on the dashboard, as though even holding it would give Brett a clue about where they were. "And now he knows we're in Breezy Sea. I led him right to us."

"Even if it's true, it's not your fault," Maddox said quickly. He peered out the window, though all he could see were the tops of the other cars in the lot. "We can't let him find the house before we do. Otherwise he'll have no reason to give Aerin back."

He moved to jump out of the car, but Madison caught his arm. "Wait. If Brett is tracking Seneca's phone by GPS, then maybe we can trick him and buy some time." She reached over and turned the Jeep's ignition. "Let's drive to another lot, turn Seneca's phone back on, and leave it in the front seat. Then we'll walk back to Sea Tern to find the house. If Brett's really tracking Seneca, he'll come to the phone, not to us."

"Good idea," Seneca said shakily. Then she cocked her head. "Should one of us stay at the lot, then, in case he *does* show up? Maybe you, Maddox?"

"No freaking way," Maddox said quickly.

"But—" Seneca protested.

"No," Maddox pleaded. "Seneca, it's not smart. We have to stay together."

Seneca glanced at Madison for her opinion. She looked torn. "I see your point, but I think there's safety in numbers. There's no way I want to be in a parking lot, even a public one, with that creep all alone."

Maddox pulled out of the lot. He found another parking area several blocks down the beach. It was equally packed, and he had an even harder time finding a spot, finally squeezing between the public bathroom and a humungous GMC that was taking up two spaces. He turned the car off, switched Seneca's phone on again, and dropped it on his seat.

Hopefully, their plan would work for a while. But Brett was smart. He'd figure it out soon enough.

They headed back to Sea Tern Lane on foot. The day was blisteringly hot—a half block in, sweat started to pour down Maddox's back as though he'd just run the 800 at top speed. The first house had several cars with Pennsylvania license plates in the driveway and seemed large enough to sleep twenty people. The second and third houses were just as opulent, with three stories, multiple decks, and pimped-out golf carts, off-road vehicles, and boats in the driveways—Maddox couldn't imagine Candace hiding in one of those. But one house stuck out like a sore thumb: It was a faded, unkempt yellow, way smaller than the others, and looked abandoned.

*Maybe?* Maddox thought, peering into its windows.

"Is this it?" Seneca whispered.

Maddox turned. To his surprise, she wasn't looking at the yellow place but a large gray two-story across the street. It looked in better shape than the yellow one did, with a nicely manicured rock garden out front and a bicycle propped up against the garage.

*"Look."* She pointed to heavy wind chimes swinging from the front porch. "Those were at the place where Brett was held, too. And there's a shed in the back."

Maddox shivered despite the heat. The shades were all closed, so there was no way of seeing what was happening inside. So they would watch and wait, then? He looked around for somewhere they could take cover. There was no way they could just stand here, staring—what if Brett drove by and noticed? But all the yards were gravel-topped no-man's-lands.

Then he spied a speedboat covered with a blue tarp parked in the driveway next door. "If we climb in there, we'll be able to watch the house without anyone seeing," he murmured, pointing at it.

Madison looked at him like he was crazy. "What happens when the owner comes out?" She gestured to the cable that hitched the boat to an SUV. "Or what if they drive away with us inside?"

"Do you have a better idea?"

"I do." Seneca walked up to Candace's door. "We're going to ring the bell."

"Are you crazy?" He grabbed her shoulder. "Candace won't just open the door for you!"

Seneca rounded on him. "Don't you remember what Brett told us? She mentioned Brett to all the neighbors. Pretended to be a normal mom. Damien might be in hiding in there, but *she* isn't. She knows what will arouse suspicion." She wrenched from his grasp and started up the path again. "We'll say we're a cleaning crew. Or anything, really. Just so she opens the door and we see that it's her."

"But . . ." Maddox protested.

"We have to do something," Seneca argued over her shoulder. "Aerin's life is at stake, Maddox. We can't just wait around!"

Suddenly, there was a loud *clonk*. They pivoted just as a large rock thudded to the ground against the house in question's front siding. Madison was brushing off her hands and stepping back. "What?" she asked, noticing the shocked looks on their faces.

"Did you just throw a *rock* at her house?" Maddox cried.

Madison nodded. "A commotion might get Candace out on the porch, too."

"Then we need to get out of here!" Maddox hissed, darting toward the boat next door. The last thing he wanted was for Candace to see them in the yard—then she'd *know* something was up.

They crouched behind the boat, relishing its cool shadow. A car whooshed past playing rap music; the driver thankfully didn't notice them. Someone's laugh spiraled from an open window. Maddox's heart thudded in his ears. Finally, the front door of the house in question opened. A woman with big droopy eyes, sunken cheeks, and thin lips stepped onto the porch and looked around, trying to figure out the source of the sound. Despite her haggardness, her features matched the pictures in the Lords' living room.

*Candace.*

Maddox gasped. Seneca made a gurgling throat sound. Madison clapped a hand over her mouth. It was astonishing that she was *here,* that this was real. As they watched, Candace frowned, grumbled, and then stepped back inside and slammed the door.

"Holy shit, holy *shit,*" Madison whispered, shaking out her hands.

Prickles were dancing across Maddox's body. "We have to get out of here. If Brett's close, we can't risk him seeing us standing right in front of this house."

"Back to the parking lot." Seneca slipped out from behind the boat and started to run. "*Then* we call Brett. We have to play this just right."

Maddox started to run, too. His head was churning. His heart was pounding fast. *We've done it,* he thought gleefully. They were going to get Aerin back. This nightmare was going to be over. But suddenly, in the calm, humid quiet, Maddox's phone started to ring. He turned it over and looked down at the screen in horror.

Now Brett was calling *him.*

# TWENTY-EIGHT

**BRETT GNASHED HIS** teeth as he pressed his phone to his ear. He was so angry he thought he might grind his teeth to pulp. Moments ago, he'd followed Seneca's blinking GPS dot to a parking lot near the beach in Breezy Sea. When he'd seen Maddox's Jeep parked there—and it had been a bitch to find, with all the freaking cars in the lot—he'd been thrilled. *Well, well, well.* His little tracker hadn't failed him. And now that he'd found where they'd stopped, he didn't need their help any longer—he'd figure out which house they were spying on and raid it on his own. He'd get his cake—Elizabeth—and eat it, too—Aerin.

So he'd crouched behind the putrid-smelling public bathroom, out of their line of sight, forming a plan. If the group was parked here, it probably meant they were watching a house nearby. He'd looked around. There was a house directly across the street from the parking lot, but there were towels hanging from a clothesline and a teenage girl talking on the phone on the upper deck. Definitely not Elizabeth's place. The house behind that one was also filled with a family, and the one beyond *that* had three surfboards stacked on a station wagon in the driveway. Those were the only two properties visible from the parking lot.

Huh.

Brett stared hard at the Jeep once more, his nose wrinkling at the stupid New Balance bumper sticker on the back. It took him only a split second to realize something strange. There weren't any shadows moving inside the windows. Brett blinked and squinted hard. The Jeep was . . . *empty*.

He sucked in a breath, then stepped closer. Nope. Not a single person inside. He peered through the windshield, careful not to leave any prints on the body. A cell phone lay faceup on the driver's seat. It was Seneca's phone—Brett remembered her mint-green case from when he'd fiddled with it in Avignon. She'd left it behind on purpose. To *trick* him.

He swallowed a scream. *Just go,* he told himself. *Get out of here. Take Aerin. They've screwed you one too many times.*

But the need to find Elizabeth taunted him. He decided to give them one more chance. And now he was calling Maddox. The phone rang once, then twice; Brett could feel his blood pressure climb with every passing second. *If they don't answer, they're going to pay.*

"Hello?" Maddox finally said.

Brett fumbled to bring the phone to his ear. For a moment, he was so blindly pissed, he couldn't even speak. "You really think you're going to outsmart me?"

"I . . ."

"Where are you? I need an address, *now*. I know you're right in front of it. The rules have changed."

"Wait." Now it was Seneca on the line. "We have the address, but there's no way we're giving it to you unless you give us Aerin. End of story."

Brett felt like the top of his head might pop off his skull. No. *No.* He wasn't giving up Aerin. The perfect outcome was one in which he pulled Aerin out of the trunk after this was over. She'd be sick from the heat and the close quarters, but he'd lay her on the backseat, put a cool washcloth on her forehead, and shush her to sleep. They'd drive and drive, maybe returning to where they'd been, or maybe going somewhere else. The sky would be the limit. He'd be free to go wherever he pleased once Elizabeth wasn't a millstone around his neck.

But the only way to get Elizabeth was to let go of that fantasy. Brett shut his eyes, despising that they'd cornered him. Still, it only took him a few moments to reach his decision.

"Fine," he grumbled. "Meet me on the boardwalk. Take the ramp in the lot where your car's parked." At this point, he didn't care that they knew he'd tracked them. "I'll be in the fun house. But if you're not here in ten minutes, you'll never see us again."

# TWENTY-NINE

**SENECA AND THE** others had stopped on the corner next to a big sign marking Sea Tern and Ocean Drive. Over the dunes, she could see the roller coaster tracks dipping and winding. Another ride rumbled, and people screamed joyfully. Something dinged at the arcade.

*He's there,* she thought with horror, staring at all the flashing and whooshing and flapping flags. *Brett is right. Over. There.*

"The fun house?" Madison whispered, her head tilted toward the boardwalk, too. "Are you kidding me?"

"Should we actually do what he wants?" Maddox asked.

"I don't see another way." Seneca rolled her shoulders back and hit the WALK button one more time. Finally, the light changed to green, and they crossed, their flip-flops smacking noisily against the pavement. Every few steps, Seneca thought she might faint. This was happening. *Really* happening. In mere minutes, she was going to *see* Brett. How was she going to control herself? How was she going to keep from pommeling him?

*You have to,* she told herself. *Do what he asks, and we'll get Aerin. Maybe we'll get him, too.*

They wove around a few beach stragglers pushing large carts full of chairs and toys up from the sand. Seneca's nerves felt as prickly as the small cacti that lined the path. She cleared her throat. "Is anyone else waiting for the other shoe to drop? Brett seems surprised for once. He's never agreed to our terms before."

"And that makes you nervous?" Maddox asked.

"Maybe," Seneca admitted. Things were never as they seemed with Brett—this might *feel* like a win, but there could be a twist in store. It felt like they were walking into a lion's mouth, its sharp teeth bared, its stomach rumbling.

Madison fanned her face. "Should we call the police? Maybe tell them what's going on, give them Candace's address? I hate for Brett to just go in there, guns blazing. What if he hurts Damien?"

Seneca had thought about that, too. "I'm afraid Brett will figure it out. He plans for every eventuality. What if he sees it on our faces and doesn't give us Aerin?"

"Let's just see what we're getting into first," Maddox decided.

They turned to the right, where the boardwalk began. People were gathered in clumps along the wide wooden slats, laughing, flirting, milling around the junky shops. Colors swirled, the scent of burned popcorn singed Seneca's nostrils, and the noisy arcade *bloops* were almost too overwhelming to bear. They walked past a strip of rides, all the stimuli blending together, everyone's faces looking shadowed and macabre in the dying light. Then Seneca peered woozily past a busy hot dog stand whose great distinction was that they made the "biggest hot dog in all of Breezy Sea." A large building next to it bore a mural of a hulking, ominous clown crouching over a set of double doors. The clown rested his hands on his knees in a lurking, Sumo sort of pose; his eyebrows were arched, his grin was nasty, and at that very moment, a little girl in pigtails was pointing at him and shrieking in terror. Written along the sides of the doors in dripping fluorescent-yellow paint read the words *Fun House.*

Seneca's heart dropped to her knees.

Madison shakily extended a finger. "Have I ever mentioned that I am deathly, *deathly* afraid of clowns?"

They wended toward the entrance, ducking around families and teenagers and a man who was inexplicably wearing a *Scream* mask. Haunting, maniacal laughter wafted from a speaker positioned just above the clown's pointed hat. Seneca stared through the fun house's doors, but it was so dark inside she had no idea what she was walking into. She grabbed for Maddox's hand and squeezed it hard. She wondered if he could feel her pulse in her fingers as he squeezed back. *Brett's in there,* her head kept hammering. *He's right there.*

"Let's do this," Maddox said through gritted teeth.

They forged into the fun house. It was cooler inside—and clammier, too, so much so that Seneca felt like she'd broken into a cold sweat. The first room was oddly narrow and strangely bright, with striped walls, slanted checkerboard floors, and a ceiling that tilted upward the farther into it they walked. *The Gravity Room,* read a plaque on the wall. They all sidestepped precariously across. The blaring, awful laugh track seemed to be on repeat, and Seneca found herself casting desperate, trapped glances at the others. Where was Brett? Was this a trick?

They passed through a second doorway and entered a room full of mirrors. Seneca stopped, disoriented. The Seneca in the mirror mimicked her movements, but that girl was warped, widened, and stretched. Then a splash of blond hair across the room caught her eye, and she spun around. Someone was lurking around a bend. Maybe *two* someones. She sucked in a humid breath.

*"There,"* she whispered to the others.

She hurried across the floor, dozens of versions of herself streaming along like colorful ribbons. When she reached the corner, she saw a brown-haired guy in a black T-shirt and black shorts reflected in the mirror. Her heart stopped. Brett looked like anyone—not menacing, not evil. He stood casually, one foot propped against the wall. One arm was wrapped around a tall girl in a black hoodie, her blond hair spilling down her shoulders.

*Aerin.*

Seneca pressed her hand to her mouth. Brett whipped around, his reflection spying hers. Their eyes met in the mirror. The corner of Brett's mouth curled up in a smirk. A sizzle traveled up Seneca's spine. For a moment, she could only gawk. She couldn't believe he'd made good on his promise. Actually, she couldn't believe Brett was here at all, real. After all this time, she'd sort of mythologized him into a demon, an evil, otherworldly creature. There was something aggressive about the way he had his arm wrapped around Aerin's waist. When Aerin saw the group, she let out a pained cry, but Brett tightened his grip and she stopped.

*He has some sort of weapon pressed into her back,* Seneca thought with dread. If Aerin screamed, she'd die. If one of *them* screamed, she'd die. Brett had every ounce of power and control, like always.

Seneca, Maddox, and Madison slowly walked toward Brett and Aerin, their eerie, warped reflections following. Brett never broke eye contact. "Nice to see all of you," he shouted over the sounds of the laugh track. His voice was like a hammer to Seneca's skull. The shape of his mouth, the squint of his eyes—it was all so *real*. "Now, do you have something to tell me?"

"Not until you release her," Seneca said shakily. She glanced at Aerin. Her friend's lips were clamped together, as though she'd been ordered not to talk, but her eyes were wide and scared. *Please help me,* she seemed to be saying. *Please end this.*

Brett shook his head. "Tell me the address, and she's yours."

"No," Seneca insisted. "Give Aerin back, and I'll *take* you to the house. I'm not going to just tell you. That's the deal. Take it or leave it."

She could feel Maddox stiffen by her side. Madison gave Seneca a look that said, *Are you sure?* Seneca really *wasn't* sure, but she didn't want Brett to trick them. She didn't want Brett to get the address, grab Aerin, and run.

A breeze wafted through the mirror room, bringing with it a scent of mildew. The clown's laughter morphed into a droning techno song. Brett stared at them for a long time, and then shifted his weight. "How can I be sure you won't take me to the wrong place?"

"Because I'll ring the doorbell. She'll come to the door. She did so for us. You'll see."

*"Seneca,"* Maddox urged out of the corner of his mouth. "This isn't a good idea."

But Seneca kept her eye on Brett, her heart shuddering, every cell in her body quivering. "Come on. Give Aerin to Maddox, and let's go. But you have to promise not to hurt the kid when you go in there, okay?"

Brett let out a note of protest. "You really think I'd hurt a kid?"

*How should I know?* Seneca thought. "You have to get Damien out as soon as you go in there. Send him to me. I'll make sure he's safe. Got it?"

"Seneca . . ." Maddox murmured.

*"Got it?"* Seneca repeated, glowering at Brett.

Brett's gaze dropped to the shiny floor. Aerin wriggled a little, the fear on her face intensifying. What was pressed into her back? A gun? A knife? Seneca took another step toward Aerin—she was so close, she could smell her floral shampoo. She was so close to Brett, too. His ordinariness scared her. The way his hair curled over his ears. The acne scars on his chin. That he'd put on shorts today, that he'd tied his shoes, that he had to cut his fingernails and brush his teeth and get a good night's sleep like every other human on the planet.

"Come on, Brett," she said gently. "I know what Elizabeth means to you. I'll take you to her. I'll let you close that chapter of your life."

The corners of Brett's mouth were still turned down, but Seneca could tell by his eyes he was starting to crack. He was going to do it. He was going to release Aerin. But suddenly, his head whipped up, and his gaze narrowed on something on the other side of the room. Seneca swiveled to look, too. A new reflection appeared in the mirrors, tall and fat and doubled and warped all the way down the line. It was the shiny badge that caught Seneca's attention first, and then the wording on the back of his jacket, reflected in the glass: *Breezy Sea Boardwalk Security.*

"Everything okay here?" the guard asked, flashing his light across the group.

Seneca froze. *Go away,* she wanted to say. *Nothing to see here.* But then she caught sight of Brett's betrayed expression. Did he think they'd set him up? *Come on, Brett. We know better!*

She opened her mouth, ready to speak, ready to fix this, but time moved both too slowly and too quickly, and her muscles didn't cooperate. The guard stepped purposefully toward them. Brett's eyes turned to slits, and he drew Aerin back, one arm slung around her tightly like a seat belt. Seneca reached toward Aerin, desperate to grab her—now that there was security present, would Brett do something crazy? In that same moment, something shiny slashed toward Seneca's body, and she saw a glint of metal and felt a jolt of pain. Maddox shouted something Seneca couldn't make out over the techno music. Suddenly, she was on the ground, stars spinning in front of her eyes.

"Freeze!" the guard cried, grabbing a gun from his holster and pointing it at Brett.

When Seneca looked up, Brett held a red-tinged knife out in front of him. She stared down in horror at the blood dripping down her arm. He'd *stabbed* her? The pain rushed in again. The world tilted, then receded. Maddox dropped to his knees next to her. "Shit, Seneca, *shit*."

Seneca pushed him away. "I'm fine, I'm fine, it's not that bad," she said breathlessly, struggling to get to her feet.

"Drop the knife," the guard repeated, gun trained on Brett. "Release the girl."

The guard's hand went to the walkie-talkie on his belt, which made Brett's knife press to Aerin's throat. Aerin let out a little screech. "Don't you dare call backup," Brett growled. His eyes were wild, and his jaw was clenched so tightly cords stood out in his neck.

The guard released his walkie-talkie, but he stepped closer, and there was a *click* of the safety switch releasing. Brett's lip twitched. Aerin whimpered. The knife blade dug into her skin. "Come on, son," the guard said gruffly. "Don't do anything stupid."

"P-please," Aerin whispered, tears running down her cheeks.

A few hot, dark, horrible seconds passed. Seneca had no idea what to do. Brett's eyes were whipping everywhere—at the mirrors, at their pockets, their hands, perhaps hyperaware that *they* might call in backup instead. But then, strangely, the next thing Seneca knew, the knife fell to the ground with a clatter, skidding to a stop against one of the mirrors. Aerin flew out of Brett's arms, staggered toward Maddox, and he engulfed her in a huge hug.

"Hey!" the guard bellowed, darting into the darkness. Seneca looked around, disoriented. Brett was gone.

"No!" she screamed, starting to follow the guard through the door. "Come back here!"

Footsteps rang out in the darkness. The pain in Seneca's arm throbbed. She exited the mirror room into an arcade full of vintage *Pac-Man* games and a bunch of claw-grabber machines. The bright lights hurt after so much confusing darkness, and she stumbled through the mayhem, searching for Brett's bobbing head among the teeming bodies. He wasn't there. She spied the guard standing by a dinosaur video game with his gun lowered. He was speaking into a walkie-talkie: "On the run . . . backup needed." Then he looked up and met Seneca's gaze. "You need an ambulance, honey?" he asked with concern.

Seneca shook her head and pivoted toward the arcade's exit, finding herself on the boardwalk again. Brett had to be here. He couldn't have gotten away so fast. She looked right and left for a tall, brunette guy, but that was the thing—there were a million tall brunette guys out here. It was like *Where's Waldo?* practically. She took a few halting steps to the left, then pivoted right toward the ramp they'd come in on, figuring he'd go back to the streets in hopes of finding Candace's house himself. She wove through the cars in the parking lot and exited onto the sidewalk, blood still dripping from her arm, head still gummy and swimming.

The streets were empty. Windsocks flapped on porches. Seagulls soared overhead. Bells rang out indicating that someone had won it big in the arcade. But Brett . . .

No. *No*. Something seemed to snap inside her, splitting her open, throwing a dark curtain over her whole world. Seneca arched her back to the sky and let out an agonizing scream.

Brett had escaped. *Again*.

# THIRTY

**THE BLOOD BOILED** in Brett's head as he ran through the streets. It felt like acid was pumping through his veins. After crossing the main beach road, he ducked behind a tree, reached into his backpack, and felt around. Took off his T-shirt and replaced it with a tank top. Positioned the long-haired wig on his head and smashed it down with a Yankees ball cap. It was a rudimentary disguise, nothing he'd use long-term, but Seneca—and the cops—would be looking for a brown-haired, hatless person in black sprinting at top speed, not a long-haired skater dude in a wifebeater out for a stroll.

He passed one house, and then another. It was still so hot; trails of sweat ran into his eyes and mouth. This house? *This* one? Maybe this one? *No, no, no . . .*

He stopped and leaned over at the waist, breathing hard. Shit. *Shit.* He started to pommel his thighs with his fists. What the fuck was happening? Had he lost? Had those idiots won? Why had he let go of Aerin? Why had that guard appeared? Why hadn't he thought to bring a gun?

He would salvage this, though. He needed to find Elizabeth—he had to. She had to be close, behind one of these doors. And now, with the mood he was in, he would take no prisoners.

He rose back up and stomped to the next block. This house? This next one? He would find it. He was *smarter* than they were. Why the fuck had he agreed for Seneca to walk him to the house? Why hadn't he just gone with his gut and forced the address out of them?

As he passed a bungalow, he nearly tripped over a shiny bike lying across the sidewalk. Bitterness swirled in his heart. *He'd* never gotten to have a bike like this. *He'd* been locked up a good portion of his childhood. He kicked it so hard that it sailed a few feet across the yard and landed with an ugly *thunk*.

And then he heard it. Distant wails at first, spiraling through the muggy air, but then they started to come closer and closer. He spun around, trying to make out their location. Flashing ambulance lights appeared through the trees one street over. Brett crept closer, walking halfway into someone's yard to get a good view. Several police cars had parked at the curb in front of a gray house. A few cops had dogs. Officers were communicating stealthily, SWAT-style. They crept, ninja-like, toward the entrance.

Brett's stomach sank to his feet. No. *No.* He tried to tell himself it might be for some other major crime . . . but how likely was that? Seneca must have called the police. Seneca must have told about Elizabeth. She'd given the cops the information that was supposed to be *his*.

He started to shake with rage. It felt like his body was ripping apart in one explosive burst. He spun around and grabbed the first thing he saw—an oar from a canoe, leaned against the side of the random house whose yard he'd wandered into. Blindly, almost involuntarily, he started to smack it against the grass, letting out a guttural wail. *They'd told. Those assholes had told.* The one thing he'd dreamed of all his life. The one confrontation he deserved, he was owed. Gone. *Gone.* He deserved to look her in the eye. It should have been his hands around her neck, repeating all those awful things she used to say to him—*this is for your own good, this is the way it has to be, I'm doing this because I love you.*

The oar started to splinter. A piece flew off, smacking against his bare calf, cutting into his skin. Another broke, skittering beneath an expensive-looking gas grill. Brett let out a grunt and flung the thing over his shoulder, feeling like he was part wild animal, part volcano, part wrecking ball. Destroying the oar hadn't satiated him in the least—he wanted to rip at something, pulverize something to pieces. He clawed at his face, not caring when he felt the prick of blood on his skin.

But then curiosity got the better of him. Gulping, half-blind, he lurched even farther into the yard toward the sound of the sirens. The ninja cops were no longer on the lawn of the gray house. An ambulance had driven up onto the grass, its lights flashing. The door to the house burst open, and a few of the ninja officers carried a young boy out. EMTs ran to the kid, covering him with blankets, doing whatever EMT stuff they did to make sure someone wasn't in shock. Brett blinked, trying to remain impassive, but he felt cracked in half. *He'd* never gotten a rescue like this.

A second wave of officers brought out a girl. She was a little taller than Damien with black hair and fine features. She looked so much like Viola that Brett did a double take. It was astonishing that Elizabeth could keep finding perfect little replicas. It was repugnant that she kept charming children into trusting her. He supposed he should feel some sense of pride that he'd helped to save these kids, but all he felt was resentment. Damien and the girl had only been stuck in this nightmare for a few months, max. They'd get their childhoods back. They'd get to see their parents. They'd get to *live.*

The door opened one more time, and several cops led a woman out in handcuffs. Bile rose in Brett's throat, but he didn't dare blink, didn't dare breathe, drinking up every moment of the thing he'd waited for nearly half his life. Elizabeth still looked the same—gaunt, scraggly, with those crazy, crazy eyes. She was shouting something, though he couldn't hear what—probably that these were her children, and that she'd done nothing wrong. She was crying, too. Unceremoniously, the cops placed her in the back of their cruiser.

And then they drove away.

Brett bit down on his lip so hard he tasted blood. His mind was whipping with fury. He had been one street away from Elizabeth. One street away from the answer. This was *his* criminal to catch . . . but there she went, disappearing down the road, seat belt on, sequestered behind a pane of glass. Months of planning down the drain. Years of searching, for nothing. What was he going to do with this anger now? What was he going to do with this hate?

A siren whooped closer, and Brett crashed back to the present. He had to get off this lawn, away from this busted oar; the last thing he wanted was to lose his freedom, too. But before he slipped away, he caught sight through the trees of a girl still standing on the kidnapper's lawn, her arms wrapped tightly across her chest, her mouth in a frown. Seneca's keen eyes searched the road, the houses, the stairs to the beach. She didn't look satisfied. In fact, she looked downright furious.

She was looking for *him*, Brett realized. He stepped back to the sidewalk, an idea forming in his mind, a tiny flicker of hope bursting in his heart. Working quickly, he called up CNC on his phone and sent off a message.

*You're sad, aren't you? So sad you didn't find me. But you will. You just have to put the pieces together. And I'll be waiting when you do.*

# THIRTY-ONE

**THAT EVENING, MADDOX,** Seneca, and Aerin sat in the waiting room at the police station in Breezy Sea.

"Here we go," Madison said, strolling back from the vending machines. She dropped bags of chips, candy bars, trail mix, and a few sodas onto the scratched coffee table.

Maddox reached for a bag of Cheetos. Aerin snatched a pack of M&M's. "I made a promise that I was going to eat less sugar if I ever went free. This seems like a bad start, but I don't really care."

Maddox chuckled louder than the joke probably deserved, but damn, he was proud of Aerin. The girl had *balls.* Other people would have gone catatonic after being trapped with Brett Grady and then threatened at knifepoint in a creepy fun house. If it were him, he probably would have requested a one-way ticket to a psych ward. But Aerin, once the hubbub in the fun house had died down and she knew she was safe and the real police were on the scene? She started tugging at their sleeves to track down Brett. "I'm going to the police station with you," she'd said vehemently. "There's no way you're leaving me out of this. Brett is going down if it's the last thing I do."

Now the sidewalk outside the police station was jammed with rubberneckers, news vans, and reporters—Maddox could hear the din even from inside. The names Candace Lord and Bethany Rose and Sadie Sage were on everyone's lips. Damien was at the back of the station with a social worker and several psychologists; his parents and Freya were on their way from New York. The girl who'd been recovered from the house, an eleven-year-old named Huntley Monroe, was also in the back, also being interviewed. Huntley had only been missing for a week. Her family had been vacationing at a nearby beach town from western Pennsylvania, and according to the news stories, Huntley had a wild streak; her parents were more worried that she'd run away or was in a terrible, freakish accident. She didn't have a clue who Candace was when Candace snatched her, which was different from Candace's normal pattern, but Maddox guessed Candace couldn't resist because Huntley looked so much like Julia, her daughter. But now, luckily, Huntley would get to go home, too.

The cops were still sorting out who needed to be interviewed, though Seneca, Maddox, Madison, Aerin, and even Thomas, from his hospital bed, were on their list. However, because recovering Damien and Huntley and apprehending Candace were the priorities, the cops hadn't gotten around to talking to them yet. Maddox and the others had agreed on one thing, though, when they *did* give their testimony: They had to tell the truth about what the guard had come upon in the fun house with Brett and Aerin. That included Aerin's kidnapping, Brett's clues, his threats, his past. Brett was gone again, and they needed everyone's efforts to catch him. Brett's rampage needed to end, *now.* They'd already called Viola about it; she was on her way from New

York to give her testimony, too. Viola had sounded so shocked that they'd found her kidnapper—but impressed. It had felt pretty freaking good to tell her the news.

"I bet the cops will find Brett," Maddox said after polishing off the Cheetos and starting on a pack of sour cream and onion chips. "There's evidence now. Fingerprints on that knife, for one. That's huge."

"I know," Aerin said as she poured more M&M's into her palm. "And there's that hair of his that I hid in the contact case. I already turned it over to them."

Maddox felt a dart of horror—to think Aerin had to scrounge for one of Brett's hairs in hopes of getting him in trouble!—but then nodded appreciatively. "Good for you."

"And don't forget the car," Madison said optimistically. The Ford Focus Brett had used to both kidnap Aerin *and* bring her to Breezy Sea had been abandoned in the parking lot where the botched exchange had gone down. A police officer was staked out near it, waiting for Brett to return, but so far he hadn't. Well, of *course* he didn't. The dude wasn't *that* dumb. Still, there could be DNA in there, too.

Seneca just rolled her eyes and kept picking lint off the arm of the couch. She was the only one who hadn't reached for any of the vending machine goodies. Not even a soda. "They're not going to find him. DNA's only useful if you actually know where the criminal *is*."

Aerin looked chagrined. "Yeah, but . . ."

"But we all saw him," Maddox jumped in. "We can describe him to a sketch artist. His picture is going to go up on the news."

"So he'll just change his appearance. And then the news will die down, and *no one* will be looking for him again, and in a few months, he'll come back and hurt all of us because he believes we double-crossed him."

"Seneca!" Maddox warned. The last thing he wanted was Seneca scaring Aerin. Seneca had been in a dark mood ever since the fun house, though. At first, she'd been great—hugging Aerin, making sure she was okay, even acting levelheaded about Brett getting away. But once the cops went to arrest Candace, once Seneca searched the entire property and didn't find Brett there, she'd begun to sink into despair.

Seneca flicked another piece of lint, then turned to Aerin. "Didn't Brett tell you he was returning to the house where he was holding you?"

Aerin sipped a Diet Coke. "He said he *might* go back. But that was before Candace was found, so who knows."

"You really don't remember *anything* about the place?"

Aerin bit her lip and stared into the middle distance. "It was a house," she said finally. "A house and not, like, a hotel or an apartment."

"You already told us that," Seneca said.

"Sorry." Aerin's eyes flashed. "I was in a room. There was no view of the outside. I got a glimpse of the hall at one point, which is how I knew we were in a house—a rather nice house. But that's it. If we *could* find it, I snipped some of my fingernails and hid them under the bed. So there will be proof that I was there."

Seneca grumbled something under her breath Maddox could hear. He gave her a cautious look, and she shrugged, her gaze trained on Aerin again. "And when you drove here, how long did it take?"

"A few hours, maybe? I tried to track the time, but he had me in the trunk. I couldn't see a thing."

"Did it seem like you were on highways or back roads?"

Maddox cleared his throat. "She just said she couldn't see anything."

"Highways," Aerin said, but then seemed doubtful. "Although this one road was kind of twisty . . ."

Seneca checked something on her phone. "My last call with Brett was at about five p.m. Then he called Maddox at about seven thirty—when he found the Jeep in the parking lot. It took you two and a half hours to get to Breezy Sea from wherever you were." She frowned. "How about when you were at his place? Did you smell anything? Hear anything? What about bugs or animals? Did you hear any weird animal sounds? Get any bug bites?" Aerin shook her head again and again. "Did you hear any strange sounds at night when you were in the room? Trucks? Airplanes? People? Music?"

Aerin's face lit up. "Actually, this one time I heard a truck. Like it was backing up. That *beep, beep, beep* sound, you know?"

Seneca seized on this. "Like a garbage truck? Or a dump truck?"

"I don't know. I just heard beeps."

"The beeps are different." Seneca scrambled to pull up two sound clips on her phone: one was a garbage truck, the second was a dump truck. She played them for Aerin. Aerin held her palms in the air. "Sorry, but they both sound the same."

"They're not the same," Seneca said forcefully. "It's one or the other."

"Seneca," Maddox warned. "They totally sound the same."

There were beads of sweat on Seneca's forehead. The only sounds in the room for a few long beats were the dull murmur of the local news on the TV screen over their heads. The story was about a strange standoff in the boardwalk Fun House . . . which then led to Damien and Huntley being found.

"Ugh," Seneca said, her face twisting. She rose to her feet and stormed out of the station, pushing angrily through a side door that led to a small side parking lot.

Maddox jumped up, too. "Wait! The cops could call us in any minute!"

"Who cares?" Seneca called over her shoulder as the door almost banged shut in Maddox's face. "It's not going to make any difference."

"Seneca . . ." Maddox followed her along a row of squad cars. The pavement was still so hot, and the air smelled like fresh blacktop and homemade fudge from the shop down the street. "What's wrong with you?"

She was hugging her body so tightly her nails dug into her upper arms. Maddox glanced uneasily at the high fence that separated the two of them from the throngs of people. Even though he couldn't see them, he could hear everyone talking, the reporters giving updates.

"Look. It sucks we didn't get Brett. I can't stand that he's still out there. But everything we said in there is true—we have DNA on him now. The cops believe us that he kidnapped Aerin. A guard saw Brett lose it with his own eyes. We have resources. We'll find him."

"No we won't," Seneca mumbled.

Maddox heaved his shoulders up and down, trying to swallow his frustration. How could she be so sure? Why was she being so pessimistic? "And also? We saved two kids today. We put a maniac in prison probably for the rest of her life. I'm proud of that, and I think you should feel proud, too. Don't you think?"

He waited for her reaction, but she didn't move. Didn't smile or nod. Suddenly, her shoulders started shaking. Maddox's stomach twisted. Was she . . . *crying*?

"Hey." He slid closer to her. "I'm sorry. Talk to me. *Please.* I want to understand what's going on with you. Tell me what's on your mind."

He touched her shoulder, but she shot away as though he'd burned her, her hip nearly knocking against the bumper of the nearest squad car. "Seneca," Maddox begged. "Please!"

It seemed like hours passed before she stubbornly wiped her eyes and looked up at him again. "Fine. You want to know what I'm thinking about? *This.*"

She shoved her phone in his face. On the screen was a message to her CNC account. *So sad you didn't find me. But you will. You just have to put the pieces together. And I'll be waiting when you do.* It was from BMoney. *Brett.*

Maddox's heart dropped to his feet. "Wh-when did you get this?"

"I saw it about fifteen minutes ago. But he sent it right around the time the cops were arresting Candace."

"You aren't actually considering . . ." But when Maddox looked into her eyes, he knew for sure that she *was* considering. "Oh, Seneca," he said. His mind tumbled. He felt a little sick. After all they'd gone through, after all the danger they'd put themselves in, she couldn't go back for more, could she?

"You can't go after him," he said, suddenly determined. "You have to show this to the police. They might be able to track him."

He reached for her phone, but Seneca pressed it to her chest. "I knew you wouldn't get it."

She sounded so hateful, and he stared at her, shocked. He felt precarious, suddenly, like he was standing on a slippery cliff and even the tiniest movement might cause him to careen over the edge. "Please don't keep playing his game," he begged. "You're going to get yourself killed." His throat felt tight. "Don't you understand that? Don't you understand there are people who want you to live?"

"You really don't get what he means to me." Seneca's voice was stony and empty. "You don't get how devastated I am that he's . . . *out there. Free.*"

"I do get it. But it's not your job to find him. It's not your job to be obsessed."

"Yes it is."

"It's *not.*" Maddox tried to touch Seneca's arm again, but once more she pulled away. It stung. Well, *more* than stung. It was like she hated him.

"You just don't understand, okay?" she snapped.

"I think I *do*. But—"

"No." She cut him off. Her eyes were dark. Unyielding. "You don't. You're not *like* me, Maddox."

"Seneca." The devastation sloshed inside him like heavy water. "This is no more personal for you than it is for Aerin or her family—he's hurt all of you. And don't you see the irony here? You're making this personal in the same way Brett made the Candace search personal. And it's going to ruin you the same way it ruined him."

Seneca's mouth made an O. She blinked hard as though he'd kicked her in the sternum. Maddox watched as what he'd said seeped into her, and he wondered if he'd gone too far. Horror and hurt passed across her features, and she clenched her jaw even tighter, angling her body fully away from him toward the chain link fence. "Well, then," she said in a small voice. "I guess Brett and I are exactly the same."

"Seneca, I didn't . . ." Maddox started.

But she held up her hand to stop him. "Maybe you should just leave me alone," she said in a dull gray voice.

He stared at her in confusion. "What do you mean?"

Her eyes were trained on her feet. The cut on her arm had been bandaged, but some blood was starting to seep through the gauze. All Maddox wanted to do was fetch her a fresh bandage. Cradle her in his arms.

"I want to do this alone," she said. "I need to *be* alone." Her jaw twitched, and she glanced at him for a millisecond, her eyes huge and dark and sure. "*Really* alone."

Maddox stepped back. A hot, messy mix of understanding and rejection and hurt churned in his gut. "Oh," was all he could say. Did she mean what he thought she meant?

Suddenly, all the frustration he'd felt this week—all the times she'd rejected his comforting touch, all the ups and downs they'd had, the little digs she'd made about his dedication, it all came banging down on his head. Maddox hadn't even realized how beat up he felt about all of it until now. She didn't want him. He'd pushed and pushed, trying to fit his way into her life, but she didn't want him. God, he felt like a fool.

He took a steadying breath. "Fine. If that's what you want."

Seneca twisted away, her arms wrapped tight. "I do."

He took a few angry steps back to the station, barely feeling the pavement beneath his feet. Once he reached the door, he swiveled back and gave her one last look.

But Seneca didn't look up. Just kept hugging herself. Didn't even register he was there.

# THIRTY-TWO

**THOUGH IT HAD** been almost two weeks since Seneca had been in her bedroom, nothing had changed. Her space still smelled like Downy and Reese's Peanut Butter Cups and that musty odor of the thrift shop where she bought most of her clothes. There was the same level of dust on her bookshelves, the same emo-rap song loaded next in her queue on Pandora. She felt, too, like she was coming back to the house the same person, even though she'd hoped to have monumentally changed.

There was something else waiting patiently for her homecoming, too. Four days after Damien and Huntley had been found in that gray house by the ocean, Seneca opened her closet door, turned on the light, and stared at the massive Brett project she'd constructed over the past three months. There were index cards mapping every case he contributed to on Case Not Closed, cross-referenced with the location and timeline of the kidnapping or murder and if Brett could possibly have been there. More index cards asked critical questions: *Does he have a plan? How does he finance all of this? What is his endgame?* And, simply, *Why?*

She knew more about those answers now. Months ago, it would have felt like a huge win. But it wasn't enough anymore.

*So sad you didn't find me. But you will. You just have to put the pieces together. And I'll be waiting when you do.*

What did it mean?

Seneca stared long and hard at the pictures of victims on the board until her eyes swam. She had been rereading all the cases Brett had contributed to on the CNC boards, and pored over psychology texts and papers about serial murderers and the lasting effects of brutal kidnapping. She'd called Viola Nevins so many times with so many questions that now Viola wasn't even taking her calls. She tried to figure out the hint Brett had given her, about how he'd kept Aerin somewhere *she'd been before*. Could it have any connection to where Brett was now?

She wandered over to her laptop and clicked on the Google search she'd kept permanently loaded on one of the browser tabs: *Jackson Brett Jones*. After a quick refresh, the site revealed that no new articles had surfaced. They hadn't found Brett yet. Big shocker.

She'd known those paltry clues the cops had on Brett wouldn't be enough for them to track him down. No one had turned up to recover the Ford in the parking lot, and eventually the city towed it to an impound lot. Forensics had tested the hair of Brett's Aerin had saved, but it didn't link to any hints about where Brett and Aerin had been hiding. Aerin's kidnapping story had blown up on the news, especially because her kidnapper might also be the person who murdered her sister. Chelsea also got to give her story, and the authorities issued her a formal apology for assuming that she was a narcissistic girl who made up a kidnapping. Both girls described Brett to sketch artists, but it hadn't done any good—the images didn't yield any tips.

Seneca had gotten a few requests for interviews, too—even big ones like *Good Morning America*. Apparently, Maddox and Madison had taken the producers up on it, but she hadn't. What was the point? Why would she want to admit how she'd let a serial killer escape? It wasn't going to get them any closer to Brett. It certainly wasn't going to bring her mom back.

She turned back to the board. There had to be something right in front of her she wasn't seeing. It was just a matter of putting the pieces together in the right way.

*It's not your job to be obsessed,* Maddox's voice rang in her head. But Seneca flicked it away as though it were a mosquito, same as she deleted all the missed calls from him on her phone. He'd texted her again and again after that night at the police station—the night when, once the police finally called them in for questioning, she'd contributed little to the discussion, and then called a cab to drive her all the way back to Maryland, which had cost a small fortune.

At first, Maddox was desperate to know if she was okay. Madison had texted, too. Though as the days went by, both had texted less and less. *Good,* she'd thought. Not because she wanted to be rid of them. She felt bad not reaching out to Madison, and it ached how she'd broken it off with Maddox at the police station . . . but both things were necessary. Since losing Brett yet again, her mind had snapped and splintered, turning into a house of horrors she didn't want them to see. She could feel the darkness settling over her like a quickly growing head of hair, strangling her, obscuring her vision. She didn't want to pull Madison or Maddox down into her abyss, too. They didn't deserve that. She *was* like Brett, making personal what was probably randomness, twisting her ruined past into a vengeful present.

But on the other hand, she couldn't stop being this way. This wasn't anyone else's fight like it was hers. Brett's atrocities hadn't seeped into anyone else's bones in the way it had penetrated her very skeleton, altering her posture, zooming through her blood. *She* needed to avenge her mother. *She* needed to find Brett. It was the only thought in her mind that got her out of bed in the day. It was like Brett's existence had left a trail of slime inside her she could never wash away, coloring everything, charging everything, dulling her senses and happiness and ambition. She was never going to be normal until she got him. She was *stuck* in this dismal Brett world, spinning in the Brett spiral until the end of time.

She still looked at Maddox's Instagram, though. His posts had returned to images of sunrises on his morning runs, and a few of his buddies at what looked like a house party, and at this very moment, one of him standing next to a girl she didn't recognize, a pretty, normal-looking redhead in a cold-shoulder blouse and dangling earrings. Maybe he'd moved on already. Good. Seneca's finger hovered over his name on the contacts list on her phone, too . . . but no, *no.*

She flopped onto the mattress, hugging her favorite lion-shaped pillow. At the foot of the bed was a stack of old photo albums she'd dug out from the bottom of the credenza in the living room. She eyed them warily; the pictures made her feel so sad, but they also made her feel close to her mom. She'd been listening to that answering machine message at her mom's old law firm a lot, too. Over and over, her mom greeting the callers, telling them to press one for this and two for that—Seneca kept thinking that the next time she listened, her mom would say something in code, like where Brett was hiding. But the message was always the same.

She chose a photo book at random and pulled it to her. The spine cracked as she opened to the first page. Her mother was lying in a hospital room with baby Seneca sprawled across her belly, fast asleep. There was a bright, ecstatic smile on Collette Frazier's face. The next photo was almost the same pose, except this time Collette was looking down at Seneca in wonder. *I have a baby,* her expression said. *This is the most wonderful thing in the whole world.*

Tears blurred Seneca's vision. *Damn it,* she thought bitterly, a lump forming in her throat. The joy and love on her mom's face got her every time.

But she kept going. She turned page after page, watching the bond between her and her mother form tighter every day. Baby Seneca smiled, then sat up, then started to walk. Collette was always in the background, grinning, cheering, clapping. There were photos of a glittery Christmas morning, Collette and toddler Seneca asleep on the couch. There was a photo of Seneca like a tiny snowman in a snow parka and boots, out to brave a February blizzard. Seneca's dark hair grew; Collette's hair went from a pixie cut to a layered bob to her shoulders. There was a photo of mom and daughter walking down a path at Quiet Waters Park, which wasn't very far from the bedroom Seneca was sitting in now. There was a picture of them having mussels—toddler Seneca scrunching up her eyes and wrinkling her nose in disgust—at McGarvey's, an Irish bar in the town square. McGarvey's was still in the town square, actually. They still served mussels. It wasn't right that a stupid restaurant and its menu had outlasted a person. It didn't seem fair that *anything* outlasted Collette.

*I let you down, Mom,* Seneca thought miserably. *Again.*

She waded through the rest of the album, looking at pictures she hadn't inspected in years—even yesterday, she'd quit a few pages in, the photos just too sad. In the last few pages, Collette, Seneca's dad, and baby Seneca—now three years old—were standing on a beach. Collette and Seneca wore matching polka-dot bikinis. Seneca's father was digging a hole. There was sand all over their knees, and they were grinning.

Seneca twisted her mouth. This picture wasn't that different from the picture she'd seen of Candace Lord's family when she'd interrogated Candace's parents. Like them, her family looked so happy. So carefree. Like nothing bad could ever happen to them.

She turned the page; there were more pictures of what looked like this same beach vacation. A trip to a mini-golf course. Seneca and her dad flying a kite. And then her favorite photo, a picture of her mother wearing a pretty sundress and an innocent smile, holding a sticky, almost-too-big Seneca on her hip. She sighed at it, touching her mother's face. She was about to turn the page when something in the photo stopped her. She and her mom were standing in front of a tree that looked . . . familiar.

She pulled the photo closer, studying it hard, her mind flicking through thousands of images. The tree had a perfect square burned into its trunk. Hadn't she seen a tree just like that somewhere recently?

She blinked hard, and then the answer appeared. *Wait.* There was a tree just like this one in the front yard of the house where Brett had been imprisoned.

Her nerves started to snap. The picture also showed a part of the house—and sure enough, it was the same reddish color as Brett's, though the paint seemed brighter, newer. On the porch were a big pot of sunflowers . . . and a set of wind chimes. Seneca would bet a million bucks they were the wind chimes she'd seen this past week.

What the hell was going on?

Seneca heard her father padding through the kitchen, probably on his way to get a snack before he went back to the TV room and watched yet another episode of *Law & Order.*

She bounded down the stairs. Her dad was in the TV room, devouring a bowl of peanut-butter-cup ice cream. When he saw her, a guilty look crossed his face. "I know. It's terrible for me. But it just looked so *good*."

"Dad." When Seneca stepped into the light, her dad's jovial expression faded into something more guarded. She thrust the photo album toward him, pointing at the picture of the tree. "Where was this?"

Her father reached for his glasses on the side table. "Oh. We took a vacation on the Jersey Shore. I think the town was called Halcyon."

Seneca's mind went numb for a few seconds. The word *Halcyon* gonged in her ears like a church bell.

She looked up at her dad. "H-how old was I?"

"Maybe two? Three? It was our only beach trip. After that, we went camping. You were too little to remember."

"And what were we doing on this street?" She tapped the background.

"I think that's the street where we were staying. Yep, that was the place we rented." Mr. Frazier pointed to a blue house on the adjacent page. "Kinda dumpy, but we had fun." He squinted at her. "Why?"

All kinds of sparks went off in her brain. She did the math. She was nineteen now. Sixteen years ago, when she was three, was the summer of 2002. That was the very same year Brett was kidnapped. She gripped the side of the armchair, feeling woozy.

"Honey?" her dad cocked his head. "What is it?"

Seneca opened her mouth but couldn't speak. This wasn't possible . . . and yet it made sense. The street where Brett had been imprisoned had resonated with her in ways that felt subconscious, suppressed. Those wind chimes, that tree. Suddenly, something Aerin said popped in her brain. She'd heard something beeping outside her window—maybe a dump truck, maybe a bulldozer, maybe a garbage truck. When Seneca was standing outside the house where Elizabeth had kidnapped Brett, she'd noticed a large dirt pile next door. Bulldozers had sat unattended when she'd been there, but in the daytime, they could have made *beep, beep, beep* sounds.

Could that have been what Aerin heard?

*I'll give you a hint. It's somewhere you've been before.*

*No.* That was ridiculous. Just because her and Brett's paths had crossed years ago didn't mean Brett had hidden Aerin in Halcyon *now.* Why would Brett have chosen to hide just steps from a house that made him miserable? Unless, of course, he was a glutton for punishment—which Seneca could see. On the other hand, maybe it was a big coincidence.

Seneca shut her eyes. In Brett's world, there *were* no coincidences.

But why had he chosen *her house* to hide in? Was there a bigger connection here, something she didn't yet get? And had he seen Seneca's family, maybe, when they'd stayed there that same summer he'd been imprisoned? Did he remember *her*?

She racked her brain for everything Brett and Viola had told them about their time with Elizabeth. They'd had fresh bread. They'd slept in the same bed. They'd been imprisoned in the bedrooms, the basement, and the shed. Then her eyes popped open with another memory Brett had painfully shared. The worst memory, actually. Something he still seemed bitter about.

She pressed a hand to her mouth. *No.* It was inconceivable. Irrational. But maybe it made all the sense in the world.

She looked at her father again. He'd put the TV on mute and was staring at her with concern, the same concern that had been building in him for a while, the same worry he'd felt for her ever since her mother died but they hadn't exactly spoken about directly. Her throat felt dry as she tried to speak. "Dad, did anything sort of weird happen when we were on that vacation? Like, with one of the neighbor kids, maybe?"

Her father's eyes searched her face. Seneca was so afraid he was going to say no, or maybe that he didn't remember, but then recognition flashed across his features. He looked startled that she'd be asking such a question—that she *knew*.

He touched her wrists and nodded. "As a matter of fact, yes."

And then he told her the story Seneca already knew was coming. The story that put all of the hideous, unthinkable pieces together. And when he was done, Seneca knew exactly what Brett was all about. She'd figured him out, after all. Just like he said she would.

# THIRTY-THREE

**THAT SAME EVENING,** Maddox sat on a splintered log in the middle of the woods in Dexby and watched as one of his track teammates, Archer, appeared through the bonfire's flames. "It's a little warm, hope you don't care," he said as he tossed Maddox a can of PBR.

"Thanks, man." Maddox caught it and rolled the smooth metal between his palms. People laughed all around him. Thumping bass played. The air smelled like bug spray and wet leaves, and a canopy of trees blotted out the view of the full moon.

It was Archer's annual cross-country season kickoff party, held in the dark woods behind Archer's house. It felt a little futile to have it this year because Archer and Maddox and so many of the varsity guys here were going off to college and there would *be* no cross-country practice tomorrow for them, but the younger guys were having fun, playing beer pong on a folding table, looking like assholes as they tried out break-dancing moves, and bragging to the girls about how much food they could put away after a long run. The whole scene reminded Maddox of that reindeer games scene from *Rudolph the Red-Nosed*

*Reindeer,* where Rudolph and his pal flirt with the does. The thought made him laugh, and he wanted to text Seneca about it, as it seemed like the kind of thing she'd get a kick out of, too. Until he remembered. She wasn't texting back. Which worried him. Worried him big-time.

"Hey."

Maddox turned his head. He thought it might be Madison, who was also at the party, abruptly having quit cheerleading and deciding to "try" cross-country for her senior year. But instead, it was Tara Sykes, who would be a senior this year as well. She settled down on the log next to him, a long-necked bottle of Rolling Rock in her hand. A few strands of her long red-gold hair curled around her ears, and her lean runner's legs were crossed at the ankles. "Hey," he said, holding up his still unopened can to clink. "What's up?"

"Long time no see." She touched her bottle to his can, then held up her phone. There was a screensaver of Tara and a couple of the girls on the team grinning after a race, their ponytails slick with sweat. "Mind if we take a selfie? I feel like it's been ages since I've seen you."

"Sure," Maddox said, leaning in. Tara smelled like sugary, girly perfume that probably came in a heart-shaped pink bottle. A totally different species than Seneca.

The flash went off in his eyes. After they both posted the picture on Insta, Tara moved a little closer. "So what have you been up to all summer? I haven't seen you at any of the group runs."

Her hand rested on his upper arm. It took Maddox a moment to remember that in his regular life, he was kind of the man. Eight million lifetimes ago, he'd had his eye on Tara Sykes. It seemed obvious that they'd be a couple, both of them the school's star runners, both of them laid-back and confident and self-motivated. In fact, hadn't Archer made a comment about Tara the first time he'd met Seneca? And Seneca had made this prissy, disapproving face, which had made Maddox feel so basic for having jocks for friends and thinking about girls. Which had then made him annoyed because Seneca didn't even *know* him and how dare she march into his life and start judging?

Of course, his annoyance totally made sense. Of course he'd wanted to impress Seneca. He'd adored her from their very first webchat. He'd wanted her to adore him, too.

But Seneca didn't love him back. She'd made that very clear; he needed to get that through his head. She'd set him free, returned him to his normal life.

So he turned back to Tara. "I've had kind of a crazy summer, actually."

"Oh yeah?" Her long eyelashes fluttered. "Crazy with parties and stuff? Or getting ready for college? Aren't you going to Oregon?"

Maddox blinked at her. Did she really not know? After he'd done the interview on *Good Morning America,* all sorts of randoms in Dexby came up to him, congratulating him. Which felt pretty cool. He appreciated the recognition for what he'd done. It rocked to be seen as something more than just the track star. Though, come to think of it, a lot of kids his age hadn't really said much about it. Maybe they didn't watch *Good Morning America* or read the local papers . . . or maybe they thought it was kind of weird. Suddenly, he was afraid it might be the latter.

In the flickering firelight, he noticed that Tara was giving him a strange, maybe-I-should-back-away-slowly look. The smell of a citronella candle wafted into his nose. Nearby, a girl happily shrieked, "Get that thing *off* me!"

Maddox let out an awkward laugh. "Actually, forget it. It's a really long story."

He stared into the leaping flames, feeling a thud of disappointment.

To be honest, this whole party was a bit of a disappointment. . . . It just wasn't as *fun* anymore, or something. Maddox wondered if what had happened with Brett and Seneca and all of them had changed his DNA for good. He couldn't just shrug it off like a coat and, like, drink beers and play beer pong and break-dance like the other fools were doing. What had happened was going to be with him during every lap around the track, during every party he attended, in his room at Olympic Village, if he ever got there. He looked around at his sheltered, innocent friends. Seneca had asked him to return to this life, but he couldn't—not entirely. He'd always be different because of what he'd gone through, and what he'd seen.

And let's face it, he'd always use Seneca as a yardstick for every other girl. Would anyone ever measure up? Did he *want* anyone to? And shit, if he hadn't said that thing about Seneca being just like Brett, would she still be talking to him now? If he hadn't pushed her to tell the cops about Brett's message, would she now be telling him about her plans?

"Anyway, good to see you," Tara said, noticing that Maddox's interest had waned. She rose from the log and squeezed his shoulder. He didn't call her back. Just stared at his unopened beer. Just moved his finger around the pull tab, debating whether to open it or head home. He could feel his sister watching him across the party, probably ready to lecture him about him dropping the ball with such a hot girl. But when he looked up, Madison's eyes were round and sympathetic. *I know,* she seemed to be saying. *She's not Seneca*. Madison was worried about Seneca, too.

When his phone in his shorts pocket started vibrating, he figured it was just comments on his Instagram story—Archer and Rory making crude, encouraging remarks about him and Tara with appropriate emojis. But it kept buzzing. And buzzing. And *buzzing.*

Finally, he pulled it out. It wasn't his Instagram that was blowing up—it was the app Madison had loaded on his phone two weeks ago, the potential malware and viruses he'd now introduced to his operating system be damned. A small, vibrating dot was leaving the spot it had been anchored to for the past two weeks. Maddox watched as the dot moved down one street, and then another—quickly, so probably in a car versus on foot. Huh. His watch said it was past 2:00 a.m.

As someone cranked the music up even louder, as a girl shouted about how she'd heard there were bears in these woods, as the unopened beer can grew even warmer on Maddox's lap, he watched the little dot move down one street, then over a bridge. His stomach started to tighten. This wasn't just a midnight run for snacks—someone was on the move.

Alone.

"Madison," he called out, standing up, feeling a sizzle of fear. His sister looked up from her conversation, suddenly alert. She hurried over.

"Is it . . . ?" she asked, as though it was written on his forehead in Sharpie.

"Yep." He set his beer can on the stump. Cracked his knuckles. Slid on his jacket. "Come on."

After he said his good-byes and jogged with Madison to his car, he watched the dot again. It was still moving . . . somewhere. *Where are you going?* he asked it. *And what are you going to do next?*

# THIRTY-FOUR

**SENECA SNUCK OUT** stealthily, leaving her father a note, taking the keys. There was no traffic on 95, and she made it to Halcyon in three hours flat. The town was just beginning to wake up: a Jeep with surfboards strapped to the top pulled out of a parking space in front of a coffee shop, a few intrepid power walkers were starting their workouts. Heart in her throat, her eyes burning from the early wake-up call, her knuckles aching from how fiercely she'd gripped the wheel the entire drive, Seneca steered the car onto Philadelphia Avenue.

The rising sun glimmered over the street, making the concrete sparkle. Many of the houses were still dark, and the sidewalk was empty of pedestrians. She held her breath as she drove past Brett's old house and the familiar tree; the place looked as abandoned and spooky as ever. Then came the lot they were bulldozing: a backhoe was there now, and the hole it had dug seemed bottomless.

She parked at the corner instead of right in front of the cheerful blue house that matched the one in her family photos. She felt like she was being controlled by an invisible set of strings. She needed to do this, no matter the outcome. She needed to *know*. She didn't even really feel afraid anymore. More like . . . vengeful. Angry. *Ready*.

The floorboards creaked as Seneca stepped up to the front porch. She hesitated at the door—knocking seemed ridiculous. What was Brett going to do, invite her in for some coffee and muffins? Was Brett even *here*? Even if he had been here with Aerin, that didn't mean he was here now. And yet, she felt like he was. He'd left her that clue, after all. And all roads led to this street, this place. All questions led to here.

She touched the knob. It turned in her hands, the door swinging open. Seneca stepped back, surprised and unsure. The inside was very dark, but she could make out a set of stairs and a hallway leading to some back rooms. Her throat went dry. Her hands trembled. But she mustered up all the bravery she had and walked in.

The house smelled pleasant, like mint. She could make out framed photos in the hallway and felt a fluffy rug beneath her feet. She listened for sounds—but there were none. Seneca's stomach began to twist. *Run*, a voice in her head screamed. But the possessed animal inside her pressed forward. She was a robot, programmed only to carry out a single task.

*Snap*.

Seneca froze. The sound had come from the left. Feeling the walls, she realized she'd missed a whole room. She took a step back and peered inside. The light was very dim, but she could just make out couches, chairs, and a TV in the corner. She cocked her head again, her ears ringing with the silence.

"I hope you're not counting on calling anyone," a voice called out in the darkness. "I've got a device in this house that blocks all cell service."

A table lamp snapped on in the corner. Brett sat on a leather couch, hands in his lap, his posture straight and erect as though he were a student in the front row of a classroom. His eyes were dark and swirling, but also bemused. A chrome bucket of ice and a bottle of white wine sat in front of him on the coffee table. Next to it were two empty crystal goblets.

Every single one of Seneca's muscles hardened to stone.

"I have to hand it to you, Seneca." An eerie smile spread across Brett's lips. "You figured this out so much sooner than I thought." He touched the wine bottle. "I think that calls for a celebration. Don't you?"

# THIRTY-FIVE

**BRETT INSPECTED SENECA** carefully. He'd seen her just days ago, but, man, had she changed. Her eyes were bloodshot. Her hair looked unwashed. Brett couldn't be positive, but it seemed like she might be wearing the same shorts and T-shirt she'd had on in Breezy Sea. *Interesting.* Brett could just picture her researching, reading, pinpointing, mapping, making lists, looking through photos, asking questions, doing all the Seneca things that brought her to the conclusion she'd come to today. He knew she'd figured it out.

Just like he knew she'd come alone. This was the Brett and Seneca game now; they were the only players.

He opened the wine with a corkscrew, poured the amber-colored liquid into the glasses, and slid one toward her. "I'd like to propose a toast." He raised his glass. "To us. To being alike in so many ways."

Seneca stared at the glass but didn't touch it. It took her a while to speak. "I figured it out, Brett," she said in a low, empty voice. "I finally know why you killed her."

The severity of her tone surprised him. The raw, painful anger shone so nakedly. Power vibrated in her quivering fists. And her face reminded him of something, though he wasn't sure what. He felt a tiny, nervous flutter in his chest, then shook it off. Okay, so she wasn't as frightened as he'd expected. He still had the upper hand here. Of course he did.

"It's why you told that story about Elizabeth trapping you in the shed," Seneca said. "When you tried to escape, that house you ran to—it was the house my family was staying in. *This* house." She swept her arm around the space. "And the woman who answered the door, the woman who didn't believe your story and walked you home and returned you to Elizabeth—it was my mother. Am I right?"

The wine soured in Brett's mouth. He stared at Seneca impassively, trying to feel next to nothing. He'd prepared for this conversation. He'd been ready for it ever since he met her in Dexby. He'd almost blurted it out to her after rescuing her from that fire in the hotel . . . but thank God he hadn't. It hadn't been time.

"Of course that's right," he said. "Good for you. You're really my star pupil."

"You've known for years." Seneca put her hands on her hips. "You've known . . . *me* . . . for years."

Suddenly, he knew what Seneca reminded him of: Occasionally, Elizabeth had allowed him to watch nature programs, and there had been one about a tiger stalking its prey, its head lowered, its eyes wide and hyperfocused. Moments later, it attacked an unsuspecting gazelle, ripping it to shreds. Seneca's determined little eyes reminded him of the tiger's just before it pounced.

"I saw you that day I came to your beach house," he said. "You were cowering behind your mom, that bitch." He enjoyed that Seneca twitched a little hearing this, though his tremulous voice bugged him. He didn't sound nearly as badass as he wanted to be. "And it wasn't so hard to track you down after I escaped. I remember an Annapolis bumper sticker on your car when your mother walked me back to Elizabeth's. It took some doing, but I eventually found where you lived. You were eleven the first time I found you in Annapolis. I'm guessing you didn't see me when I watched you at your swim meets?"

"Nope." Seneca stared at him, dead-eyed.

"I was the one sitting on the top bleachers, looking bored. But I wasn't bored. I watched you backstroke to the wall. I watched your mom clap. I really wanted her to see me and remember me as the kid she *didn't save*, but she was focused on you." He shrugged, waving a hand. "She forgot about me so fast. But I didn't forget her. I just had to wait for the right time to do what I needed to do."

Seneca's gaze was like a wall of stone. It seemed like everything he was saying was bouncing right off her. "So you killed my mom all because she took you back to Elizabeth's that day, is that right?"

"Of course it is."

She snorted. It was an ugly, mocking sound. "I've been thinking about that the whole drive here. Don't you realize how irrational you are? How self-centered? How was she supposed to know your situation?"

The old rage flared inside him, volcanic-hot and spiny. *Irrational? Self-centered?*

He shifted forward on the couch. "Your mother turned a scared, desperate kid away. It was like she didn't hear me. She didn't care that I was afraid. She just walked me back to that house, *la, la, la*. Didn't want to destroy her peaceful vacation with a messed-up kid in her house, did she? Didn't want to mar any of the memories! So she delivered me straight back into the nightmare." He looked hard at Seneca, his heart jumping, his throat contracting, feeling the sudden urge to either roar or sob. "You and your family got to go on, blissfully unaware, while I rotted away. That wasn't fair. So I vowed I was going to do something about it—make her pay."

"Yeah, and did it make you feel better?" Seneca's eyebrows rose. "After you killed her, Brett, did all your problems vanish, just like that?" She snapped her fingers.

He scoffed, annoyed. What kind of question was that?

"It didn't. That anger was still inside you, putrid as ever, wasn't it? That drive to make things *right,* to settle your score—maybe it got even *worse* after you killed people, am I right?"

She searched his face, but Brett looked away.

"There was a hole inside you that you needed to fill, so you kept finding more to fill it with," she went on. "Except nothing you did made you feel better. No matter how many people you killed, no matter how much *revenge* you got, you were always your same, shitty self when it was all over. Well, I have news for you, dude—you're never going to change. You're always going to be you. You're always going to be a mess."

"Of course I'm always going to be a mess!" Brett groaned. "My freaking childhood was taken away!"

"You're not the only person that's happened to!" Seneca roared right back. "And all those other kidnapping victims in the world? They don't turn into murderers!"

Spit flew out of her mouth as she spoke. She was leaning so close to him now he could see the freckles on her nose, the flecks of yellow in her wide, furious eyes. *She isn't afraid of me,* he realized. *Not one bit.*

Enough of this. He needed to get control back. He splayed his arms across the cushions and took a leveling breath. "So then why are you here, Seneca? What do you want to know? Do you want me to *explain* it to you? Would you like to know how I tracked Collette? How it all went down that very last day she was alive? What I did to her moments before she died?"

Seneca froze. She opened her mouth, but no sound came out.

"Maybe you'd like to hear what else I did besides kill her? Or how scared she was? Or what she *said* to me?" He grinned. "I remember every word she said. Some of it was about you."

Seneca stepped back like he'd just taken a swing at her, but she didn't spit out a quick and decisive no. *She's curious,* Brett thought deliciously. In a dark, messy corner of her soul, she wanted to know every last detail.

"Or maybe we should instead talk about how I kept tabs on you after it was all over?" Brett asked, feeling his confidence rise. "I saw up close how *broken* you were about her death. How shocked you felt that your mommy had been taken away from you. It felt good to see that, you know. Finally you were feeling pain like my pain. I saw that necklace of hers you started wearing. And I knew your little secret—that you stole it off her body. She'd been wearing it when—you know." With a grin, he placed his hands around his neck, pantomiming someone getting strangled. "I also noticed how inquisitive you were, how desperately you wanted answers about what happened. God, it plagued you for *years,* didn't it? You barely got through high school! You dropped out of college! In fact, I knew the moment you signed on to Case Not Closed. I was watching your e-mail—I saw the Welcome letter they sent you."

Seneca swallowed hard. She was trying hard not to react, but he had to believe that each new realization was shocking her like a bucket of ice to the face.

"So of course I joined that site, too. And we became friends, didn't we? Just casual acquaintances at first, but I really wanted to get to know you. See what made you tick. See what you were *thinking* about—because you held your cards pretty close to your vest when it came to your mom, and I wanted to know more of that sadness. I just couldn't get enough—I was like an addict. So I saw who you were friends with on the site—good old Maddy Wright. I met him, too—in person, though, and wow, did we hit it off." He belted back another swig of wine. "And what a coincidence, Maddy Wright was from Dexby, *another* place I knew well. It all got me thinking: How fun would it be to have *two* people related to my victims in one room . . . with me in the middle? Even better, what if we were trying to *solve* a case . . . together? Really . . . *become* friends?" He heard his voice crack again and felt a pang in his chest. "The more I planned it, the more I wanted it to happen."

Seneca blinked at him. "So you encouraged Maddox toward the Helena case. And then he invited me. And you."

Brett nodded. "I said he should get a crew together. I knew he'd pick you . . . and me."

"But why? I mean, if you knew where I was, if you were still so angry at my entire family, why put us through all that? Why not just kill me?"

"Because . . ." Brett shrugged, knocked a little off-kilter again. "You're the gift that kept on giving. If I couldn't hurt Elizabeth, at least I had you."

"Hmm." That tiger stare, that condescending tone, it had suddenly returned in her.

Brett clenched his fist. "What does *hmm* mean?"

"I think you did it because you wanted to control something. Control *people*, because you'd been controlled your whole life. You were a puppet, but you wanted to be the puppeteer. So you found us. You used us to work through all your pain."

Brett twisted away. "Since when did you become a shrink?"

"You're not that hard to figure out, Brett. Sorry."

"Yeah, well." Something squishy and vulnerable pulsed inside him, making his cheeks flare, making his hackles rise. "I *also* needed you to find Elizabeth. I was going to leave you alone after that. Except it didn't turn out that way, did it?" He felt a darkness settle over him again. "You robbed me of that chance. But I'm not angry at Elizabeth anymore. I don't feel vengeful toward her—she'll get what's coming to her. But I do feel vengeful toward *you*."

Brett rose to his feet. Seneca stepped back a little. As he stood, he noticed a small, faint light glowing from within her shorts pocket. It was her phone, making a perfect, neon square beneath the cotton. At first, he figured she had an incoming call or text—but that was impossible. He'd installed the cell phone jammer he'd bought from a shady guy he'd met on Craigslist, and all cell phones were disabled the moment they crossed the threshold.

So what was still running on that phone? It took him only a moment to make the mental leap. Then he dropped his wine glass to the floor, where it shattered to pieces, and leapt for her. Seneca jumped back and screamed.

Brett grabbed her by the shoulder and pulled the phone from her pocket. Just as he thought, the video function was on—the timer at the bottom said the video had been running for more than five minutes.

"You *recorded* us?" he screeched.

Seneca tried to grab the phone back, but Brett was too quick. Roaring, he hurled the phone across the room. It slammed against the wall and dropped to the wood floor with a thud. It felt like a betrayal, a slap across the face. Seneca hadn't just come here for a play-by-play, she'd come to *trap* him, the stupid bitch. She was as heartless as her mother.

Seneca ran to the shattered phone, but he caught her by the shoulders and spun her around, catching her unawares. Suddenly, in the dim light, she looked just *like* her mother—that heart-shaped face, those big blue eyes, that pouty mouth. If he squinted, he could picture Collette Frazier standing in the doorway of this very house all those years ago, unmoved by Brett's story, apathetic about his plight. All the pain he'd held in years ago, all the agonizing worthlessness, all the regret and fury, it rushed back in a flaming, sparking fireball, exploding from his limbs, spewing from his mouth. He saw himself scared and frantic as he rang the doorbell to Seneca's family's rental house. The relief when her mother answered flooded him anew, as though it had only happened moments before. Here was his hero. Here was the person who was going to make everything right.

Why hadn't he just run from her when she'd walked him back home? Why hadn't he bolted down the sidewalk and hid? But Brett knew why: Elizabeth had brainwashed him. A refrain rang in his head, over and over: *Your parents don't love you. Nobody loves you except me. The world thinks you're a piece of shit.*

"Your mother was supposed to save me," Brett hissed at Seneca, digging his nails into her skin. "I will never forgive her. And I will never forgive *you*."

He closed his hands around her neck. Inhaled her slightly sour scent. Felt her whole body tremble. It gave him a rush, really—here she was, Seneca Frazier, finally within his grasp. It felt like a circle was finally being closed. He'd set out to ruin a family, and now he was doing it.

"You're getting what you deserve," he whispered, and closed his hands around her neck tighter, squeezing and squeezing, just wanting it to be done.

# THIRTY-SIX

**SENECA FELT BRETT'S** strong hands crush her neck, and something in her chest gave. He pressed on her windpipe, and her lungs screamed with panic. She grappled to move his hands away, but his grip was too strong—and then, suddenly, she was on the ground, her head slammed into the round rug, the weight of Brett's body on top of her.

*Oh God, oh God, oh God,* she thought. This wasn't how it was supposed to go. She was supposed to run out of the house after she got his confession. Or if Brett did try to get violent, she'd stashed a Taser in her bag. She noticed it in the doorway out of the corner of her eye. It was almost within reach of her foot, but Brett was pinning her thigh, so she couldn't quite snag it.

Brett twisted her head to the side with a jerk, bringing tears to Seneca's eyes. There was an ecstatic grin on his face, a look so evil and diabolical that Seneca roiled with fear and let out a small whimper. Brett moved a little closer to her as though to listen, his grin broadening. "That's right," he cooed.

He *wanted* her to be afraid, Seneca realized. It was like he was feeding off it.

She couldn't give Brett more power, then. He might kill her, but she wouldn't let him get everything he wanted.

"Whatever," she managed to cough out. "Kill me. But that confession of yours? It's already uploaded to my cloud. You broke my phone for nothing."

A flare of panic passed over Brett's features, but it quickly submerged. "You're bluffing. That recording is gone. Maybe you shouldn't have come here by yourself, huh? But you had to, didn't you? No one had your back. And now you're going to die alone."

He squeezed harder. Seneca couldn't hold on for much longer. *Come on,* she willed herself, feeling her heart straining against her chest. But her field of vision was narrowing. She could feel herself growing weaker, giving up. Was this really how it was going to end?

When she shut her eyes, a thin column of light appeared. *Death?* she thought with horror. Was it really already here? But then, stepping through the light, literally bending it sideways as though it were a column of beads, a figure appeared in her mind's eye. The face sharpened into view, and she gasped. She would know those big blue eyes, high cheekbones, and silky blond hair anywhere. It was her *mother.*

*Honey,* her mother demanded. It was her voice, clear and clean—but also kind of bossy, exactly as her mom used to be. *Honey, get up. You got this. You have to.*

Seneca stared at her mother helplessly, wordlessly, *breathlessly.* How was she here? Why was she just staring at her with that faint smile? Why was she making rising motions with her hands?

*Your hands are free,* her mother instructed, gesturing to Seneca's hands, which flailed at her side as Brett strangled her. *Grab his ear and twist.*

"Huh?" Seneca whimpered.

*You heard me. Grab it. Come on. You're a badass. I didn't raise a wimp.*

"But I can't!" Seneca whimpered.

*You can.* Her gaze upon Seneca was steady and strong. *I'm right here.*

And then, before Seneca knew what was happening, lightness began to fill her, a golden column dripping from her head down to her feet. With a burst of unexpected energy, she lifted her shaky hand, grabbed Brett's ear, and twisted it hard. He let out a screech of pain, jolted back, and released his hands from her neck. Coughing, Seneca scrambled away and shot to her feet. Brett grabbed for her ankle, and for a moment, she started to stumble, but she was able to shake him off and got in a swift kick to his face. Brett wheeled backward, clutching his nose. "What the *hell*?" he screeched.

*Keep going,* her mom's voice thrummed inside her. *Keep going.*

Brett was on his knees now, so she shoved him with a force that surprised even her until he was flat on his back. He hit the floor with a terrible *crack*. Blood gushed from his nose. He was swearing under his breath. Seneca wiped sweat from her face, trying to figure out what to do next—should she run for her purse and the Taser? But it was several steps across the room—if she hesitated even slightly, Brett was going to get the upper hand again. He was so much stronger and bigger.

*That doesn't matter,* her mother urged. *Bigger isn't always better.*

Then something on the coffee table caught her eye. The corkscrew's sharp, shining tip was pointed straight at her. She lurched for it. Brett noticed, and his eyes popped wide. He grabbed at her leg again and tried to take her down, but she kicked him in the stomach and he retreated, a strange, gurgling sound emanated from his throat. Brett tried to scramble backward, and Seneca saw as his gaze whipped around the room, probably trying to find his own weapon. But Seneca marched over to him and stood on his chest hard, pressing her weight into his sternum. That same superhuman strength filled her. She felt buoyed, *powered* by her mom. She could do this. She *was* doing this.

The corkscrew shook in her hand as she raised it over her head like a knife. Tears streamed from her eyes. The pale, vulnerable strip of skin on Brett's neck shone in the pale light. He stared at her imploringly, his lips trembling, and then shut his eyes and grimaced.

"Do it," he said. "I know you want to. Though if you do, we really *will* be the same."

Seneca's palms were so sweaty, it was getting tough to hold on to the corkscrew. Sobs rose in her chest. She didn't want to kill him. She didn't want to be anything like him. His death wouldn't solve anything. It would probably make everything worse.

Suddenly, there was a loud *crack*, startling both of them. Brett rolled over. Seneca jerked back against the wall. Four figures burst into the house and surrounded them, guns raised, voices shouting things her garbled brain couldn't quite process. But as her vision cleared, Seneca could make out HALCYON POLICE printed in large block letters across their jackets.

"Stay down!" they screamed at Brett. "Hands where we can see them!"

Brett stared at the police, then at Seneca, his mouth twisted in fury. Abruptly, he pushed to his feet, turned, and tried to make a run for it, banging sloppily against the coffee table and shattering the wine bottle. He disappeared through another darkened hallway that led to a different part of the house.

The officers stormed after him. "Stop or we'll shoot!" they bellowed.

Seneca peered into the darkness, her teeth chattering, her lungs burning. Loud *bangs* rang out down the hall. She heard bodies knocking into walls and heavy grunts. "No!" a voice that sounded a lot like Brett's screamed out, and then there was a loud *thud*. She heard the *click* of handcuffs snapping together; footsteps rang out down the hall once more. The officers burst into the room again, this time flanking Brett, forcing him to walk. Brett's head snapped up when he saw Seneca still standing where he'd left her. His bottom lip curled, and his eyes narrowed to slits. He looked plaintively at the police. "Arrest *her*. She's the one who broke in here and attacked *me*."

The cop just snorted. "And she had good reason to, kid."

They continued to drag him out. Brett snarled at Seneca just before he passed through the door. "They weren't supposed to follow you. They weren't supposed to *believe* you."

Seneca's lips parted. She didn't understand what he meant. Follow her? Believe her? Who?

As if in answer, the officers parted to shove Brett through the door, and Seneca saw two figures hanging back, half in shadows, half dazzled by the morning light. Madison's hands were in her pockets. Maddox was staring at her with his mouth wide open, blinking and blinking as if he couldn't believe what he was seeing.

Seneca felt a jolt. "What are you guys doing here?"

Maddox and Madison took a few tentative steps toward her. At first, Seneca was too stunned to do anything, but then she ran to them and dove into their arms.

"Oh my God," she whispered, hugging them tightly. She could

feel their shuddering sobs matching hers. "How did you . . . ? What made you . . . ?"

"I was going crazy not talking to you," he moaned into her neck at the same time. "And when I heard you scream, I thought . . ." But then he looked at the front door, where the cops had just taken Brett. "Except I was wrong." He stared at her, impressed. "You were doing just fine all on your own."

"But what are you *doing* here?" she cried. "How did you know to come?"

"Don't be mad," Madison said. "We were both really worried. I helped Maddox keep tabs on you, and when we saw you were on the move, we had to follow. Once we were sure this was Brett's place, we called the cops."

Everything was moving too fast. Seneca's mind was unable to grasp all the swirling pieces. "S-so you've been stalking me, then?"

Maddox wiped his eyes and laughed self-consciously. "No. I mean, we were just . . . well, watching your movements really carefully. But from a totally loving, totally concerned place." Seneca felt a rush of defensiveness, but he put up a hand to stop her from protesting. "I *understand* why you had to find him. As best I can, anyway."

Seneca shut her eyes. "That's good, because I'm not sure *I* do anymore." She looked up at Maddox, then Madison. It was still hard to believe they were actually *here*. They loved her this much. They cared even when she pushed them away. There were no words for that kind of devotion.

Maddox held her arms tightly and looked deeply into her eyes. "Actually, let's not talk about that right now, okay? How about you explain how you basically single-handedly took down a criminal mastermind with your bare hands?"

Seneca ducked her head. "Well, my hands weren't *bare,* exactly." She held up the corkscrew. *And some other help, too,* she added in her head. *Of the supernatural kind.*

The vision of her mom rushed back to her. Had it really happened? She didn't see her mom's image anymore, but all the same, she still felt her presence nestled inside her, filling her with strength. She swore she heard her mom whispering something new into her ear, too: *Honey, stop pushing Maddox away. He's a good one.*

Who knew if it was really her mom or just the lack of oxygen to her brain? But in that moment, Seneca believed. Her mom's voice was like a bell, loving and kind and utterly right. Choking back a sob, she gave Madison a tight squeeze, then turned to Maddox, feeling a little nervous. "Thanks," she whispered.

"For what?" Maddox asked, astonished.

Instead of answering, she leaned forward and kissed his lips. As he kissed back, she closed her eyes and sank into the kiss, relishing the fact that she was okay, and that Maddox was with her, and maybe, just maybe, a door in her life had finally closed.

And another door had opened, too. From now on, Seneca would take her mom's advice. She would let Maddox in.

# THIRTY-SEVEN

**TWO DAYS LATER,** Aerin and a recovering Thomas sat in a booth at the Dexby Pizza Trattoria. It was probably the least fancy restaurant in all of the upscale Connecticut town where she lived, though that wasn't saying much—the bartender wore a sleek dark suit, appetizers started at fifteen bucks, and the gourmet pizza offered toppings ranging from truffles to pancetta to beluga caviar, which Aerin thought sounded extremely gross.

The waiter, a pimply kid named Ross she had almost hooked up with two years ago, delivered them a Margherita pie, and Aerin and Thomas dug in. "Oh my God," she murmured, letting the oozy cheese melt in her mouth. "I dreamed about this when I was stuck in that room. I thought I'd never get to taste real food again." Thomas's face clouded over, and she petted his arm. "Sorry."

"Don't apologize." Thomas set down his slice with his good arm, the one that wasn't in the sling. "I just want to make sure you're processing what happened . . . and that you're okay."

Aerin shrugged. Part of her hadn't wanted to talk about the kidnapping around family and friends. Her story to Brett about Mallorca wasn't a lie: Her whole MO was to escape when shit got hard. It seemed so much easier just to act like it never happened.

But there was no way she could do that, not with Brett still on the loose. So she'd mustered up her courage and took charge in that interrogation session in Breezy Sea, explaining exactly what Brett had done to her and who she was. She showed the detective the bruises on her neck from where Brett had hurt her. Kind women on the forensic team had gently combed over her body, asked her a zillion questions. She unearthed the hair from the contact lens case. She told them about hiding her fingernails under the bed. She told them about Brett holding her at knifepoint, even though it still sent spasms through her body.

It had been a godsend when that security guard had rounded the corner at the fun house. Well, terrifying at first—Aerin had really though Brett was going to kill her—but when he released her, her heart had exploded with relief. From what Aerin could gather, it was completely random that the guard was in there in the first place, though she had to wonder if it was somehow Helena's guiding hand at work, keeping her safe. Combined with his report of Brett's crazed actions with the knife and the Reeds Hotel's surveillance footage they were able to obtain that showed Aerin getting into Brett's vehicle, then struggling to get out, and then Brett locking the doors, the detectives believed her story. It made the rush to find Brett even more of a priority.

But when it *really* did some good was after Brett was caught. With his kidnapping charge already in place, Brett went straight to jail. Even better, after the cops took his prints, they matched an unidentified print they'd found on Seneca's mom's vehicle years before *and* a print the cops had recently pulled from the Dakota when investigating Helena's death. Together with Brett's confession to Seneca, the police were able to charge him with both murders.

So many dominos tumbled after that: Marissa and Harris Ingram, the husband and wife previously accused of Helena's murder, were freed from jail. The police re-interviewed Chelsea Dawson, showing her a lineup of potential men who could have kidnapped her—she chose Brett out of the group immediately. Brett's prints were also located on the balcony railing at the Ocean Sands condos, where he'd shoved Jeff Cohen over. The coroner had even exhumed the body of the guy they thought was Gabriel Wilton, Brett's alias, who everyone presumed had died in a car crash up the coast. Obviously, it wasn't Gabriel but a young Danish tourist who looked a lot like him.

So many bodies. So much destruction. And as Aerin glanced at Thomas again, it chilled her that he could have been hurt much worse. Finally, Brett was getting what he deserved . . . and Aerin had helped make that happen. So maybe there was usefulness in telling your story after all.

Aerin took another bite of her pizza. The only teensy problem was that it had been hard to sleep since she'd returned. She kept waking up in the middle of the night covered in sweat, certain she was back in that room with Brett, unable to move, unable to scream. On the fourth day of insomnia, she'd finally confessed to her mom that maybe, just *maybe*, she needed a shrink.

Aerin wasn't sure if she liked Dr. Cindy Fowler yet—the woman had a thing for cats, and she wore way too many ugly jangling charm bracelets—but she swore like a sailor and didn't look at Aerin like she was an idiot screwup. And, okay, it was actually *helping* to talk. A little, here and there, at her own pace. She kept getting the urge to hide, to suppress those memories of being locked in that car trunk, and that woozy feeling she'd had the moment she'd woken up and realized Brett had taken her, and the fear that any moment, Brett could burst into her room and kill her, but when she did tell someone something, she felt a little lighter and freer. Not that she was suddenly the poster child for therapy or anything. But right now, it was doing some good.

Of course, she had Thomas, too. Besides his broken arm and healing bruises on his face, he was doing fine. The burns on his body had healed. He'd cracked a rib, so it still hurt to inhale, but that would heal in time, too. She reached across the table and took his hand. "I think we're both going to make it," she said with a wink.

"I think so, too." He gave her a look of love that made Aerin's heart do a triple flip. She desperately wanted to tell him how she'd pined for him while in Brett's clutches, how the only thing that kept her going those nights was knowing that she needed to get to him, make him better. It scared her to say it, though—she hadn't really trusted anyone since Helena went missing. Though maybe, after enough sessions with Dr. Fowler, she could work up the guts.

Thomas's attention moved to the TV over the bar. A news report had come on, and an image of Candace Lord flashed on the screen. Though the sound was off, Aerin knew what the reporter was saying: Candace's pretrial hearing was today, and because she'd pleaded not guilty—*lunatic*—the case was moving to trial and she was being held without bail.

Aerin watched as the camera panned across a haggard-looking woman in a baggy orange prison jumpsuit being led out of the courthouse in handcuffs. *That's the woman who made Brett who he is,* she thought with a shiver. The memory of sitting on the bed in Brett's house, listening to him talk about what Candace did to him, slid through her like water, filling her with an unexpected rush of empathy.

She swallowed another bite of pizza. "Is it weird I feel bad for Brett for having gone through that with her?" On the screen, the cops were shoving Candace into a squad car. Candace didn't look repentant for what she did. Maybe she didn't even know it was wrong. "Is it also weird that I feel bad that she lost her kids?" She laughed self-consciously. "Maybe I'm losing it, right? I'm supposed to hate these people."

"I think it makes you human," Thomas said. "And, I mean, it *is* awful. That's the tragic thing about all of this."

The news switched to a weather update. Aerin turned back to the pizza and Thomas, suddenly feeling a bolt of contentment. It was so good to be here with him, not even doing anything special, but getting to live and eat and enjoy. The feeling had struck her a bunch of times since Brett had been arrested and she knew she was truly safe. Was it weird that it took her being kidnapped to appreciate all she had?

"Honey?"

Mrs. Kelly stood over her, offering a sheepish smile. "Do you mind if I sit with you guys?"

Aerin curled her toes. The last thing she wanted was her mom staring nosily at her new boyfriend. They'd talked about a lot of things they'd avoided before—Helena's freaky affair with Harris Ingram, what Aerin knew about Brett, and even about *Thomas*. It felt good, because how long had it been since Aerin actually had a real mom? But it was also a little weird . . . especially explaining the Brett stuff. Sometimes, all Aerin wanted to do was zone out on the couch and watch *Dancing with the Stars*.

But then she let out a breath. Her mom looked so *hopeful,* like all she wanted was to be a small part of Aerin's life. One of the things they'd talked about was how broken Mrs. Kelly had been after Helena's death, too—she just handled it differently than Aerin had, throwing herself into work, trying to forget, and accidentally ghosting Aerin in the process. But she'd made a renewed promise—a real, solid, genuine promise—to change her ways now for the better. They were going to talk, they were going to have each other's backs, they were going to try—because life was short, wasn't it? One day, you were on a private plane; the next, you were a kidnapping victim imprisoned in a small room. Aerin supposed you really didn't know what you had until it was gone.

She let her shoulders relax, then smiled and wriggled over a little to give her mom room. And with a smile, Mrs. Kelly plunked down and signaled the waiter. Ross hurried over with three glasses filled with white wine. At first, Aerin figured her mom was going to drink them all herself, but then she passed the other glasses to Aerin and Thomas.

"That's for us?" Aerin asked.

Mrs. Kelly nodded. "I thought we needed to have a toast."

She raised her glass, but then seemed at a loss at what to say. Aerin watched delicate emotions cross her features, and the reality smacked her all over again—everything they'd just gone through, it was *brutal*. But now they were seeing the light at the end of the tunnel. Now they could heal.

"To family," she said, raising her glass.

Mrs. Kelly's smile wavered, then grew broader. "To family," she answered, clinking it with Aerin and Thomas. And then all of them drank. It was the best wine Aerin had ever tasted.

# THIRTY-EIGHT

**WHEN MADDOX WALKED** back into Seneca's pretty living room in Annapolis, she was grinning at him, her laptop on the table. "I have a very, very important question for you," she said.

"Shoot," Maddox said. Though when he moved to look at the screen, she turned it away, a mischievous smile on her face.

"What would you say your dorm room style is?" she asked. "Rustic adventurer? Preppy chic? Oh wait, this is totally you—casual and athletic." She finally turned the laptop around. IKEA's website was on the screen. She was looking at dorm décor.

Maddox groaned. "I'm going to lose my mind if I look at any more pillows and comforters."

"You only have a week left before you're going to Oregon. You have to choose something, and you might as well have some style." The mouse hovered over a hamper in an optical-illusion print. "This is a cool laundry bag, right? It's called the *Snajda*." She giggled. "How do you even say that? SNODz-da? IKEA is so weird."

Her pink lips parted, and her bright blue eyes shone. Would

Maddox *ever* get sick of seeing her beautiful eyes looking at him with such affection? He was psyched he'd come down here for a few days before leaving for school. Madison, Thomas, and Aerin were taking Amtrak here this afternoon, and they were all going to take Seneca out for her birthday. Actually, they were going to celebrate *all* their birthdays—not just because the school year was starting soon and they were going to be separated in the months to come, but because the saga with Brett had taught them that life was fleeting, and they should party it up while they had the chance.

He closed the laptop and put it on the coffee table. "I have to admit, I'm not as excited about college as I used to be."

Seneca stared at him. "Because of this summer?"

He nodded. "I just feel so . . . different now. I'm not sure it's going to be enough for me to be on a track team, go to classes. I'll always be thinking about what we went through. Chelsea. Damien and Huntley. Helena. Even Brett's messed-up story." He brushed a hand through his hair. "I mean, even *Madison's* different from all this. She quit cheerleading. I never thought I'd see the day. She said the girls seem sort of . . . vapid." He chuckled. "You must be rubbing off on her. She would have never used that word before."

Seneca absorbed this for a beat, laughing about Madison, and then nodding thoughtfully. "But isn't college about figuring yourself out? Getting a broader view of life? Finding people that *do* get you?" She folded her hands. "You won't get that staying in Dexby."

"I know . . ."

"And what are you saying, you're going to give up running?" Now Seneca seemed angry. "You're an Olympic hopeful! What other reason do I have to watch the next Summer Games?"

She moved to smack him on the arm, but Maddox ducked away,

grabbing her instead around the waist and pulling her close. God, she smelled good—like chocolate, and soap, and just . . . *Seneca*. How could he explain what he felt for her? Did she even understand the emptiness he'd felt those few days without her when they'd broken up—or, going back even farther, the extreme *rightness* of the moment they'd first kissed?

"I'd never give up running," he admitted. "If only knowing that you'd be in the stands, watching me at the Olympic trials."

"Good," Seneca said.

"But how can I go across the country?" he moaned. "I'll miss you too much."

Seneca leaned back against the pillow and stared out the window. Her house had a view of the Chesapeake, and the water was dotted with sailboats and fishing vessels. "You can't quit your dreams because of that," she scolded.

"It's not just because of you." Maddox considered propping his feet up on the coffee table until he remembered he wasn't in his own house. "I mean, yes, it's *mostly* you, but this summer changed me. I didn't run last week when we were looking for Aerin, and I didn't even care. There are things out there that are bigger than running, you know? It put things in perspective."

"Yeah, but hopefully we won't have to deal with those big things anymore, right? It's all behind us."

She looked so chill when she said this. Not maniacal. Not crazed or obsessed like she'd been in Breezy Sea after they'd found Damien. Maddox thought about that crazy-awesome-awful day for a moment. A few days after their blowup, he'd gotten it—really *gotten* what she was trying to tell him. Brett was like a sickness in Seneca's head; if she didn't treat that sickness, it would grow like a weed, choking out everything else. And the only way she was going to get rid of the weeds in her head was to find Brett.

That, combined with the note he knew she'd received from him, was why he'd watched her so carefully. He knew she was searching. He knew, too, that she would hit upon the answer in time. Like Brett had said, she already had all the clues.

When he looked up, Seneca looked giddy, like she was working hard to hold in a secret. "What?" he asked.

She bit her lip, her eyes sparkling. "Okay. I was going to save this for closer to you leaving, but I guess I'll tell you now."

"Tell me what?"

Her gaze fell to the couch, where a few crumbs of the pita chips they'd devoured earlier were scattered. "I've been talking to my dad. Like, *really* talking. He's pissed at me for not explaining what I was up to, and he was livid that I tracked Brett down alone—but that's not all we've been talking about. We've been talking about *her*, too. My mom." Her gaze drifted to the big book of photo albums on the coffee table; she'd been showing Maddox them nonstop since he'd arrived. "For so long, my dad hasn't wanted to—he said he was trying to protect me from his grief. And I think I didn't want to talk to *him* about her because I was trying to protect him from my rage. But anyway, we've been telling stories about her—fun, funny stuff that I'd forgotten. It's been really nice."

"That *is* really nice," Maddox agreed.

"That's not all. Knowing what we know now, about Brett? It really helps. Both of us feel closure in a way we haven't felt since her death. Before, at the University of Maryland, I was so unsettled, still stuck on my mom's mystery. It was why I couldn't focus on classes—or *anything,* really. Even relationships." Here she looked up and gave Maddox a half-sly, half-sheepish smile. "But now everything has changed."

"That's great." A boat drifted across Maddox's field of view, and for a second he wished he and Seneca could be aboard, wearing skimpy bathing suits, listening to hip-hop. Then he turned back to her. Seneca was grinning as though the best part of her speech was yet to come.

"I think what's held me back is staying in the same town where my mother was killed." She swept her arm around the living room. "Even hunting down these other mysteries and getting out of my bubble really helped. And then, the other day, right before you got here, I got accepted into a criminal justice program. *And* I'm going to volunteer with the college's local PD."

"Wait, *what*?" Maddox exclaimed. "All this happened and you didn't tell me?"

Seneca looked sheepish. "I needed to think about it first. It's such a big step. But the college was impressed with the work I did finding Helena and Brett. So that helped with my applications." When she looked up at him, her face was full of hope. "I really want to do it."

"Then you *should* do it! You definitely should!"

She sat back. "See? You support me in my dream. Of course I'm going to encourage you to follow yours as well."

Maddox rolled his ankles and felt both joints crack. He *was* dying to get back into running and racing. And, okay, missing the Olympics was more than he could even bear. Who'd pass up the chance to walk in the opening ceremonies with Michael Phelps and all those hot women volleyball players?

"I just hate that we're going to be separated, you know?" he said softly.

A sneaky smile appeared on Seneca's pink lips. "But I haven't even told you where I was accepted." Her eyebrows shot up and down. "How does the University of Washington work for you?"

Maddox stared at her. "Washington . . . as in State?"

"DC's way too close to home, baby."

"As in only a few hours from the University of Oregon?" Maddox grabbed her arms. "Are you kidding me? Are you seriously kidding me?"

"Nope," Seneca said as he pulled her in for a bear hug. "And I'm going to intern at the Seattle PD."

Maddox stared at her for a long while, then put a finger to his temple. "Mind, *blown*."

"I thought you'd like it," Seneca murmured into his ear as he held her close.

"I don't just like it," Maddox said, pulling her back and looking deeply into her eyes. He wanted to freeze this moment, put it in a jar, and keep it always. "I love it."

"And I love you," she said softly, kissing his lips.

# THIRTY-NINE

**THAT NIGHT, AFTER** Madison, Aerin, and Thomas arrived and Seneca got them settled in her house's creaky third-floor guest rooms—which were a bit dusty and serving as a Holiday Inn for a few spiders—the group set off down the road to Lowry's, one of Seneca's favorite crab cake joints in all of Annapolis. The restaurant had a noir-slash-pirate vibe about it: It was very dark inside, the floors were original from the 1940s and littered with peanut shells and wood shavings, the bartender was an old, grizzly dude named Sven, and the dock outside for boats bobbed and shook and had death-trap planks with nails sticking up every which way.

Everyone barreled inside, and the hostess, Fran—a cranky older woman who'd been there forever—led the group to a booth. But before Seneca followed, she held up her finger to Maddox, stepped out onto the back porch near the decimated dock, and peered out at the bridge in the distance.

There was another reason why she was drawn to this restaurant over the years: It held a vista across the water of where her mother was found. If Seneca squinted, she could just make out the marshy inlet where the police had recovered her body. She hadn't been on the scene when that happened—she hadn't known, actually, until hours later, when an officer came to the house to ask her to ID her mother's corpse—but after she found out the details, her mind had worked to fill in the holes. How on earth had her mother gotten there? Who had done this to her? Why had this happened?

Now she had those answers. Every single part; she'd even put Collette's killer behind bars.

Seneca pushed her hair behind her ears. Not long ago, she'd assumed that when—not *if*—she cracked the case, she'd feel a huge weight off her shoulders. Her life would immediately be happy and peaceful; everything would change for the better. But that wasn't exactly what had happened. In learning about what had happened to her mother and why, Seneca had peeled back the layers of so many terrible events. Tragic car accidents. Descents into madness. Stolen childhoods. Hideous violence. The world could be so senseless and cruel. People were so fragile, so easily ruined, so quickly haunted.

Brett had been right—they *were* alike in a lot of ways. They were both marred by what had happened to them. They were both victims of life's hideous cruelty and randomness. But unlike Brett, Seneca wasn't going to turn her tragedy and misfortune into evil. By studying criminal justice in Seattle, maybe she could help even one person get closure on something that was haunting *them*. She hoped it would make a difference.

The wind kicked up, making ripples across the water. The rickety dock swayed noisily, knocking the lone moored boat against its side. Seneca stared hard at the inlet across the bay; she'd always thought of it as her mother's true grave, not the St. Anne's Cemetery, where they'd buried her. *We did it, Mom,* she thought, feeling tears prickle at her eyes. *We got him. I'm just sorry he did this to you in the first place.*

She closed her eyes, wishing for an answer. If only her mom could talk to her just one more time, but since that day at Brett's house, her voice hadn't returned. What more did Seneca need her to say? That she loved her? That she was sorry? *Was* Seneca mad at her mom for sending Brett back to Elizabeth's lair all those years ago? Brett certainly was. If you looked at it one way, her mom's decision set off a toxic chain reaction that led all the way to her death. But if you looked at it the rational way, who would ever have thought evil could lurk two doors down in a peaceful beach town? Seneca wouldn't have. Most people wouldn't have. She couldn't fault her mom for that.

"Hey."

Maddox stood in the doorway, his head cocked to the side, his eyebrows were raised in question. "Hey," she said, walking back to him. He put his arm around her. "I really love this view."

Maddox smiled. "It's pretty, especially with this sunset."

Seneca nodded. Then she turned to him, feeling a little shaky and uncertain that she should ask the question that was swirling in her mind. "Do you ever think about Brett in prison?"

Worry flashed across Maddox's face, and Seneca was afraid he was going to give her another lecture about too much Brett on the brain. But then he nodded. "Actually, yeah. It's hard to imagine him actually confined somewhere, you know? I can't quite picture it."

"I keep thinking he's going to escape." Seneca laughed self-consciously. "I've called the prison every day to make sure he's still there."

Maddox chuckled, then took her hand. Seneca leaned her head on his shoulder, considering asking him another thing that had been weighing on her mind—if he was going to go to Brett's trial. *She* had to. Aerin did, too, because of the kidnapping. The prosecution would only call Maddox as a character witness, though. Seneca figured he would, but the two of them had avoided talking about Brett over the past few days. It was so much calmer that way. So much less charged.

But she was still thinking about Brett. Not obsessively, not in an I-need-to-find-him-or-I'm-going-to-explode sort of way. Now, to her surprise, her thoughts about him were tinged with something complex that she couldn't quite name. She knew it made no sense, but the only thing it reminded her of was how she felt when she'd come home from the hospital after getting her tonsils out—the surgery had hurt, the hospital bed was lumpy, and a couple of the nurses were unfriendly, but it had been memorable and transformative. In a completely bizarre way, she had Brett to thank for setting off her life in a thrilling, purposeful new direction—meeting new friends, meeting Maddox, finally feeling ready for college. She'd always remember Brett for that. Not with fondness . . . but definitely with significance.

"Helloo?" a voice trilled. Madison poked her head around the door, hand on her hip. "There's a big plate of fried clams with your name on it, Seneca!"

Seneca squeezed Maddox's hand and stepped back inside the restaurant, sliding back into the booth with the four friends who were probably the most important people in her life. Aerin sat against the wall, her glossy mouth smiling wide, so unlike the cranky, closed-off girl Seneca had met months before, when she'd come to Dexby to search for Helena's killer. And Thomas was squeezed next to her, still looking thrilled that he was even *with* Aerin but also providing a comforting stability. Madison, picking up a clam strip with the tips of her fingernails, which were decorated with polka dots and glitter, ribbed Maddox about wearing a freaking Under Armour T-shirt to his girlfriend's twentieth birthday party. "I mean, *honestly,* Maddox?" She took his sleeve between her fingers. "Could you not have put on something a teensy bit fancier?"

"It's okay." Seneca leaned into Maddox. "I like his sporty gear. Which is kind of funny, because the very first time we met in person, I thought, *Ugh, a jock.*"

Maddox poked her. "Actually, the very first time you met me, you were surprised I wasn't a girl."

The table roared with laughter, and Seneca did, too. She wouldn't have a few months ago—maybe even a few *weeks* ago. She used to be so prickly about her mistakes, so defensive about any critique someone made of her. But she was starting to get over that. She *wasn't* always right. And that was okay, as long as someone had her back.

"Here," Madison said, pushing something wrapped in tissue paper across the table at her. "A birthday present."

Seneca frowned. "I said no gifts, guys." But she peeled away the filmy tissue paper anyway. Inside was a small white box. Seneca lifted the lid, then gasped. Her mother's *P*-initial necklace lay on a small satin pillow. The gold shone. The charm was no longer bent and charred. Tears came to her eyes.

"Guys," she whispered. "How did you do this?"

"Madison knows a jewelry guy," Maddox said. "He fixed it right up."

She ran her fingers over the gold disc. The memory flashed back of pulling it off her mother's body, desperately needing something that was hers. She lifted it from the box, and Maddox helped to secure it around her neck. The *P* charm settled at her throat in that old, familiar way she remembered. Her fingers instantly started to fiddle with it, and she felt her heart slow. When had her friends even had time to do this? She'd never felt so touched in her life. "Thank you. I don't even know what to say."

Maddox held his water glass up in a toast. "Happy birthday, Seneca."

"We love you," Aerin said, raising her glass, too.

Seneca clinked her glass to theirs. She couldn't help but get a twinge of the *last* time she'd heard a toast—in that dark, spooky living room in Halcyon, with Brett leering at her from his couch. A shiver went through her, filling her with dread and even a little worry. But that was crazy, of course. Brett couldn't scare her anymore. Because of her—because of *them*—Brett would never hurt anyone again.

# AFTER

THE WAY JACKSON Brett Jones saw it, if he'd lived through years of being locked up with a madwoman, prison was going to be a piece of cake. He'd learned a thing or two since escaping from Elizabeth. Like how to manipulate people. Like how to slide into any role he needed to play. *Fake it till you make it,* and all that. And so Brett walked into the Garden Plaza Correctional Facility not the scared little twerp who let himself be kidnapped or the careless dude who'd misjudged an amateur crime-solver named Seneca Frazier, but the confident, ballsy, mad-genius badass he knew he was.

And it had worked—so far, anyway. He'd already gotten privileges to have shoelaces, decent shampoo, and fresh rolls in the cafeteria. He'd schmoozed with enough inmates and did enough favors—which typically involved hacking contraband cell phones to contact the outside world—and people gave him a wide berth. He was escorted to the front of the phone call line every Wednesday afternoon, and he always got hot water for his shower. Basically, he had it pretty good, all things considered.

The best part? He'd charmed the guards into giving him a choice job in the prison library, which put him around tons of books . . . *and* computers. And sure, the prison *thought* the internet's server only accessed a handful of sites the staff thought appropriate, but that was before Brett got his hands on the thing. Like it was really so hard to bypass their flimsy firewalls. He almost wanted to write an open letter to the taxpayers of New Jersey, spilling how their hard-earned money was going to a lot of uselessness. Then again, he had more useful endeavors for his web-surfing time.

He sat at the computer terminal now, his fingers wiggling over the keys, trying to ignore the fact that the room smelled not like musty books but like sweat, piss, and burned hair. The first thing he did was Google *Jackson Brett Jones*. Not so long ago, there were no results except for those buried stories about a missing boy from Tallyho Island, but today? Today, he was a freaking Twitter trend.

Every news outlet known to man was speculating on his upcoming trial, trying to figure out how he was going to plead, hedging their bets on whether he'd get the death penalty—which, *duh,* he wouldn't, because Brett was hoping all the cases would be thrown out on technicalities or insufficient evidence. There were timelines of the murders he'd pulled off, essays from psychologists diagnosing him with various mental illnesses, a big splashy story about how he measured up to some of the serial killer greats, and an interview with Viola, who'd seemed so stunned and blindsided through the whole thing that Brett's heart broke a little. The CNC forums were full of questions: how he'd gone unnoticed for so long, how he'd chosen his victims, and how he'd gotten the cash to sustain himself all these years.

Brett would love to answer that last question—would anyone believe the story? Who knew the old-fashioned scion Vera Grady, one of the very first women he killed—*and* the woman he claimed to be his grandma to Seneca and the others—was paranoid about banks? It wasn't even why Brett killed her—he'd been working as a bagger at a high-end grocery down the street from her in Greenwich, and she was bitchy to him every time she came in, and he'd snapped one day, still so wounded and touchy from the agony of Elizabeth. But he considered it a lovely little perk.

He'd found money stashed all over the house. A safe with an easily crackable code contained over one hundred thousand dollars in crisp hundreds. Not even her housekeeper, Esmerelda, knew about Vera's little nest egg, because the press didn't report anything missing. It also helped that Brett had left everything *else* in that safe—a lot of gaudy jewelry, some deeds to some properties, an old, sappy love letter—untouched.

Clicking out of Google, he leaned back in the chair and cracked his knuckles. Now on to the real reason he surfed the internet. He looked right and left, making sure Joseph, the head librarian who acted like he was a force to be reckoned with, still had his nose stuck in a Le Carré novel. He did. Smiling, Brett typed in the link to Case Not Closed.

The site came up quickly. Brett signed in under the new handle he'd created, JCoin—a little twist on BMoney, get it?—and watched as the screen loaded. It was comforting how the old, badly designed homepage never changed. Neither did the losers who weighed in on the cases.

He clicked on a tab, then found himself staring at Helena Kelly's name. *Case Closed,* read a red stamp over the thread. He clicked to Collette Frazier next; Seneca must feel so good that her mommy got a shiny new *Case Closed* sticker, too. The thread was still open, though, and he clicked on the thread, scrolling all the way to the bottom. Some of the regulars had weighed in after Brett had been arrested—*and* the press had made public that he'd been posting on CNC as BMoney for years. HE'S NOT ONE OF US, some bitch named MizMaizie wrote in all caps, peppering the post with skull emojis and a GIF of a burly dude pounding his fist into his palm. *I hope that guy rots in hell.*

*Sigh,* Brett thought. You couldn't please everyone, could you?

His gaze drifted to the little message window in the corner. There was no number superimposed over the image, meaning he'd received no new messages—no one knew who JCoin was, and no one cared. He hadn't weighed in on any cases yet. He was dying to, though. There was a girl in Arkansas who'd been found in a barn, slashed from throat to belly button. There was a set of twins who vanished from their Texas home and cleaned out their parents' doomsday prepper's stash of gold bullion in the basement. There was a missing little girl in Phoenix, a murdered college student in New York, a brand-new housewife found dead in her trailer in Michigan and her husband nowhere to be found. Every day, dreadful things rolled onto this site, too many cases, too much work for the cops, deaths and disappearances that got shoved in a closet and forgotten about because there were just too many of them in the world.

Of course he wanted to dive into one of them. And hell, maybe he could be helpful. An insider's perspective, if you will. But it was kind of lonely to solve cases by yourself. What Brett really wanted was a team.

He opened a new message window and hovered the mouse over the recipient line. Going for it, he typed in *TheMighty.* Her name autofilled in the space, which meant her handle was still active on the site. Brett felt a little tingle in his bones. That was a good start.

*I miss you, pal,* he typed. And then, because he was afraid to write anything more that might give him away, he pressed the little blue SEND button. The message disappeared into the ether; Brett imagined it scrambling up, zooming through electronic tunnels, only reshaping once it reached Seneca Frazier's inbox. It was a pleasure to shut his eyes and fantasize the first moments she read the note. Would she instantly know who it was, or would it take her a moment? Would she be afraid . . . or maybe a little bit thrilled? And most of all, would she write back?

Brett hoped she would. He really did. The world was much more fun when they were playing the game.

# ACKNOWLEDGMENTS

**THE AMATEURS TRILOGY** has been a fun ride, and I am hugely grateful to those at Alloy Entertainment who helped hammer out this world and the mystery, characters, and much, much more from start to finish, to really make this series shine: my old friends Lanie Davis, Sara Shandler, Josh Bank, Laura Barbeia, and Les Morgenstein.

Kieran Viola, your editorial input really elevated this novel from an entertaining read to something I'm really proud of. Thanks also to the rest of the Freeform group: Mary Mudd in editorial, Whitney Manger in design, Holly Nagel in marketing, and Cassie McGinty, my tireless publicist, for your attention, support, and enthusiasm. And I'm lucky to have Andy McNicol on my side to shepherd this series to a close. I'm so happy to have such a great team.

Also thanks to my father-in-law, Mike Gremba, who has provided a lot of behind-the-scenes police procedure details that I otherwise would have made up (and gotten wrong). Much love, too, to Michael, Kristian, and Henry. And of course Clyde, for eating out of my trash can while I wrote this book.

And finally, thank you, all my readers, for enjoying, commenting, discussing, posting, blogging, Booktubing, Bookstagramming, and messaging me about what you think about this story. Connecting with readers is one of the best parts of this job, and you guys make it all worth it.